## "Have you had ⟨...⟩ life?"

Marley snorted with laughter.

He pushed up on one elbow to stare down at her. "You're an attractive woman. Has something bad happened to put you off men?"

"No, I've just always been that girl next door who fades into the woodwork."

He laid a hand on her cheek, preventing her from looking away. "Stop putting yourself down."

"But—"

His mouth closed over hers and she gasped, surprised. He took advantage of it to taste her more deeply, and a strange sound she identified as a moan escaped her throat.

"Relax, Marley," he murmured. His hand roamed from the back of her knee up her thigh, and darned if her legs didn't obey him and fall apart. His hand slid up by inches...

"What are you doing?"

"I'm establishing that all the guys who failed to ask you out in the past are complete idiots. Are you okay with that?"

Okay? No, she wasn't okay with this. She wanted more...

\*\*\*

# HIGH-STAKES PLAYBOY

### BY
### CINDY DEES

Published in Great Britain 2015
by Mills & Boon, an imprint of Harlequin (UK) Limited,
Eton House, 18-24 Paradise Road, Richmond, Surrey, TW9 1SR

© 2015 Cynthia Dees

ISBN: 978-0-263-25348-1

18-0115

Harlequin (UK) Limited's policy is to use papers that are natural, renewable and recyclable products and made from wood grown in sustainable forests. The logging and manufacturing processes conform to the legal environmental regulations of the country of origin.

Printed and bound in Spain
by CPI, Barcelona

**Cindy Dees** started flying airplanes while sitting in her dad's lap at the age of three and got a pilot's license before she got a driver's license. At age fifteen, she dropped out of high school and left the horse farm in Michigan, where she grew up, to attend the University of Michigan. After earning a degree in Russian and East European studies, she joined the US Air Force and became the youngest female pilot in its history. She flew supersonic jets, VIP airlift and the C-5 Galaxy, the world's largest airplane. During her military career, she traveled to forty countries on five continents, was detained by the KGB and East German secret police, got shot at, flew in the first Gulf War and amassed a lifetime's worth of war stories.

Her hobbies include medieval re-enacting, professional Middle Eastern dancing and Japanese gardening.

This RITA® Award-winning author's first book was published in 2002 and since then she has published more than twenty-five bestselling and award-winning novels. She loves to hear from readers and can be contacted at www.cindydees.com.

# Chapter 1

Marley Stringer crouched in front of the movie camera, checking it one last time, even though she'd already checked it twice. Everything was ready to go. But that didn't keep her stomach from doing nervous flip-flops. This was her first big break in movie cinematography and nothing could go wrong.

Not to mention she didn't like flying. She'd arrived at the airport this morning to find that her camera had been taken off the usual helicopter she flew in and mounted on this tiny, two-seat bubble-cockpit-thingie she'd never flown in before. Why the last-minute change to this mosquito of an aircraft, she had no idea. But she had a bad feeling about it. What if the camera mount came loose? Or the helicopter crashed and killed her? Or...

"Ever fly in one of these puppies?" a husky male voice asked from directly overhead.

She lurched, startled, and promptly banged her head into the belly of the helicopter. *"Oww!"*

Big, tanned hands reached past the spots dancing in her eyes and lifted her to her feet. "You okay?"

"No, I'm not okay," she snapped, embarrassed. "The damned helicopter whacked me on the head."

A chest came into view, clad in black leather. An aviator's jacket. "Bad, bad helicopter," the laughing voice chided the offending aircraft.

Scowling, she looked up at the face to go with the jacket…and stared. *Whoa.* Rugged jaw, complete with sexy, dark, whisker stubble. Generous mouth and a dazzling smile. Lean, male-model's cheeks. Dark, slashing brows. And then her gaze met his. *Hoo, baby.* His eyes were as black as midnight and so hot she was fairly sure she felt her extremities threatening to catch on fire.

"Are you one of the actors in the movie?" she asked breathlessly. Lord. Where did all the oxygen in Northern California go all of a sudden?

He tapped the name patch over his right breast. "Wings. Pilot. It's my bird that attacked you."

She looked back and forth between him and the olive-green helicopter. "You need to take that thing to obedience school before it really hurts somebody."

His mouth curved up in a sinfully hot smile. "Once I've got my hands on her, she's the soul of cooperation. She does whatever I want, whenever I want it."

Her gaze riveted on his mouth as he formed the words. She'd bet all the girls did whatever he wanted whenever he wanted it once he had his hands on them. She finally managed to tear her gaze away from his *GQ* face, and it slid downward past the broad-shouldered leather jacket to the black jeans cupping his family jewels... *Please, God, let there be truth in advertising behind that bulging zipper.*

Her face did catch on fire then. She tore her gaze away from his fascinating anatomy, but not before she glimpsed long, powerful thighs and black leather cowboy boots.

She stammered, "Where's Gordon Trapowski? I'm supposed to fly with him today. You're not him."

"Gee. Thanks for noticing," the god replied, as unlike burly, rough Trapowski as a man could get.

"I checked around the hangar," she elaborated breathlessly, "but he's not anywhere to be found. Do you know where I might find him?"

"No idea where he's got off to. He's going to be flying the combat-drop bird that's being filmed today, I think."

*Oh.* Alarm filled her gut. As much as she disliked flying, she'd come to trust Gordon's piloting skills over the past few flights with him. He was crude, a chauvinist and an all-around ass, but he was a competent, if jerky, pilot. Apparently, she would be filming him today instead of riding with him. Who was this guy, then?

"Any idea where I can find the cameraman who belongs to this camera?" the new guy in question asked, his voice rich with amusement.

"I'm him. I mean, I'm her. I'm your cameraman. Woman. Camerawoman." *Dammit.* Did she have to stutter like a thirteen-year-old talking to her first boy?

"Ready to take a wild ride with me?" he murmured low, his voice charged.

Trepidation rattled through her. She sincerely hoped not. Wild was not high on her list of favorite flavors. That was, not until she'd turned twenty-five and realized abruptly that she was becoming a boring cat lady about to live the same tired routine for the next fifty years.

Hence the shift from early-morning local TV news crew to action-movie camera operator—a choice she was *deeply* reconsidering right about now. This pilot and all his raw sex appeal were scaring her to death.

That and his vicious attack helicopter.

On a movie set, she supposed she had to expect to be around sexy studs. She just hadn't expected one of them to actually notice her. Good news was the stick jockey would lose interest in her soon enough. She would hide behind her camera until he hooked up with one of the hot, young starlets roaming around the set and forgot about her.

If her sister, Mina, were here, she would be all over this guy. But then, Archer would be all over Mina, too. He would never have given mousy little her the time of day. Which would have been a relief. Although for once, she wasn't so sure she wanted this magnificent male specimen to look right past her.

Part of her—the part that didn't want to end up alone, eccentric and smelling funny—wondered what it would be like to have his hands on her, and do whatever he wanted whenever he wanted it.

If only she wasn't completely jinxed when it came to men. If this poor guy actually took a second look at her, no telling what horrible fate would befall him. Her last almost-boyfriend had nearly died of food poisoning on their first real date. And then there was the guy who found out on a picnic with her that he was deathly allergic to bee stings...

"You didn't answer my question. Ever been in one of these puppies?"

Startled back to the present, she risked a peek up at

the sexy pilot. "I've been up with Gordon in a big helicopter with two engines." Two nice, safe engines. If they lost one, they still had a second one to land with, everybody in one nice piece.

"But you've never been up in a fast maneuverable bird like this one?"

"No. Never."

"Ah. A virgin. Excellent."

Her jaw dropped. *How did he know...* Oh. A *fast helicopter* virgin.

His eyes widened for a shocked instant and then narrowed speculatively. *Damn, damn, damn.* Please let that be him planning how to scare her in his helicopter. Please let that not be him picking up on what she'd almost given away.

"In you go," he instructed. He was holding the passenger door for her, and damned if he still didn't have that thoughtful look on his face. Swearing silently, she climbed awkwardly into the seat. A dizzying array of dials and knobs covered the dashboard in front of her. But then she spied the viewfinder for her camera. Familiar turf. Mounted on a swivel, she pulled the wide metal tube in front of her face and rested her forehead on the rubber face-piece. She felt a little faint.

"Slow down, darlin'. Gotta buckle you in first."

She jerked her face away from the view box as hands touched both of her shoulders and knuckles skimmed down over her breasts. She lurched in shock at the intimate contact. *What the...*

*Oh.* He was feeding the shoulder harnesses down her body. Through her thin T-shirt and thinner bra, her nipples leaped to attention. Of course, his gaze went straight to them and heated up a few hundred degrees more. Did he *have* to look like a volcano about to blow?

Although, in fairness to him, the way her own face heated up as his avid gaze took in her breasts was pretty volcanic, too.

She watched him, practically panting as he reached across her and ran his hands around her hips. They ended up at the juncture of her thighs and commenced fumbling around there. "What are you doing?" she squeaked.

"Seat belt," he explained smoothly. A metallic click punctuated the word. He yanked at the loose ends of the nylon web strapping, tightening the restraints. Looking straight at her chest, he muttered, "Is that too tight?"

Her chest did feel mashed by the shoulder straps, but she wasn't about to say so. And wasn't snug supposed to be good...when it came to seat belts? "It's fine," she managed to croak.

He reached over her head to a hook and put a pair of clamshell headphones over her ears. She felt about six years old, the way he was treating her. He even pivoted the microphone down in front of her mouth.

"All set?" he murmured.

"I guess so." It was considerate of him to hook her in like this and make sure she was secure. But it was deeply unsettling having a man's hands all over her like that. Her brain said it was bad unsettling, but her lady parts declared it definitely good unsettling. She pressed her knees tightly together and tried to ignore the sudden throbbing in said traitorous lady parts.

He slipped into the left seat and strapped himself in quickly. His hands flew across the dials and switches as he read aloud from the checklist Velcroed to his left thigh. His strong fingers were mesmerizing as they pressed and flicked and twisted the controls.

There was something almost unbearably intimate

about having his voice piped directly into her ears as he announced, "Radio check. One, two, three, four, five. How do you copy?" He looked over at her expectantly.

"Uh, was that for me?" she mumbled.

"I hear you five by five. How about me?" he repeated a little impatiently.

"Well, obviously I hear you because I'm answering you," she replied testily.

He grinned and, on cue, her stomach did a picture-perfect, double-twisting layout. He responded drily, "The usual response is 'Loud and clear,' or a numerical description of volume and clarity, each rated on a scale from one to five."

"Um, okay. You're five plus five."

His grin widened. Swear to God, the guy looked like a male fashion model as he replied, "Roger."

"I'm not Roger. My name's Marley." She knew what *roger* meant, but she couldn't resist making him smile again. He gifted her with a big, beautiful one that made her insides melt a little more.

"Hi, Marley, I'm Archer."

"Archer what?"

"Just Archer. And you're not supposed to interrupt the pilot in the middle of a checklist. I might miss something important."

"Oh. Sorry. I didn't mean to—I'll be quiet now."

That million-dollar grin flashed again as he reached up to push and hold a fat button. The big rotor overhead started to turn slowly, and the sound of a jet engine revving up grew louder and louder. Her heart pounded as he completed the engine-start checklist and ran something he called a before-takeoff checklist. He radioed for clearance to lift off. A voice answered, clearing them to proceed on their filed flight plan.

"Sure you want to do this?" he asked grimly.

What was she missing? He was conveying something significant with that dark tone of voice. Something unspoken. A question, maybe. But she had no idea what it was. Confused, she nodded, and then belatedly remembered he might not be looking at her. "Um, roger wilco."

"*Wilco* means you will comply. I haven't given you an instruction to comply with." A pause. "Yet." He pushed forward on the throttles with one hand and eased back on the stick thing between his knees with the other.

And just like that, the ground fell away from her feet and they were rising straight up into the air. It was exhilarating. She'd never flown in a nearly all-clear helicopter before. It was like flying inside a bubble. A very thin, fragile bubble. But the visibility was incredible. It was easy to forget she was inside an aircraft at all. She felt as if she was levitating above the earth. Guess she could check that off her bucket list. Not that it had ever been *on* her bucket list.

The helicopter's nose dipped slightly and it eased forward, picking up speed, slanting into a turn that took her breath away.

"What's your last name, Marley?" her pilot—Archer—asked.

"Stringer. Marley Stringer."

"Nice to meet you. I'd shake your hand, but mine are full at the moment."

She looked down at his hands, so comfortable and capable on the controls. The kind of hands a girl could put herself into and trust him to know what to do…

Dang, she was getting horny in her spinsterish old age.

"Is Archer your first or last name?"

"Both."

O-*kay*. Was he some kind of aviation rock star who only needed one name? "Your parents named you Archer Archer? Did they hate you or something?"

"Something like that." His eyes went dark and turbulent, and her photographer's keen eye detected sadness. Regret. Rough childhood, huh?

Trees were streaking by below their feet now, fast enough to make her nervous. She blurted, "Did your folks give you some horrible first name like, I don't know, Eugene?"

He laughed, a little reluctantly if she wasn't mistaken. But interestingly enough, he didn't elaborate on his actual name. *Ooh*, a mystery. She never could resist those. Somebody in the payroll department for the movie would know his full name. She could stroll over there after they landed…

He interrupted her scheming with "We'll reach the shoot site in about fifteen minutes. Pretty quickly after we get there, we'll make our run down the valley. You'll get one shot at this. My boss reported before I headed out to Minerva that all the pyrotechnics are ready to go."

"Who's Minerva?" An ugly spike of regret poked her in the side. Of course this cover-model guy had a gorgeous, confident, sexy girlfriend with an exotic name.

He patted the top of the dashboard. "This is Minerva."

"You named your helicopter?" Ahh. He'd named it after his gorgeous, confident, sexy girlfriend, then.

He shrugged. "Yeah. I call every 'copter I fly after my grandmother."

His grandmother? That was so sweet! Although he emphatically struck her as the kind of guy who wouldn't appreciate being called "sweet."

"She took me in and forced me to get my head together when my mom died."

"Oh," Marley said cautiously. But she didn't have a chance to ask him about it.

"Five minutes to target," Archer announced in a businesslike tone. He got busy on the radio talking to the film's DP—the director of photography—and she turned her attention to her camera.

She pulled her viewfinder in front of her face once more. Beside her right knee, a small joystick remotely moved her camera on its nose mount outside. She tested it carefully, and it responded like a charm. Tall stands of pines skimmed past as the helicopter raced across the mountainous Northern California landscape toward the site of today's shoot. The crew had spent all morning wiring the pyrotechnics and explosions, and it had taken most of the afternoon to position all the tanks, personnel carriers and extras dressed as soldiers. Which was why the director, Adrian Turnow, was having to race to get in this shot before they lost their light.

As it was, she had to adjust the light aperture to capture more of the late-afternoon sun's lingering rays. The quality of the light out here was extraordinary, though. The sky was a deep cerulean blue, the trees a rich, lush evergreen with gray and blue undertones. And the mountains themselves, the northern end of the Sierras northwest of Lake Tahoe, were dark and forbidding, a few even topped with caps of snow. So stark and majestic. She'd love to photograph them sometime.

The helicopter slowed, topped a ridge, and hovered at the head of a long, narrow valley. Its granite walls were silvery gray, the valley floor a carpet of green. Cattle had grazed this valley for long enough that the trees were mostly gone. It made for a perfect movie battle-field, level and open with sweeping views.

"You good to go?" Archer asked her.

"Yup," she muttered, her eyes glued to her view-finder. She'd gone over computer simulations of this valley with the DP and the ground camera crew, and she'd chair-flown filming this sequence in her head a hundred times, but seeing it in the flesh was still different. And once the tracers and fake missiles started firing, all bets were off. It would be up to her to see and adapt to capture the best possible shot on film. The footage she shot today would likely determine whether or not she continued to work on this project.

Adrian Turnow's voice came over her headset. "I'm turning over control of the shoot to Steve Prescott, head stunt coordinator. Whenever you're ready, Steve."

She listened as Prescott got thumbs-ups over the radio from a dozen stuntmen and explosives operators. He was the ex–Marine officer who'd set up this combat scene to be as realistic as possible. And then he started checking off the cameras. Finally, he announced, "Heli-cam?"

"Ready," she replied as snappily as her knocking knees and trembling hands would allow.

"On my mark, everyone," Prescott ordered. "Three. Two. One. Go for explosion one." His orders came hard and fast as wave after wave of gunfire, tanks rolling, soldiers charging on foot, fake missiles, tracer rounds and who knew what else was put into motion. Hundreds of actors, extras and stunt coordinators launched into the complicated ballet that was a big action scene. A dozen cameras rolled, catching the action from every conceivable angle.

Prescott's voice came on again. "Archer, start your run on my mark. Three. Two. One. Go."

Beside her, Archer slammed the throttles forward and shoved Minerva's nose down. The helicopter swooped down into the valley in a stomach-dropping dive that threw the bird at the treetops with dizzying speed.

She felt Archer tense beside her, but her concentration was riveted on her viewfinder. *Wow.* All hell had broken loose before her. So much was going on she wouldn't have known where to point her camera had they not gone over it carefully in the simulations. She chanted the sequence in her head. *Pan left slowly, zoom fast to the line of soldiers charging. Tank explosion. Hard bank right by the helicopter...*

"You're supposed to bank right," she mumbled to Archer.

"I'm trying," he ground out.

A tracer whizzed by wicked close, and although she jerked in surprise, she doggedly held her camera steady. The projectile streaked by dramatically, leaving a trail of sparks and smoke that the helicopter blasted through. That was going to look *awesome* on film. Good call by Archer to delay the turn.

They were on top of the action now, and deafening explosions rocked the helicopter. Hard to believe these were fake charges. She couldn't imagine what the real deal must be like. Hell on earth if she had to guess. Her camera mount had inertial stabilizers built into it, so her shot remained steady in spite of the concussions slamming into Minerva.

"Time to turn, Archer," she called out loudly enough to be heard over the war zone outside.

Columns of smoke rose around them and Archer dropped the bird even lower, skimming across the ground barely above the grass. They buzzed a line of extras dressed as soldiers low enough that some of them hit the dirt in fear of getting brained by the helicopter's skids. The grunt's-eye view from her camera was unplanned, but amazing. She went with it, panning across the field of fire and zooming toward the enemy line as Archer raced toward it.

Something exploded directly in front of them, rocking the helicopter violently. They weren't supposed to get that close to any pyrotechnics! She lifted her face from her viewfinder to glance over at Archer. "You need to pull up higher and turn the helicopter," she said distinctly. "All I'm going to be shooting in a minute is dirt."

He didn't in any way acknowledge her. His concentration was one hundred percent on flying. He looked to be fighting hard with the helicopter controls. Was that normal? She knew pilots tended to be fit, muscular guys. Was this why? His jaw was clenched and his knuckles were white on the controls. As well they should be. Minerva was tearing along only feet above the ground.

"Archer?"

*No response.*

She glanced outside, and the end of the valley was coming up. Fast. *Damned* fast. A sheer granite cliff rose in front of them.

"Archer!"

*Nada.*

"Hey! What's going on?" She slapped him on the upper arm to get his attention. But it was as if he was on another planet. He ignored her completely. She let go of her camera controls and tried to turn in her seat, but the tight harness stopped her. She ripped at the belt buckle frantically, but to no avail. She was strapped in tight. The mountain loomed directly ahead, and it was getting bigger by the second. She could make out individual trees racing toward them. They were going to slam into the cliff in a few seconds!

"Help me pull," he grunted.

Shocked, she grabbed the stick between her knees and pulled back on it. It moved a bit as Archer pulled on it, too.

"*Harder, Marley*. We're going to *die*."

Panic slammed into her as full realization of how much trouble they were in finally registered. Something was wrong with the helicopter, and if they couldn't turn it in the next few seconds, they were going to crash head-on into that cliff.

She stood on the rudder pedals and pulled for all she was worth on the stick, straining every bit as hard as Archer. It wasn't working. Frantic, she started shaking the stick side to side in a desperate effort to break it loose.

The stick gave way all of a sudden, slamming her back into her seat so hard she hit her head on the cockpit wall. Archer flung Minerva into a violent turn that slammed Marley against her door next.

The bird banked up onto its side, and all she saw in her windscreen was granite and more granite. They were so close to the cliff that she saw individual clumps of grass clinging to its face. Frankly, she was amazed the skids didn't scrape the rocks as it turned. The helicopter shuddered as Archer hauled it around, creaking under the strain. He gave a tug back on the throttle, and it moved easily, slowing the bird's breakneck speed.

As quickly as the crisis had come, it passed. The helicopter flew forward sedately as if nothing had ever happened.

She became aware of somebody shouting in her ears.

Steve Prescott. "What the hell was that, Archer? Report to me when you land." She winced. Archer's boss sounded *pissed*.

"Copy," Archer replied tersely.

Silence, broken only by the steady thwacking of the rotor blades, filled the cockpit. Archer was as pale as snow in the seat beside her in stark contrast to his black leather jacket.

"Are we okay?" she asked in a small voice.

"You tell me," came the grim reply. He flew low and slow back up the valley toward the airport.

She took stock of the current situation. They were alive. The bird seemed to be responding to normal control inputs. Archer's knuckles were no longer white. That was all good, right? "What happened back there?"

"Did you get your film?"

"I got a few of the planned shots. Then you went off course."

His jaw rippled as if he was clenching it, and damned if it wasn't one of the sexiest things she'd ever seen.

*Stay on point, Marley. You want to know what just happened and why you nearly died just now. You're not drooling over the pretty pilot.*

"Can you review your footage right now?" he asked. "Those digital cameras have instant playback, right?"

Confused, she jammed her face to the viewfinder and watched the raw footage she'd captured in their wild ride down the valley at weed height. The images looked about like she'd expected for the first part. The boys in postproduction would need to push the light a little in editing, but that was no biggie. And then the footage got interesting. The tracer ripped past. The trail of sparks looked as great as she'd thought it would. And the perspective from so low, moving so fast, was gripping.

And that violent pull-up at the end—the camera had continued to run while they'd fought to break the controls free from whatever frozen state they'd gotten stuck in—was outrageous. Any director worth his salt would be orgasmic over it. Adrian Turnow was all about being as realistic as possible. He was going to *love* this stuff.

Feeling a little surly that her near-death had resulted in such spectacular footage, and unreasonably ticked off at Archer for getting footage that she would never have gotten herself, she admitted, "Yeah, I got my film."

"All right, then. Let's go home."

She didn't like that he was blowing off the fact that they'd nearly died mere moments ago. Shouldn't he be upset? Freaking out at least a little? But he was acting like it was just another day at the office. Like this kind of stuff happened to him all the time.

Well, it *didn't* happen to her all the time. And she didn't like it one bit. He'd scared the living hell out of her back there. The least he could do was apologize or offer her some explanation of what had just happened. But nope. He just flew along, looking around outside and every now and then glancing over at her like they hadn't just nearly splattered like bugs on a windshield.

The ride back to the airport was dead quiet. Plenty of time for her to consider how flipping close she had just come to dying. A second or two at most. Had the stick not broken loose and Archer managed to haul the helicopter into that violent turn like he had, they'd have crashed into the side of that mountain for sure. Had she not helped pull, not shaken the stick in panic like she had, she couldn't bear to think about what would have happened.

By the time Archer set Minerva down gently, Marley's entire body was shaking. Adrenaline surged through her and she felt as though she could flap her arms and fly all by herself. As scared as she'd been before, this aftermath was weirdly exhilarating. She was *alive*. Gloriously, vividly so. Now that she wasn't roadkill on a mountain, she supposed it might be described as exciting in retrospect. But she'd about peed her pants when it was happening.

She didn't know what the hell had happened back there in that valley, but she knew one thing. She'd never done anything that intense in her entire life.

Never again would she listen to the crew's war stories about near-misses with disaster the same way. Having experienced near-death up close and personal, now she would hear the harrowing reality behind their tales told laughingly over cold beers. These pilots were crazy!

The door beside her opened. Archer reached for her lap. But she looked up at him and made eye contact for the first time since he'd nearly killed them both. His stare was dark. Turbulent. Suspicious, even. Shouldn't he be apologizing to her in some way for nearly killing her? Shouldn't she be the one staring accusingly at him? Perplexed at his wary distrust, she moved restlessly beneath the confining seat belts. Trapped. She felt trapped.

Maybe he wasn't as unaffected by their almost-disaster as he was letting on. Maybe the suspicion bit was just him covering up his own reaction to nearly dying. It wasn't like she'd had anything to do with the damned helicopter refusing to turn.

His hand stilled, nestled in the junction of her thighs, as his gaze shifted. Heated with fiery intensity as she stared up at him. His stare scorched parts of her that were not at all used to scorching. And all of a sudden any thought of suspicion flew right out of her head.

"Admit it," he murmured low and rough, "you liked that a little."

That was nuts. No sane person enjoyed cheating death. Or was he right? The rush of heat between her legs, the hot pulse throbbing there, said he was. She tingled to the tips of her fingers and ends of her hair. Felt restless. Hungry. Alive.

Shocked, she examined this rush of new feelings more closely. Sought out their source. And reeled mentally when it dawned on her that she was attracted to her death-defying pilot.

So this was lust, huh? She finally saw what all the fuss was about.

# *Chapter 2*

Archer couldn't have lifted his hand away from Marley in that moment if a dozen men tried to drag him away from her. She probably wasn't aware of it, but her hips were pulsing lightly against his knuckles, and it was so sexy he could barely breathe. His male parts abruptly swelled hard and painful enough that he had trouble standing upright.

Man, that had been a close call back there. What the hell had happened to his aircraft? He'd never seen a complete flight-control failure like that. The collective—the stick that steered the bird—and the throttle were two completely separate pieces of equipment, not related to each other in any way. It was simply not possible that a single mechanical issue had caused both systems to freeze up simultaneously.

Which left only one glaringly obvious possibility. Sabotage.

When Steve had called and asked him to come home on emergency leave, to help figure out what the hell was going on with a string of accidents around the movie set, he'd thought the guy had finally given in to his paranoid tendencies. Apparently not.

Marley shifted restlessly beneath his hand, her body radiating the heat and taut energy of a turned-on woman.

His throbbing erection blessedly distracted him from the alarming directions his thoughts were headed and he was glad to let it. It didn't help matters that she was staring at him as though he was some kind of conquering hero. Her lips were parted and moist, her pupils dilated so big he could hardly see their bright blue color. Hell, he could *smell* the lust on her, sweet and needy.

Was she seriously a virgin? The thought riveted him. Not that he was the kind of sleazeball who ran around looking for virgins to debauch. Actually, he liked his women experienced. Worldly. The kind who knew the score and didn't expect commitment or the whole emotional-involvement thing. The kind who wouldn't freak out when he loved 'em and left 'em. He'd learned very early in life how bad it hurt to be the one left behind and not the one doing the leaving.

But damn. A virgin. She had to be, what? Midtwenties? Who, in this day and age, hadn't had sex by that age? He examined her closely. She wasn't wearing a stitch of makeup, but she was still a pretty girl. Really pretty, in fact.

She had that whole old-school, movie-star glamour thing going. Bedroom eyes. Lush lips. Not to mention she had soft, creamy skin and curly blond hair pulled back into a short ponytail. Kinda looked like a poodle tail, but it was cute. Seriously, those big blue eyes of hers made a guy want to dive into them and go for a swim.

Abruptly, she seemed to shake herself out of her sexual trance and batted ineffectually at his hand. Bemused, he stepped back and let her unlatch her seat belt. She stumbled on the skid in her haste to get out of the helicopter, though, and staggered forward. He caught her up against him.

Her belly slammed into his zipper, and she couldn't fail to feel the gigantic erection straining against the denim. Her eyes went wide and her fair skin blushed bright pink. Yup, she'd noticed his hard-on.

"Easy, there, Grace," he muttered.

She was as light as a bird in his arms. He'd registered her as being reasonably tall the first time he'd seen her. But in fact, she barely reached his nose. Must be the mile-long legs in tight jeans that had given him the false impression. His heavy leather jacket prevented him from feeling her breasts smashed against him, but the view as he looked down the V-neck of her T-shirt was compensation enough. Marley Stringer was stacked.

"I'm such a klutz," she mumbled self-consciously.

"I'm pretty sure Minerva tripped you. She's the jealous type, you know."

Marley smiled up at him a little and his heart did something strange in his chest.

"Archer! My office. Now." Steve Prescott's voice carried clearly across the ramp, low and hard.

"Been nice knowin' ya," he muttered to Marley.

"You think he'll fire you?" she asked, her expression dismayed.

"Hell, yeah. *I'd* fire me." He had to act like just one of the guys—not a special operator brought in to find and stop whoever was causing accident after accident on the movie set. Film crews were among the most superstitious of all professions, and if the problems didn't get resolved soon, this film—heck, the whole studio— was in serious jeopardy.

Frankly, the timing of Steve's private call for help couldn't have come at a better time for him. He was on sixty days' forced leave from his unit overseas—thirty days of regular leave and thirty extra days of medically directed leave by his unit's flight surgeon.

If he had to sit at home staring at his toes all that time, he was going to lose his mind…or do something really dumb. Last thing he needed to do was actively tank his career. Or his life.

Besides, it wasn't like he really believed that there was a saboteur running around a movie set trying to kill people. It was a *movie, for crying out loud*. Not real life. It certainly wasn't anything like the war zones he'd been operating in for the past decade. Now those were places where people were overtly out to kill a guy.

But this—he looked around the quiet airfield with its orderly rows of toy airplanes, all neatly tied down and waiting for their wealthy owners to come play—this was not the kind of place that harbored dangerous killers.

Maybe he should consider retiring. Stunt flying in the movies. It was a sweet gig, after all. The pay was great, and the wild flying was every chopper jock's dream.

Nah. He was an adrenaline junkie at heart. Truth be told, he got turned on by being shot at. By cheating death.

He took off walking toward the hangar where Steve's on-set office was located.

The good news was that it would take almost his whole two months of leave to do the movie shoot. God knew, he could use the distraction. He'd been more relieved that he cared to admit when Steve had called to ask for his help.

"I'm coming with you," the girl declared, falling into step beside him.

His gut twisted unpleasantly. Was she inserting herself into this confrontation to find out if anyone suspected a saboteur yet, perhaps?

Aloud, he asked, "Why? You like having your butt handed to you in a sling?"

"No, but I'm still coming."

It wasn't like he could stop her from trailing along beside him to Prescott's office. Hell, maybe her presence would tone down the epic ass-chewing he was about to receive—for the benefit of the plentiful mechanics and crew hanging around in the hangar, no doubt to eavesdrop on the reaming Steve was about to lay on him. The one thing more distinctive about movie crews than their superstition was their love of gossip. They were veritable hotbeds of it. And Steve was no dummy. He would know full well that this conversation would, in effect, have an audience.

The two of them would talk more tonight. In private. But for now, for public consumption, he was in big trouble.

The idea behind today's change of flight crew/camera operator matchup had been to test Marley. To see if she would actually go up in his helicopter with him. They'd gotten an anonymous tip that Archer would be targeted today.

And Steve's investigation to date had uncovered that she had been seen in the vicinity of every one of the half dozen near-disasters the movie had experienced so far. She was the only crew member who had been.

As unlikely a saboteur as she seemed at a glance, the facts all pointed at her.

Today's plan had never included actually taking her up flying with him, particularly since she'd been seen fooling around near this bird earlier this morning.

Steve was going to be rip-snorting mad that Archer had had an impulse to go through with the flight, to see if she would actually put her neck on the line. His logic had been that no sane saboteurs put themselves into a position to die, after all. He'd assumed that, since she was willing to go up with him, she either wasn't the saboteur or knew his helicopter was not tampered with. *Wrongo, buddy.*

What the hell had happened to his bird back there, anyway? Steve was sure to ask, and he didn't have a clue. He'd headed down that valley, the explosions had started and the next thing he knew, none of his flight controls were functional. There hadn't been any noises like something had broken. The helicopter hadn't lurched as if something related to the flight controls had given way. Nothing had hit the aircraft to his knowledge.

Frankly, he was eager to tear into the guts of the bird and figure out exactly what *had* happened. He'd gotten an aircraft mechanic's license in his spare time a few years back that helped him to converse with his maintenance crews intelligently and diagnose and deal with mechanical problems while airborne. But he'd never even heard of something like this, let alone seen it.

How in the hell did Marley know to shake the stick from side to side like that to break loose whatever was obstructing its movement? Was she the saboteur, after all? If so, why would she cut it that close? He'd barely managed to turn the bird in the nick of time. Were he one iota less strong or less quick in his reflexes, the two of them would have died in a blazing fireball against that cliff. His rotor blades hadn't missed the mountain by more than a few feet.

All of a sudden, he became aware of his legs feeling weak as he walked to the back of the hangar. His knees were shaky, and his whole body felt like a rag doll's. And he was thirsty. So thirsty that it was abruptly all he could think about. Startled, he put a name to his symptoms.

*Shock.* He was in mild shock. Jeez, that had been close. The adrenaline that had gotten him home in an unnaturally calm, hyperaware mental state deserted him all at once, leaving him wrung out and wobbly as hell. His breathing was too fast, his pulse too shallow, as he opened the door to Steve's office and ushered Marley inside.

No surprise, Prescott didn't offer him a seat when he stepped into the ex-Marine's office. Aww, hell. Theater though this might be, this was gonna suck.

Archer stood at attention out of habit, not that he'd often stood at attention to get reamed out during his military career, which had been exemplary to date.

Prescott asked grimly, but with admirable restraint, "Care to tell me what happened out there?"

Archer glanced at Steve to see which one of them Prescott was addressing—him or Marley. *Him.* Yup, Steve was planning to keep up the charade of acting like she wasn't a suspect.

Too bad he had no idea how to answer Steve's question. He opened his mouth with the intent to say something brief like "No excuse, sir" or "Lemme tear apart the bird and I'll get back to you," but Marley dived in before he could get a single word out.

"He just did what I asked him to. When I saw the combat unfolding, I saw an opportunity to push the shot and get a more extreme perspective on the battle. The footage I got is spectacular. I'm so grateful he followed my instructions to the letter."

Archer didn't know if his jaw or Prescott's fell open farther. What the hell was she doing? He didn't need her to take the fall for him like this. Steve wouldn't actually fire him. After all, he was here at Steve's request to help the guy with an urgent problem. And Steve couldn't fire her. She wasn't in his chain of command. She worked for the director of photography, not the stunt crew.

Glaring at her, Archer bit out, "I take full responsibility for going off our flight plan and off course, sir. She had nothing to do with…"

Marley interrupted, "If Mr. Turnow doesn't love the footage we got, *I'll* take full responsibility for it."

Prescott looked back and forth between the two of them suspiciously. Archer knew better than most just how smart a man Steve Prescott was. And the guy smelled a rat. He thought Marley Stringer *was* behind the near-crash.

Thing was, he wasn't about to talk openly with Steve about the mechanical failure in front of her. For now, his hands were tied. They had to fake out Marley and pretend the flight control failure wasn't out of the ordinary. That no one was thinking about sabotage.

"Archer, if you ever pull a crazy stunt like that again, regardless of what your camera operator asks you to do, I'll fire you so fast your head spins. You got that?"

Wow. Steve had really mastered that whole quiet, menacingly restrained thing since the last time they'd been together. In his younger days, Steve would have yelled his head off. Archer sincerely hoped Marley was taking note and figuring out that now would be a good time to lie low for a while and cut out the shenanigans.

The ex-Marine growled, "Get out of my office. I'll take this up with Adrian. He can decide what to do with you two mavericks."

Marley opened her mouth to say something—whether an apology or more arguments on his behalf, Archer couldn't tell. But he recognized all too well the tight set of Steve's jaw. It was time to make like the wind and blow. He gripped Marley by the elbow and hustled her out of Prescott's office in spite of her protests.

He hauled her all the way out of the hangar and out of their boss's earshot before turning her loose and demanding, "Why did you leap to my defense and not tell him what really happened? What the hell was that?"

"That was me saving your ass," she snapped.

"But— Why?" If she was the saboteur, why didn't she let him take the hit for not finding the flight control problem before they took off? Wouldn't it hurt the movie more to have a highly experienced pilot like him get fired? If she wasn't the saboteur, he'd nearly *killed* her, for God's sake.

One thing he did know, she'd been legitimately scared to death up there. He might have called her bluff, and she might have called his, but she understood full well just how close they'd both come to dying today.

"Give me just one reason why you covered my ass like that," he demanded.

"I have no idea why I did it." She gazed up at him, and she did, in fact, look genuinely perplexed. Almost as perplexed as he was. He shoved a hand through his short hair.

"The footage I shot really is phenomenal," she offered. "Adrian Turnow's going to go nuts over it. It's one of a kind."

"For good reason. No rational pilot would ever do what we did today."

"What happened up there?"

Right. Like he was going to talk with her about it. No way was he giving her the satisfaction of watching the aftereffects of her handiwork. He was not going to admit that she'd scared the bejeebers out of him, or that he was now genuinely worried about the future of this movie. Was she a nut ball operating alone? Or was she working for someone who'd hired her to do this? "No clue what happened, babe."

"Oh."

*Yeah. Oh.* "Hey, I've got to put Minerva to bed. After I'm done buttoning her up, though, do you want to get a beer or something? I could meet you back at the motel in a few hours."

He could already see it coming now. Steve's next assignment for him was going to be to get close to Marley. Win her trust. Hell, maybe even to convince her he was hot for her. Not that something like that would be too much of a stretch for him. She really was an attractive woman. But he couldn't take her to bed for a little out-of-school pillow talk. Even he had his limits. He would have to find another way to make her talk.

He was startled out of his grim thoughts by her unsure answer to his invitation. "A beer? Um. I guess so. Yeah. Sure."

She was cute when she got flustered. "Great," he replied, a little startled to realize he really meant it. She was about as far from his usual type as a girl could get. And yet, there was something about her…

\* \* \*

Marley watched Archer stride away. She figured she'd earned the right to admire the hot ass she'd just saved. Truth be told, she wasn't that worried about the director's reaction to their unscheduled filming. Turnow was going to love the footage she'd shot, or she wasn't half the photographer she thought she was, and he wasn't half the visionary everyone said he was.

"That man has one fine caboose."

She looked up sharply at the tall, lean, African-American man who'd stopped beside her to ogle Archer. "Hi. I'm Marley. Camerawoman."

"Tyrone. Makeup. Damn, girl, you got good taste. Everyone on the crew's talking about the new, hot-stick helicopter pilot. Did I hear him invite you out for drinks?"

"It's just a beer. A guy like him would never be really interested in a girl like me."

The makeup artist threw her a withering glare. "Why the hell not?"

"Look at me. I'm as plain as mud and he's…he's… godlike."

Tyrone studied her critically. Reached out to grasp her chin and turn her face side to side. "Good bones. Great skin. Best features are your sweet eyes and those divine lips. With a little Tyrone magic, you'd be pretty smokin' hot, yourself. You've got a Marilyn Monroe quality to you."

She didn't know whether to laugh aloud or snort in disbelief. She settled for asking, "Are you high?"

"Did you just diss my artistic mojo?"

She wrinkled her nose. "C'mon. A guy like him would go for one of the lead actresses. Or a high-fashion model. Someone sexy and spectacular."

"You ain't never gonna be tall enough for the runway, sweetie. But you could definitely give any model a run for her money in the sexy-thang department. My room—number 208. Six o'clock. Be there." With a snap of his fingers, the makeup artist turned and strode away.

Was Tyrone right? Did she maybe have a shot at Archer, after all? But then reality slammed back into her. She was a cat-lady-in-training. She wore baggy sweatpants and played computer games in her free time. Every guy she knew thought of her as a little-sister surrogate. She had no social life, heck, no social skills. She watched life through her cameras, she didn't actually live it.

Mina was the adventurous sister. The one who grabbed life by the horns and wrestled it into submission—for better or worse. As for her, she was the...other...sister, as quiet as Mina was loud, as shy as Mina was brash.

A psychologist would probably have a field day analyzing her and Mina. He would probably say she was compensating for her out-of-control sibling.

Marley shrugged. After all her bad luck with guys, she was seriously starting to wonder if *she* was the sister with something wrong going on.

Six o'clock came and went, and she sat on the bed in her motel room, morosely munching on chocolate-covered raisins. The crew would be gathering at the buffet downstairs to eat dinner—the production company had rented out the entire motel for the next two months—and then most of them would adjourn to the motel's sports bar. It was the only drinking hole in this godforsaken corner of nowhere. Only the folks with early showtimes or those handling explosives would skip what had become the daily happy-hour routine.

No way did she need Archer buying her a beer in front of the whole crew. They would rib her about it forever, and there was no need to embarrass him, either. With her luck, he'd keel over dead from an aneurism as soon as she got near him.

No, she would just stay in her room. Some hot actress would move in on him this evening, and by tomorrow he'd have forgotten his offer. It was for the best this way.

Angry pounding exploded against her door and she leaped about a foot straight up in the air. "Girl, you in there? Open up, you scrawny little white-meat chicken!"

*Tyrone.* Crap.

"Tell me again why you think this girl is your saboteur?" Archer asked Steve skeptically.

"Our security guys have gone over the footage from the security cameras. Every single time there's an accident, she was seen immediately before the accident in the exact place the sabotage occurs. What are the odds that it's a coincidence six—no, seven times now, if you count your helicopter today?"

Archer frowned. It just didn't feel right. She was pleasant, struck him as a little naive, if anything, and didn't seem to be the type to be hiding a thing. Either he was right, or she was one *hell* of an actress.

"What about someone high up in the movie's production? If this film shuts down, the insurance company would have to make a hefty payout to the producers. Isn't Adrian Turnow the executive producer on this project?"

Steve frowned. "He doesn't strike me as the type."

"What? And this girl strikes you as a vicious saboteur? Have you done a background check on Turnow?

Or Marley for that matter? Found anything that would explain why either of them would do all this stuff?"

"She's got a juvie record," Steve replied.

"What did she do?"

"No idea. It's sealed."

Archer shrugged. "I've got a sealed juvie record. After Mom died, I had a pretty wild stretch there for a few months."

Steve pulled a face. "Yeah, I remember, little brother. I did everything I could to straighten you out."

"Is that what you called pounding on me like your own personal punching bag?"

"We all had anger issues to work out."

"You just figured out yours faster than the rest of us."

His brother snorted. "Nah. I was just told by a justice of the peace to join the Marines or go to jail sooner than the rest of you."

"Yeah, well, Shyanne and Lyra turned out okay." Not that his younger sisters didn't still drive him crazy, of course.

"They were too little when Mom died to be messed up by her choosing drugs over her own kids."

Archer didn't want to talk about his mother. He'd put her in a mental drawer and slammed it shut a long, long time ago. Locked it and thrown away the key, too.

Had his grandmother not taken in the five young Prescott children, there was no telling how badly they all would have turned out. As it was, with the help of her fierce love, they'd all gotten their lives together. The oldest Prescott, Jackson, was a movie star and part owner of the studio producing this movie. Brother number two, Steve, was a retired Marine officer and stunt coordinator in the movie business now.

In an effort to get out from under Steve's long

shadow, Archer had joined the Army and become a search-and-rescue pilot. It satisfied his need for reckless living. Channeled his wilder impulses into a profession where they were an asset and not a problem. Hell, somewhere along the way, he'd grown up, too.

Archer took a pull from the cold beer Steve had served him. "Okay, so she's got a past. That doesn't necessarily make her our saboteur."

Steve commented, "I've got a guy looking into peeking into that sealed record. I want to know if she has a violent past or not."

Archer had a very hard time picturing sweet, innocent-seeming Marley Stringer hurting a fly, let alone another human being.

"Are you interested in this girl?" Steve demanded.

"No!" he lied.

"Then why are you defending her so damned hard?"

"Hey, bro. I'm not defending her. I'm just not declaring her guilty and convicting her in my mind before I hear her side of the story."

Steve stared at him long and hard. "You willing to make a run at gaining her trust?"

Ha. Steve *did* want him to get close to her and see what he could learn about her. "You want me to sleep with her and get her to pillow-talk with me?"

"Jeez, no. I just meant you should make friends with her. Put yourself in a position to keep a close eye on her. But I need you to take a suspicious mind-set into the project. Keep your head in the game. This girl could not only be dangerous, but *very* dangerous."

"How about I agree to keep an open mind about her guilt or innocence?"

"Fine. Just keep your zipper closed, eh?"

Archer raised his beer bottle to his brother. "I dunno, dude. She's not a horrible-looking girl."

"This is important, Archer. Serendipity Studios is a young company, and they've invested a crap-ton of money in this movie. If it fails, the studio could go under. We've got to find out who's screwing with this film. And fast."

"Yeah, yeah. I got it. She's not as innocent as she seems, and we've got to nail her if she's behind the accidents."

Marley threw open her door, indignant, to admit Tyrone. "Who are you calling chicken? I about died today, I'll have you know, and I didn't even pee my pants!"

The makeup artist was pulling a rolling suitcase behind him and barged into her room without invitation. "Sit your butt down on that chair, and don't give me sass. And get that nasty sweatshirt off. Put on the shirt you're gonna wear on your date so you don't smear my art."

Overwhelmed and out-attituded, she headed for her closet. And froze. What to wear? "It's not a date," she mumbled as she stared at her horrible clothes.

Tyrone peered into the closet over her shoulder and, tsking, eventually pulled out a simple white, oxford button-down blouse. "Here. Wear this. I've got a scarf that'll make it less dreadful."

She went into her bathroom and slipped on the shirt. She peered at herself in the mirror, and a plain, mousy, faintly academic woman stared back at her. *This was crazy.* Archer would never give her the time of day, let alone seriously consider dating her. Who would ever be interested in that unexciting girl in the mirror? She emerged reluctantly, only because she was convinced

Tyrone would bust down the door and drag her out if she didn't come out voluntarily.

"Sit. Close your eyes and no talking. I'm an *artiste* and I need to concentrate on my work," he announced.

Never in her life had anyone applied makeup to her, and it was a strange sensation. Tyrone sprayed some sort of defrizzer on her hair and put it up in hot rollers—a first for her—and kept up a running commentary under his breath, discussing with himself how not to overwhelm her fragile coloring, how to pull together the gold tones in her hair with the pink tones in her skin and how best to highlight her eyes. It must have taken him close to an hour to finally be satisfied with his work. He alarmed her mightily for most of the last half of it with his patter about channeling Marilyn Monroe, how Marley was a retro flashback to fifties pinup girls and the possibility of her being the reincarnation of the sexiest woman in movie history.

Marley tried to get a word in edgewise and make an argument for Elizabeth Taylor as the sexiest actress ever, but Tyrone silenced her so he could outline her lips with an outrageously red liner pencil. The man did not fight fair.

Finally, he announced, "There. Done. Observe my masterpiece."

Marley opened her eyes and looked in the mirror.

*Who. Was. That?*

She stared at the stranger before her in complete incomprehension. Tyrone wasn't kidding. She *did* look like Marilyn Monroe. Her blond hair fell in the same soft waves around her face, and with that dramatic eyeliner, light eye shadow and scarlet lipstick, she totally looked like a poster child for the 1950s. There really was something of the wide-eyed, sex-kitten innocence of Marilyn Monroe about her. Freaky. She even had dimples like the movie icon.

She gestured a hand at her reflection and declared in shock, "But I don't look like that."

"Girl, I didn't transplant a new face onto you. That's you. All I did was decorate your assets."

"But…"

"But you look fantastic. Get over it. I'll teach you how to do it for yourself, and then you can always look like this."

Her entire being cringed at the idea of walking around looking like a sexpot all the time. Mina did that. Not her. Although Mina went more for the leather-and-lace look.

Everyone—okay, *men*—would pay far too much attention to her like this. Attention that made her acutely uncomfortable, thank you very much. Because…well, because of the whole virginity thing. But a little voice at the back of her head whispered that it had nothing to do with her virginity. Her dirty little secret was that she wasn't even the least bit interesting or lovable.

"Now put on the shortest skirt you've got and go get you that flyboy. If you don't have screaming-hot sex with that man tonight, I'm going to be deeply disappointed."

The idea of screaming-hot sex with Archer sent her brain into blank, blue-screen-of-doom overload.

Was it possible? Could she once and for all ditch her damned virginity and shut up that nasty little voice in her head? Goodness knew, Archer was the hottest prospect for doing the deed that she'd ever run across. Much hotter than she'd dared hope for, truth be told.

All she managed to get out in response to Tyrone was, "I don't own a miniskirt."

He just shook his head. "Me and some of the girls are taking you shopping the minute we get back to LA. Jeans, then. You got any tight ones?"

Actually, she did. When she was sitting on a camera boom, she couldn't afford to catch her clothing on the lift or wiring. While she rooted around in a drawer for a pair of clean jeggings, Tyrone rooted around in her closet. She pulled on her pants, and he held out a pair of slouchy ankle boots to her.

"We're getting you some proper heels when we get back to L.A., too," Tyrone announced as she stomped into the soft leather boots. He looped a narrow, sparkly scarf casually around her neck and stepped back to survey his work. "Mmm-hmm, now we're talkin'," he declared, wagging his chin and wearing a *bitch, please* face.

"Okay, Marilyn. Go have yourself the mother of all hot flings."

# Chapter 3

Marley stood outside the motel's bar listening to the raucous shouting inside. A professional football game was on the big screens and, judging by the catcalls and booing, an unpopular call had just been made by the officials.

"Do I have to go in?" she wailed under her breath at Tyrone. The makeup artist had insisted on escorting her downstairs to see Flyboy's reaction to her grand transformation. Which meant she couldn't make a run for it. Genuine panic clawed at her throat. Damn Tyrone, anyway.

"Go on. He won't bite you...or maybe he will...you lucky bitch."

With a last glare at Tyrone for making her go through with this, she took a deep breath, waited until another shout went up and slipped into the dark bar. It was crowded and she eased around the edges of the mob to wedge herself into the darkest corner she could find and bellied up to the bar.

Please let no one see her in this clown makeup. Please let them not laugh their heads off at her bad Marilyn impersonation. Please let her become invisible in the next ten seconds. A flashback to the one and only time she'd tried to doll herself up in high school and had been laughed out of the dance in about two minutes flat came back to her in all its humiliating detail.

Film crews were notoriously quick to pick on one another, particularly on the new kid on the block. Mean girls in the ninth grade had nothing on a bunch of stuntmen, lighting techs and grips. She'd been crazy to think this might be the place where she finally got to experience sex. *Please let no one laugh at me. Please let them just ignore me.*

It took her about two seconds to pick out Archer's tall, perfect profile. No surprise, he was surrounded by a bunch of fawning women, most of whom Marley recognized as actresses. Her heart sank. She could never compete with those beautiful, bold women flirting so openly with him. Archer didn't look too heartbroken at their attention, either. Not that Marley blamed him. Why wouldn't he go after the gorgeous girls?

Relief actually coursed through her. She was off the hook. She could slide back into her safe anonymity and not put herself and her fragile heart on the line tonight.

But that darned little voice was at it again. This time it whispered in disappointment. *If not now, when are you ever going to break out of your plain, boring shell?* She ordered it to shut up and pulled her shell a little more tightly around herself.

Glumly, she ordered a soft drink on ice. The bartender took pity and stuck an umbrella in her glass to disguise her wimpiness. Marley had never been drunk and didn't plan to do *that* for the first time in front of her coworkers, either.

She might look a little like Marilyn Monroe, but she completely lacked the sex symbol's innate hots. The essence of what had made Marilyn who she was had been that effortless heat she'd exuded. Men just looked at her and lusted after her. No one would ever react to Marley Stringer, rookie camerawoman, like that.

A couple of guys she'd never seen before drifted over and introduced themselves—a prop guy and a pair of set constructors. She mangled small talk badly enough with them that they drifted away before long. See? No sex appeal whatsoever. She was the anti-Marilyn.

Heck, even that much attention from strange men had been intensely uncomfortable for her. How in the hell was she ever going to have sex if she couldn't get over this stupid shyness? Were it not for Tyrone throwing her encouraging looks and glares by turn from his table a few yards away with the other makeup artists, she'd have bolted already.

Adrian Turnow appeared in the bar entrance and a shout of greeting went up to him. He was an interesting man. Brilliant eye for visual art. Bit of a loner himself. When she'd met him briefly a few weeks ago, he'd put her at ease more than anyone else on the crew. She sipped idly at her soda as he advanced into the room, looking around for someone.

She was startled when he made eye contact with her and even more startled when he did a hard double take. She looked down quickly, fiddling with her drink's lime-green umbrella. How much longer until she could slip out of here without Tyrone dragging her back in?

"Marley?"

She looked up, startled. "Uh, hi, Mr. Turnow."

"I had no idea you look so much like Marilyn Monroe."

"One of the makeup artists was fooling around and tried the look on me."

"It works. Very cinematic. You should stick with it."

Um, okay. Did major film directors all talk makeup with their crew members?

He continued. "I just wanted to tell you that the footage you shot today was incredible. Best stuff I've seen in years. You've got a real future in this business. Gordon Trapowski was spot-on to recommend you to me."

*Gordon* had recommended her for this gig? She did not know that. Color her shocked.

She'd only met him once before she started flying with him on this movie shoot. He'd flown her in his chopper as a freelance pilot a few months back so she could film a big fire back at the local news station. He'd made a half-hearted pass at her but had backed off when she mentioned all her dates coming to disastrous ends.

He must have been impressed enough with her work to recommend her to a hotshot film director. Rumor had it Gordon came from old film industry money but that his family had fallen on hard times. That must be how he knew Adrian.

Speaking of which, the director was talking to her. "...you keep bringing in footage like today's, I can't justify yelling at you too hard. Still, in the future, I expect you to follow my instructions. If you have an idea for shooting something differently, tell me in advance and we'll talk it over."

"I promise it won't happen again."

"It took *cajones* to pull a stunt like that on your first shoot. Good job, Miss Stringer."

The director moved away, and she could only stare in shock at his shaved head retreating across the bar.

"Are you okay?" a voice asked from beside her. A concerned *male* voice with a familiar, husky timbre.

*Archer.*

Hovering protectively over her, looking grim. "He didn't fire you, did he?"

"No. He told me he loved the film we shot."

She fully turned to face Archer, and he inhaled sharply. "What the hell happened to you?"

*Oh, God.* She *did* look like a clown. Distress slammed into her. "Do I look ridiculous? I knew I shouldn't have let Tyrone play around with my makeup."

A big, warm hand came to rest on top of hers. "You're fine. Better than fine." Then he added a little menacingly, "Who's Tyrone?"

"He's one of the makeup artists," she explained hastily. "This retro thing was his idea."

"You look unbelievable."

"Unbelievably good or unbelievably bad?"

Archer smiled and leaned in close enough that she caught a whiff of his cologne. It was as sexy, masculine and designer-cool as the rest of him. "Trust me. It's good. I just didn't expect you to be such a chameleon. You look really different."

Her breath fluttered nervously as she ventured a peek his way. Lordy, that man was easy on the eye. Smooth talker, too.

"So tell me, Marley. Do you have any acting experience?"

"God, no." She stirred the ice cubes in her drink around with her little umbrella. "Why do you ask?"

"That's quite a transformation you've undergone in a very short time. I was just curious."

She had no idea how to answer that. If she wasn't mistaken, she heard a note of something strange in his voice. Almost like the suspicion from earlier.

"Hey, Archer. Who's the hot chick?"

Marley looked up sharply at a burly guy with enormous biceps. Gordon Trapowski. He'd been her regular pilot on the movie shoot until Archer, today.

"Holy moly. Is that you, Marley?" Gordon exclaimed. "Day-umm, you clean up good."

She supposed she ought to be complimented by the blatant shock on the guy's half-drunk face. But it did make her wonder a little just how awful she'd looked before this makeover.

"You should stay away from this guy, Marley," Archer warned under his breath. "Especially when he's been drinking."

"This sissy boy feeding you a line of bull?" Gordon retorted belligerently. He did, indeed, smell like a few too many whiskey shooters and Marley didn't like the truculent glint in his eye. He looked like he was spoiling for a fight.

"Archie tellin' you all about how he's a glorified delivery boy? Lying about being a real warrior?"

"I've seen more combat than you ever will, Trap," Archer commented casually.

Gordon made a rude gesture to show what he thought of that. The temperature between the men cooled off a few more chilly degrees. No love lost between these two. "You say the word, and I'll take care of 'im for you." Gordon's words were just slurred enough to send chills down her spine.

"Archer's not bothering me," she said nervously.

"Yeah, well, he's bothering me," Gordon declared. He shoved Archer's shoulder roughly. "Go back to them skinny actresses who're too snooty to talk to the rest of the crew."

*Crap, crap, crap.* Marley held her breath in panic. She *so* didn't need to end up in the middle of a bar fight. She *hated* violence. She hated confrontation in all forms, for that matter. This was all her fault. Her damned jinx was going to get Archer killed in a bar fight. She said frantically, "Really, it's okay, Gordon. We were just talking about work stuff."

For his part, Archer had gone silent. And deadly. He'd turned into a panther, waiting, ready to strike, right there beside her. Dark eyes narrowed, he followed every move the bigger man was making with lethal intensity. How on earth was Gordon missing the threat?

"I don't want a scene, Trap," Archer said low and even. "You don't want to upset the lady, do you?"

It wasn't a stretch for her to look completely freaked out as the big man stared hard at her as though multiple images of her were swimming in his bleary gaze. A shout went up as one of the teams on the big screens scored a touchdown, and it seemed to momentarily distract him.

She looked around in panic for help. Gordon was going to break Archer in half. The motel didn't employ a bouncer that she could see, and the bartender was not much taller than she was and probably didn't top a hundred and forty pounds soaking wet. *Crap.*

But then she spied Steve Prescott across the bar. He looked like the kind of guy who could handle himself in a fight. And he was the boss. If anyone could diffuse a brewing brawl, it would be him.

Gordon stepped up to Archer and literally chest-bumped him. Archer took a casual step back, smiling slightly. "That all you got, Trap?"

She hopped off her stool and headed for Prescott as fast as the crowded space would let her. Visions of Archer's head cracked in half and him lying unconscious on the floor in a pool of blood spurred her to shove rudely past a half dozen crew members.

Finally, Steve Prescott loomed in front of her. *Thank God.* "Mr. Prescott," she gasped. "Gordon Trapowski's trying to pick a fight with Archer. You have to stop him. He'll kill Archer."

"Trap and Archer, you say?" the big Marine asked casually. "You've got that backward. Archer will kill Trapowski."

"You have to stop them!" She laid a beseeching hand on his arm.

"I'll mosey on over and have a word with them if it's this upsetting to you. But, Miss Stringer—that's right, isn't it? And you look nice, by the way—Archer knows how to avoid a fight, and he can sure as hell handle himself if he ends up in one."

Prescott started across the bar, sauntering far too casually for her, and she followed nervously in his broad-shouldered wake to where Gordon was snarling, and Archer looked as unperturbed as before. But that air of cold menace clung to him even more strongly.

"How we doing, fellas?" Steve asked lightly as he bellied up to the bar between them.

"Fine," Archer answered casually. "You?"

"Good, thanks."

"Buy you a beer?" Archer offered.

"Sure," Prescott replied.

"Want one, Gordon?" Archer added.

"I'm gonna break your head in two, you arrogant sonofabitch," Gordon snarled.

"Power down, Trap," Prescott said mildly.

"Damned Prescotts," the big man muttered under his breath. "You think you own the whole damned world." He might be drunk, but he seemed to have enough sense left not to slug his boss. Trapowski shoved away from the bar and stomped off into the crowd, still muttering.

"He's not done, Arch."

"I'll watch my six."

"I've got your back."

"Thanks."

"Anytime." Prescott picked up his beer and strolled away.

Marley had no idea what had just transpired, but as quickly as the ugly confrontation had blown up, it had settled down. For now.

"What was that all about?" she asked Archer.

"Just Gordon being Gordon."

"That's some temper he's got."

"Trap and whiskey don't mix," Archer commented. "Didn't want to get into a fight over you before I had a chance to buy you that beer I promised you."

Was *that* what the two men had been snarling over? Two dogs fighting over a bone? Or, more accurately, her? The notion wouldn't compute. Men did not fight over her. Especially not hot ones. Not that Gordon was her type at all. He was too burly. Too gruff. Too rough around the edges.

"Bartender, a beer for me and another one of what the lady's having for her."

"A beer and a soda coming up," the guy replied.

"A soda?" Archer looked amused. "Let me guess. You've never had a real drink."

"I have so," she replied defensively. "I just don't want to get drunk in front of my coworkers."

"Fair enough. Let's go."

"I beg your pardon?"

"C'mon. Let's get out of here. I'll take you somewhere you can have a drink in peace without these jokers crawling all over you." He looped a protective arm around her waist and drew her close to his side. His muscular, hard, totally sexy side. He guided her toward the exit and she happened to catch Tyrone grinning like he'd just won the lottery. Okay, she owed the guy one. But then the makeup artist pointed at her and mouthed, *Screaming-hot sex.*

*If only.* But in the tight gossip mill of a movie set, and with the demigod of sexiness that was Archer? And *her*? So not happening.

Archer led her outside to a big, brand-new-looking, extended-cab pickup truck. He opened the passenger door and helped her up into the seat as he had with Minerva, only this time he let her fasten her own seat belt.

A rush of excitement took her by surprise as he closed the truck door behind her. Omigod, she was in a truck with a cute guy, driving off somewhere private to drink beer and do who knew what. In high school, she'd imagined a date like this almost every Friday night she could remember. But she'd been the shy girl the boys never looked at and the cool kids didn't even bother to scoff at.

Her rotten luck with boys had squelched the few attempts she'd made at socializing—she'd literally fallen on her face the first time she tried to talk to a cute boy. She'd broken her nose and given herself two massive black eyes in the process. But who in the hell put a foot-high brick wall right next to a sidewalk like that, anyway?

The only reason she hadn't been laughed entirely out of high school was because she'd been the yearbook photographer, camera always plastered to her face, at every school event, but never participating. In some ways, her camera had been her shield against being a social outcast. It had made her merely invisible instead of embarrassingly boring.

Film school had been better. All the students there were artists, creatives who'd never fit in elsewhere. She'd figured out fast, though, that the television and film industries were fiercely competitive, and if she wanted to get work upon graduation, she needed to spend every waking minute perfecting her craft.

The jinx had asserted itself more strongly there, though. At first, she'd put it down to bad luck or just bad taste in guys. But after a while, mishap after dating mishap started to mess with her head. She'd researched jinxes on the internet…and read way too many articles about fathers who never gave their daughters approval—Lord knew hers had barely noticed her existence, let alone taken time to tell her she was beautiful or a princess. Whatever.

Ultimately, she'd stopped trying to date in film school. It had been easier and safer to cast herself as the sister-confessor type. Not datable material, but a great sympathy and advice giver. Professional jealousy had kicked in among her classmates as graduation neared, though, and even her little-sister shtick had worn thin. She'd given up on having any social life at all and just concentrated on her classes.

Her focus on learning had paid off, too. She'd gotten work filming at a local news station when most of her classmates went into the exciting world of fast-food preparation and sales. And hey, her life wasn't all bad. She had a really cool career in a field she loved. There was more to life than sex. Right? So what if she'd never made out with a guy and steamed up the windows of his car.

"Why so quiet over there?" Archer asked, startling her. He turned on the ignition and a snazzy electronic dashboard lit up.

She smiled mentally. His truck looked at least as high-tech as Minerva, and obviously had all the very latest bells and whistles. "I was just thinking."

"About what?"

"Making out and steaming up the windows."

He glanced over at her, looking distinctly startled. And disappointed, if she was reading him correctly. "Direct, much?" he murmured. "I pegged you for the type who would let the guy make the first move. Silly me."

Her cheeks heated up. Good thing the dashboard was already casting hellish red light up at her face. "Sorry. That came out wrong."

"I thought it came out just fine."

She gulped. Yeah, but she wasn't necessarily prepared to follow up on her inadvertent proposition. It was one thing to wish to get rid of her incredibly inconvenient virginity. It was another thing altogether to do the deed.

"I probably ought to warn you that I don't have very good luck with guys."

He glanced over at her sharply. "Why not?"

"They tend to, um, have accidents." She added in an embarrassed rush, "I think I may be jinxed."

"Good thing for you I don't believe in magic, then."

"I'm serious, Archer."

"So am I." He turned the truck off at a scenic overlook, and she was surprised to see the film set sprawling under huge banks of work lights in the valley below. "What are they building?" she asked curiously.

"Fake city. Adrian's going to blow it up day after tomorrow."

She looked over at him sharply. "Are we going to have to fly over it and film the explosion?"

"That's the plan." His voice was clipped, but otherwise emotionless. Still, she thought she felt tension emanating from him.

"Tell me about your job."

"You've seen my job. I fly camerawomen over movie sets."

"The way I hear it, you were a military pilot in a former life."

"Where did you hear that?"

She'd heard it from Tyrone, who'd been a veritable fountain of information and gossip earlier while he'd been doing her makeup. She shrugged at Archer. "You know how movie sets are. Everybody knows everything about everyone."

"Lord, I hope not," he muttered fervently.

She chuckled in commiseration.

He reached behind the seat and emerged with a six-pack of brown longnecks in a cardboard carrier. He opened one and held it out to her. "I did promise you a beer."

She reached out to take it and her fingers wrapped over his. *Strength. Heat. All man.* An image of her body entwined with his the way their fingers were right now blazed across her brain. Skin on skin. Naked bodies tightly pressed together. Lust and sweat and—*holy cow.* She let go abruptly. He lifted the beer higher and she grasped the bottle below his hand. God, she was such a klutz. A freaking horny one.

"I'm a search-and-rescue guy."

"Which means what?" She was a total civilian. She knew zilch about the military. Sure, she got that he searched for people and rescued them, but she had no idea what that entailed.

"SR pilots insert troops into hot zones and extract them when they're done. Sometimes they deliver urgent supplies, or fly generals to their golf games. It's a little of this and that."

"Do people usually let you get away with baloney answers like that?"

He grinned around the mouth of his bottle and finished taking a pull on his beer. "Yeah, actually. They do."

"Maybe they haven't flown with you recently. I've never seen anyone come that close to dying and be so completely unaffected by it afterward. Did you come that close to dying all the time in your military work?"

His face went tight. Closed. Even so, he was beautiful to look at, but the stress around his eyes was palpable.

He spoke tightly. "I wasn't unaffected by today. That was a hell of a serious mechanical malfunction we had. You and I both came damned close to dying. And no, I don't usually flirt with death quite that intimately. Sure, missions go bad from time to time. It's the nature of flying in war zones. But I've always done my damnedest not to endanger myself, my crew, my passengers or my bird, if I can possibly help it."

"Tell me about the scariest mission you've ever had."

If possible, his face went even more tightly closed against her. "I'd rather not."

"Fair enough. How about this? Rate today's flight on a scale of one to ten in how scary it was to you."

"Pilots don't think in terms of being scared. We are trained to believe we can fix any problem, survive an emergency, save any plane. I'm too busy doing my job when something like today's mishap occurs to be afraid."

"Not even after it's all over?"

He grinned. "Ahh, well, that's different. Then we go out with the prettiest girl we can find, get a little drunk and celebrate still being alive."

"There were a whole bunch of girls in that bar prettier than me, Archer Archer," she declared.

He grinned broadly. "Yeah, but I figured that after your scare today, you needed to get a little drunk and celebrate being alive, too."

No kidding. "Thanks. It was kind of you to think of me."

He shrugged. "It's no big deal."

Hah. It might be no big deal to him, but it was a huge deal to her. "Do pilots ever talk to people after they have a really close call? I've seen a lot of stuff in the news about post-traumatic stress disorders. Do pilots get that?"

He snorted. "Hell, yeah, pilots get PTSD."

"After a near-miss like today, is that the sort of thing you should talk to someone about before you fly again?" Oh, Lord. She was already back to doing the shoulder-to-cry-on thing. Would she never learn to shut the hell up?

"I'm talking to you." And he looked none too happy about it, either.

She rolled her eyes. "I mean a counselor or someone professional."

"A shrink?" He sounded genuinely horrified. "Not if I want to keep my pilot's license."

"I don't understand."

"Any pilot who goes to see a shrink is automatically grounded. And it's a bitch to get your ticket back from the FAA once it's been pulled. You have to jump through all sorts of hoops. Pain in the ass."

"What's the FAA?"

"Federal Aviation Administration. Regulates all flying in America and by American pilots."

"It doesn't make sense that they would prevent you from talking out your fears. Wouldn't the FAA want pilots talking to counselors if they need to? Why wouldn't they make it easy for you to do it?"

He shrugged. "Government bureaucracy. Just the way it is."

"Well, it's dumb."

"Amen." He reached over to clink his beer bottle against hers.

This was nice. Just sitting and talking with him. Maybe Tyrone had the right idea, after all. Maybe she should go for the mother of all flings with this guy. God knew, she was more than ready to be rid of her stupid virginity. He seemed pretty coordinated and not inclined to eating tainted shellfish.

He leaned across her to adjust an air vent to blow warm air at her side window, and she gasped as his sleeve whisked across her thighs. Her hips wanted to rise to meet his forearm against her jeggings, and her pulse leaped as his palm skimmed across her knees on its way back to his side of the car. "There. Now your window won't steam up no matter what we do in here."

*No matter what—omigosh.* Excitement and panic wrestled for supremacy in her tummy. "Do you like flying?" she asked breathlessly.

"Love it. I thought for a long time that I wanted to go

fixed-wing and fly fighters—Mach two with my hair on fire shooting stuff down. But then I got a ride in a helicopter and was hooked. I loved being down in the weeds where the action was. And all the fighter jets are going to end up being drones flown by remote control before too much longer, anyway. Me, I get to work directly with the guys I support. I can change and adapt what I'm doing in the blink of an eye depending on conditions on the ground. I never know what's going to happen next. It's a hell of a rush..."

He broke off as if he was a little embarrassed by his burst of enthusiasm. Personally, she thought his passion was sexy as hell.

"So you're an adrenaline junkie?" Maybe that explained the wild way he'd flown.

He gestured at her with his beer. "Like you aren't? Job like yours has to have some pretty crazy moments."

Yeah. Like when frozen-up flight controls nearly got her smashed into the side of a mountain. "This is my first movie shoot. I'll let you know how wild it gets."

"What did you do before this?"

"I was the overnight camera operator at a local news station. If breaking news came in, the on-call anchor and I would come in and do a special report. And I filmed the early-morning news. You know, the stuff at 5:00 a.m. that nobody watches."

"Except for the occasional blooper that goes viral?"

She grinned. "Exactly. And 5:00 a.m. weather girls in Podunksville aren't exactly the cream of the meteorological crop."

"What's your favorite part of your job?"

That was a no-brainer. "Capturing real emotions in a way that makes viewers experience them, too."

He studied her speculatively. "Spoken like a true photographer."

"How about you? What's your favorite thing about your job?"

He answered promptly and with a broad grin. "The hot groupie chicks."

She rolled her eyes. "How do you ever get a date with an attitude like that?"

Archer stared at her in what looked like genuine surprise. She supposed he didn't often have to resort to sparkling conversation to get women into his bed. He merely had to turn those bedroom eyes and mega-watt smile on them. "I got a date with you, didn't I?"

It was her turn to stare at him. "If this is a date, I have to warn you that your life is in grave danger. I've hospitalized no less than three guys on previous outings."

He looked startled. As well he should. But when he replied, his tone was light. "Honey, my mind boggles wondering what you did to put them in the hospital."

"I'm not kidding when I say I'm jinxed..." she started.

"There's no such thing as jinxes."

"Spend a little time around me. Stuff like today's problem on the helicopter will happen over and over. I'm just saying..."

"What kind of stuff?"

She shrugged. "All kinds of things. Little stuff mostly. But sometimes it's bigger stuff. Dangerous stuff. I used to think I was just a klutz. And I suppose that's part of it. But over time, I've come to realize it's more than that." She lowered her voice, confessing reluctantly, "Sometimes I wonder if I'm never supposed to be happy, and if that's why bad things keep happening around me."

"Stop talking like that," he bit out.

She blinked, shocked. "Like what?"

"Stop putting yourself down. You're beautiful. Smart. Funny. Gutsy. There's no reason you shouldn't be happy." He added forcefully, "None at all."

He thought she was all of those things? "It's okay, Archer. I know I'm not in your league. It's really nice of you to spend time with me like this, but you don't have to flatter me."

"What the hell are you talking about? I enjoy being with you. You surprise me. On top of all that, you're hot and make me think about sex."

Well, okay, then. He made her think about sex, too. A lot. She drank more of her tepid beer in search of a little liquid courage. If she was not mistaken, he'd just announced that he was amenable to a relationship with her. They'd have to be careful. Keep it secret. But that wasn't impossible. The little voice in the back of her head let out an excited *squee*.

"So tell me, Marley. Why'd you jump in this afternoon to save my hide with Prescott?"

"Why wouldn't I? I work with you, and I could get you off the hook with a few words. Wouldn't you do the same for your coworkers?"

"Depends on who we're talking about. Most guys, yeah. A guy like Gordon Trapowski...I might let him swing in the wind."

"Really?" she asked in disappointment. She'd thought better of him than that.

He made an exasperated noise. "No, I'd probably save even his double-wide ass." He finished his beer and tossed the bottle behind the seat. "I just didn't expect a civilian like you to understand why I'd do it."

"Are you saying I don't get the ethics of it because

people don't routinely shoot at me, or because I'm a girl? Answer carefully because I'd hate to have to break this bottle over your head."

He laughed aloud. "That's what I'm talking about. You surprise me. And for the record, don't ever try to break a bottle over my head. I'd hate to react reflexively and hurt you by accident."

Warmth coursed through her. She surprised him, huh? That could be the foundation of a beautiful one-night stand. "How long are you here for?"

He answered evasively, "As long as Steve needs me."

"I think we're supposed to be done filming in about four weeks," she replied.

He shrugged. "Stuff happens to extend shooting schedules. Bad weather, refilming shots."

Which she would duly commence praying for so she had more time to build a relationship with Archer. She would also pray that it ultimately led to sex. People had *no* idea how socially crippling it was to be a virgin at her age.

"So tell me, Archer. Did anyone figure out what happened to Minerva this afternoon? Why did she refuse to turn like that?"

He shrugged again. "Some sort of mechanical malfunction. A widget hung up on another widget, most likely. Apparently he mechanic didn't find anything wrong when he took a look at her."

He said that so damned casually. If she were a pilot, she would bloody well want to know exactly what had happened up there and why before she flew in that aircraft again. Heck, even if she *weren't* a pilot, she would want to know what happened before she rode in that helicopter again!

"It was just a one-time anomaly?" she asked.

"Guess so."

"And we're supposed to get back in that helicopter and fly in it like nothing ever happened?"

"Minerva behaved just fine all the way home. The maintenance guys wrote it up as a CND. And before you ask, that stands for Could Not Duplicate. The bane of pilots and mechanics. A one-off problem that never repeats itself."

"I can't believe you're just blowing it off like this."

"Honey, I'm not blowing off a thing. But stuff like what happened today is all part of taking machines built by human beings up into the air and going very high and very fast. Or, in our case today, very low and kind of fast."

She just shook her head. No way could she be as cavalier about nearly dying as he was. She wasn't at all used to men who were quite so sure of themselves.

What would it mean when it came time to sleep with him—jeez, she was pretty sure of herself all of a sudden. *If* she slept with him. She had to catch the fish before she could eat it.

"When do you have to show up for work tomorrow?" Archer asked.

"I've got an 8:00 a.m. call. We're shooting close-ups to go with today's footage. Since I have experience at fixed-camera facial stuff, I'm on deck for that."

"It's probably time to get you home, then. It's getting late." He reached for the ignition.

Mentally, she sighed. Note to self: the girl who was interesting to talk with didn't get kissed. Maybe if she had bored him to death, he'd have run out of other things to do up here and would have resorted to making out with her. She so *sucked* at this dating stuff.

The drive back to the outskirts of the tiny town of

Serendipity, California, only took a few minutes and he parked behind the motel. "What room are you in, Marley?"

"Room 305."

"I'll walk you up."

"You don't have to."

He came around the truck to open her door for her. "I know I don't have to. But my grandmother didn't raise a total heathen."

"You mean the human Minerva?"

He did an odd thing, then. It was as if his entire being shut down for a moment. Like she'd opened his soul to have a look around and some powerful emotion had tried to break out. Instead, he'd slammed the door shut on it. Hard. And now he was waiting to see if she poked again where she wasn't welcome.

She hadn't been everyone's little sister for nothing. She knew a raw nerve when she saw one and backed off immediately.

He opened the motel door and held it for her. She moved past him, and his hand touched the small of her back as he ushered her in. A shiver of delight rippled up and down her spine from the spot he'd made contact with her.

"Is your grandmother still alive?"

He did it again. Whatever emotion had wanted to escape him was rounded up, captured and stuffed back into its little box inside him. The guy was seriously repressing something. His voice was stripped of all emotion when he replied, "Alive and kicking. Doesn't mean we're on the best of terms at the moment, though. She's on this big kick for all of us to get married and start giving her great-grandchildren. None of us are keen on the idea except for one of my brothers, who's a damned overachiever. He and his fiancée are expecting a baby any day now."

"Uncle Archer. That has a nice ring to it."

He scowled and ushered her into the elevator. "I'm just glad she's lived long enough to see me get my wings and to know I didn't end up in jail."

"That was in some doubt?" she responded drily.

"For a while there, it looked highly probable."

"What turned you around?"

"The military," he answered without hesitating. "It provided the discipline and structure I needed and all that rot."

"All that rot" sounded like a highly charged topic that he also was suppressing hard. But who was she to judge? She figured everyone had crap in their past they'd just as soon not think about.

They reached her door and she fumbled at the lock with her key card, but tanned knuckles appeared on the door handle and blocked her attempt to finish unlocking her door. She looked up, startled.

"Thanks for spending this evening with me," he murmured in a low voice as rough as the stubble on his jaw. "I enjoyed it." And then, *omigod, omigod,* he touched her chin with his finger, tipped up her face and his lips touched hers.

She inhaled sharply and tasted the yeasty tang of beer. It was arguably the sexiest thing her tongue had ever experienced. His hand crept around behind her head to cup her neck as his mouth slanted across hers, deepening the kiss.

She leaned forward, breathless, for more. Her entire body swayed toward him like a magnet drawn to its natural pole. Finally. Kissed by a real man. The roughness of his jaw stubble and the silky softness of his hair passed under her fingers. The faint tang of sweat and the woodsy musk of his cologne went straight to her head and made it whirl. And his mouth. Holy smokes, his mouth. It was firm and smooth, wet and hot, and totally in command of her, body and soul.

Her mouth opened beneath his and he wasted no time tasting her, his tongue sliding seductively across her lips. Her sex throbbed so hard he might as well have been licking her there instead. She moaned in the back of her throat and he devoured the sound, sucking it out of her mouth and into himself greedily.

She surged up against him, bumping into him awkwardly. His arms tightened around her with effortless strength, steadying them both. He backed her against her door and her lust soared at being sandwiched between its cold wood and his hot steel.

Her right leg crept up around his hips and she shamelessly rubbed her female regions against the hard bulge of his male regions.

"Oh, baby," he groaned under his breath. "That feels so good."

He had *no* idea how good it felt to her. Liquid heat erupted in her core, making her standing leg so weak she had to throw her arms around his neck to stay upright. At least until he grabbed her rear end in both hands and lifted her entirely off the floor. Her left leg, that hungry wench, whipped around his waist, opening her completely to him. His hips rocked forward once, twice.

Shocks of pleasure ripped through her and she cried out into his mouth. "Yes. Yes," she gasped. "More."

"How much more?" he gritted out, his hips rocking more urgently now, his denim-covered erection driving her out of her freaking mind.

"All the way. Right now. Please."

He let go of her tush with one hand and fumbled for the door handle. Omigosh. This was really going to happen. She wanted to be with him so bad she could hardly see...

The elevator dinged and a spate of male voices erupted at the end of the hall as the doors slid open. Archer dropped her to her feet abruptly and she staggered, so disoriented she could barely stand upright.

He stepped back and smiled down at her ruefully. "Good night."

*Damndamndamndamndamn.* So. Damned. Close.

She mumbled something completely inane akin to "Hum-a-duh, hum-a-duh" before she finally managed to fumble around and get her door unlocked, then slip into her room. She closed the door and leaned against it, panting and cussing like mad until the building orgasm taunting her mercilessly finally drained away enough for her to stand unaided.

*Hot sex, thy name is Archer...and here I come.*

# *Chapter 4*

Archer observed sourly that, after Marley had shown up at the motel bar last night looking like a million bucks, the guys in the crew were sniffing around her today like a pack of horny dogs.

And after the smoking-hot kiss she'd laid on him last night, he was freaking *not* about to share her with any of them.

Interesting girl, Marley. She'd all but told him she caused accidents to happen around her. That bad stuff happened to men she dated. That dangerous accidents were known to happen to people near her. How had she put it? *Sometimes I wonder if I'm never supposed to be happy, and if that's why bad things keep happening around me.*

But as much as his brain saw the evidence stacking up against her, his gut argued that no way was she a psychopathic saboteur. Maybe because he'd had a rough youth, made some mistakes along the way, he was too eager to see the best in her. To believe that she wasn't responsible for the movie's accidents. Or maybe he was really just so antsy to get in her panties that he couldn't think straight.

He spotted her the second she walked into the motel dining room—he'd been lurking here for nearly a half hour waiting for her—and she had at least a half dozen hopeful bastards trailing along after her drooling. If only they knew how she could kiss. They'd be tearing their shirts off and worshipping at her feet.

Today, she sported a toned-down version of last night's full Marilyn getup, but the effect was still hot enough to give him an erection of granite. That sexy-innocent vibe hummed off her so hard he could barely see straight. Her blond curls were tucked behind her ears, and it was all he could do not to grab her and take a bite out of a cute, pink earlobe. Since when had he developed an *ear* fetish, for crying out loud? Of course, if she didn't quit chewing on her kissably full lower lip like that, he was going to develop a lip fetish, too.

He'd intended to keep his distance from her today. If she was as cunning an actress as Steve thought she was, she would be scared off by too aggressive an approach by him. And if she was as innocent as his gut said she was, too aggressive an approach would still scare her off.

But then he spied Gordon Trapowski moving across the dining room toward the buffet line. And the bastard's stare was targeted in on Marley like a laser designator. *Stay away from her. Turn around and walk away.* No way could he stand idle and let that guy get his hands on a sweet kid like Marley.

Gordon moved to stand right behind her in the buffet line, openly crowding her, and she got a panicked look in her eyes, like a baby bunny cornered by a big, bad fox.

Swearing, Archer stood up. He had no choice but to act. Painful erection notwithstanding, he managed to stride across the dining room to her side. He rested a light, but unmistakably possessive, hand on the small of her back.

"Hi there, beautiful," he said to Marley before nodding at Gordon. "Hey, Trap."

"Scram, Archer," Trapowski growled. "I'm talking to the girl."

"She's not your property, buddy."

"She ain't yours, neither."

Archer glanced down at Marley's plate, and it had enough food on it for her to politely walk away from the buffet. "Would you like to sit with me, Marley?"

"I'd love to." She smiled brilliantly at him, and in that moment, rescuing damsels in distress leaped high on his list of favorite things in the world to do.

He was pretty sure he heard Gordon's teeth grinding together as she leaned into his encircling arm. Over her head, he flashed the guy a triumphant grin, and Trap actually growled aloud. *Too bad, jackass. The girl's mine.*

The thought jolted him.

*Hell, no! Love 'em and leave 'em,* his gut chanted at him. *Before they walk out on you.* His mother had given up on him, on life, and died rather than deal with her grief and failures. He had always been the kind of guy whom women used for his body until they got bored and moved on to the next gigolo wannabe—unless he beat them to the moving-on bit.

Marley deserved better. *Screw Steve and his admonition not to get emotionally involved with her.* His gut said she was no way, no how, guilty of the crimes of which she was suspected.

He led her to the corner of the dining room and a cozy table for two. Their knees bumped and the heat leftover from last night's good-night kiss abruptly flared like a supermassive solar storm between them. Her gaze jerked to his face, and her breasts lifted sharply on a gasp. His male parts leaped against the tight confines of his jeans.

"I can't remember the last time a woman made me react like this."

"I know what you mean."

Just watching those glossy red lips form words made him think about how they'd feel on his flesh. All warm and soft and tight. He groaned and tore his gaze away from her mouth. They were in a cafeteria full of people, for heaven's sake.

She looked down, blushing nearly as red as the strawberries on her plastic plate. He studied her face as she concentrated on her food, slicing it into precise little chunks that she proceeded to push around on her plate like toy cars. Too sexually frustrated to eat, huh? He knew the feeling.

Yup, he made her nervous. Really nervous. Like she was seriously hoping to sleep with him and didn't know what to do about it. It was one of the sexiest damned things he'd ever seen, watching the struggle play out on her sweet face. A weird, nameless thing…moved…in him. It was more than sexual attraction. Different than simple lust. Deeper than mere possessiveness. But putting a name to it completely eluded him.

One thing he knew for sure. He wasn't going to let his brother or anyone else railroad her out of this job without proof positive that she was the culprit behind all the accidents.

"Uh, how are you today?" she asked awkwardly. She peeked up at him shyly, caught him studying her and looked down hastily. She was adorable when she was all jumpy and unsure of herself like this.

"Turned on. You?"

"Same."

"How'd you sleep last night?"

She pushed her green-pea salad in fast little circles around her grilled chicken breast. *Yesss.*

He leaned close to murmur, "I dreamed about you, too. Woke up so hard I had to take a shower in the middle of night to relieve my discomfort."

*What the hell are you doing, buddy? She's not your type.*

"Really?" she blurted. Her cheeks turned bright pink. Bonified all-American-girl material. *You don't do pure and sweet. You don't break innocent hearts. Stop flirting with this girl...*

He answered, "You and I were in an outdoor hot tub. And it was snowing. The stars were out and we were naked. And then we..."

Her soft fingers pressed frantically against his lips, halting the tale. "Someone will hear you!" she whispered in panic.

*Damn, she was beautiful. Mesmerizing. Irre-freaking-sistible.*

"Tell me about your dream," he murmured against her fingertips, "or I'll keep telling you about mine." He touched her fingers with the tip of his tongue. She jerked her hand away like he'd burned her with a hot iron. He was being a jerk. He should get up from this table and walk away right now, and instead he was flirting in the most openly sexual way with her. He wasn't her type any more than she was his. They really, really shouldn't do this. And yet, he wasn't standing up. Wasn't walking away. Correction: he was an idiot and she was...not.

"Um, I dreamed we were camping," she stammered. "In the woods. And there was a tent."

"Were we in it together?" She was too innocent for him. Deserved a real relationship to go with her first sex.

She nodded.

"Inside one of those double sleeping bags?" *Shut. The hell. Up.*

"No. On top of one."

"Naked?" *Stop leading her on.*

She looked around the dining room guiltily. *Hah.* She'd *so* dreamed about the two of them together. His mouth curved up into a knowing smile. "We were making love, weren't we? Was it hot? Wild? What did we do? I've got a few things I'd like to try with you..."

"Hush!" she whispered urgently.

She was breathing fast and her tongue kept darting out to moisten her lips. She was rocking her hips forward and wiggling in tiny little pulses she probably wasn't even aware of. Triumph roared through him at how bad she wanted him. Nearly as bad as he wanted her. *Double jerk.*

Gritting his teeth against the lust pounding through him, he changed subjects. "Are you shooting this afternoon?"

"Yes. We're finishing the close-ups and then we're shooting stills of the fake city that's getting blown up tomorrow."

"What time will you be done?"

"Around dark, if I had to guess."

"I'll pick you up at eight, and we'll go somewhere private so you can tell me the details of your dream." *You did not just ask her out again.*

"Are you for real?" she asked earnestly. She sounded like she couldn't believe he was actually attracted to her.

*Smart girl. Run away, Marley. Far, far away as fast as you can go.* Jesus, he felt like a tennis ball bouncing back and forth between lust and sanity. And unfortunately, lust was a much better tennis player.

"Why are you the slightest bit interested in me? You barely know me, and Lord knows, I barely know you."

*Good thing.* If she did know him, she'd leave him, just like every other woman he'd ever given a damn about. Ouch. Sanity had just served an ace. The thought was a bucket of ice water on his raging libido.

"How do you suggest I remedy that, other than spending time with you?" he asked reasonably.

"I just don't get what you see in me."

A thousand deeply sexual images flashed through his mind, but what came out of his mouth was, "Let's find out together, shall we?"

She shook her head and finished her meal in frustrated silence. He could relate. Honestly, he didn't have the faintest idea why he was so attracted to her. For years, he'd honed his expertise at spotting the kind of woman who just wanted empty sex. The kind who would treat him with as much indifference as he treated them. Marley Stringer was emphatically not one of them. No matter how hot she was, she would want the whole ball of wax. Sex. Romance. Intimacy. Hell, a real relationship.

Granny Minerva used to talk about kismet, and he'd always thought it was a load of crap. But maybe she'd known what she was talking about, after all. Fascinated, frustrated and thoroughly appalled with himself, he watched Marley bolt from the dining room.

Gordon bit out from beside him, "She ain't your type."

Archer looked up at Trap. She might not be his type, but no way was he turning her over to this brute. Women talked, and Gordon had a reputation in the sack for being a bull in rut. "I already called dibs on her, Gordon."

"The hell you did. She's hot, and I'm goin' after her." Trap poked him in the chest. Under other circumstances, Archer might have taken grave exception to such an act. But he had the girl's attention and Gordon didn't. He could afford to cut the guy a break and not rip his finger off.

"I'm turning the Gordon-ator charm on her whether you like it or not, jerkwad."

Archer pushed past the larger man nonchalantly, but a frisson of worry tickled the back of his neck. Gordon was right: he wasn't Marley's type any more than she was his. Would she actually fall for a guy like Gordon? Was she that naive?

He had no choice but to save her from Trapowski. And of course, he'd promised Steve that he would try to find out if Marley was behind the sabotage, but that was as far as it went. After he did those two things, he was walking away from her.

Period.

Marley paced her room in panic. She'd left an SOS on Tyrone's cell phone, but the makeup artist had yet to respond to her urgent call for help. Tonight wasn't a gratitude beer with Archer. It was a continuation of that volcanic kiss last night and, good Lord willing, *The Night*. Her first time.

A knock sounded on her door and she leaped for it, threw it open and all but cried in relief to see Tyrone standing there, makeup suitcase in tow.

"Hey, girl," Tyrone said breezily. "A real, live date with Flyboy, huh? You gonna have that screaming-hot sex you promised me tonight?"

"God, I hope so. I'm so ready to finally…" She broke off. The last rumor she needed getting around the set was that the new camera girl was a virgin. At her age, leprosy was a lesser curse than the big V.

"Drink this." Tyrone shoved a glass of wine into her hand. "You need it more than me. Sit, girlfriend. And pay attention. I'm not always gonna be around to turn you into Marilyn the Second."

She did watch what he did closely, and Tyrone was generous with explaining the tricks of the trade. But then the makeup artist surprised her by saying, "What's this I hear about your guy going commando on you yesterday?"

She frowned. *Huh?* "What are you talking about?"

"A few of the stunt men were talking about Archer nearly taking their heads off with his helicopter during the shoot. I guess he got way too low and scared the bejeebers out of them."

*Oh. That.* "I asked him to go lower so I could get a better shot. I was trying to impress Adrian Turnow with my first action scene."

"Did you?"

"I've still got a job."

Tyrone seemed to accept the explanation but still frowned a little. "The way I heard it, Archer might have a screw loose. He's fresh out of some heavy combat apparently. They thought it looked like he confused movie combat with the real thing."

Was *that* what it had been? The movie had gotten a little too close to reality and he'd busted into real combat maneuvers? Why, then, had the flight controls frozen up? Nah. Archer wasn't crazy. They'd had a mechanical malfunction. She didn't think he would be held responsible for that, but she wasn't sure. She didn't know a blessed thing about flying, after all.

Worse, rumors could get Archer fired. Maybe she could redirect the gossip mill a little. She said as casually as she could, "Well, of course I wanted him to fly like it was the real thing. How else was I going to get realistic footage? Everyone knows Adrian's a stickler for authenticity."

"True." Tyrone brushed her entire face lightly with setting powder. Based on the name, Marley guessed it would keep her makeup from smudging. The makeup artist commented, "As long as that boy don't kill you, I guess it's okay if he flies a little crazy. Promise me you won't make him do anything really dangerous, though. A good camera shot's a nice thing, but not worth dying over. 'Kay?"

"'Kay," she answered meekly. As if she had any control over how Archer flew.

"I'm gonna skedaddle before Romeo shows up. Don't do anything with your man that I wouldn't do." Tyrone went off into gales of laughter at that one, finally gasping, "God, I crack myself up."

Her motel room felt silent and empty after the ebullient makeup artist left. There was nothing to distract her from recalling every detail of last night's near-sex in the hallway. But before she could freak herself out too badly over how she was going to maneuver Archer into her bed without looking like a total newb, a firm knock sounded on her door.

She flung it open and gasped to see him standing there so tall and gorgeous and smiling back at her. "Wow, you're handsome. I forget just how much so when you're not here."

"Guess I'll just have to stick around all the time, then," he replied, smiling like he was genuinely pleased at the compliment. He leaned down to kiss her cheek and murmured, "Every time I see you, I swear you're more beautiful. Hungry?"

*For him? Hell, yes!* "Mmm-hmm," she managed.

He installed her in his truck and pulled out of the motel parking lot. In a few minutes, only the silent silhouettes of mountains and the starry sky were visible in the dark night. Dammit. She was going to have to endure eating before she ravaged him.

She tried to enjoy the grandeur of the Sierras, but it was hard to do, given the way her nerves were jumping all over the place. She was alone with the hottest guy she'd ever met, and she was disguised as a woman who knew what to do about it. Sure, she'd read her fair share of romance novels. But translating a general idea of how this whole seduction thing worked into reality was turning out to be more daunting than she'd imagined. If only she could be sure he wouldn't die laughing at her clumsy efforts.

"Where are we going?" she asked over the purr of the engine.

"Rancho Colombo," he answered. "I hear they've got a rib restaurant that's crazy good. I've been craving barbecue for months."

"Not a lot of barbecue in central Asia, huh?" she asked sympathetically.

"Not so much."

She laughed. "What else do you miss when you're over there?"

He shrugged. "Pillowcases that aren't full of grit. More than one football game on a Sunday afternoon. Good deli pizza. And women, of course."

"I thought lots of women are deployed overseas these days."

"They are. And they're soldiers. The military has strict rules about fraternization, and everyone works long hours and lives in a state of constant exhaustion. Not to mention, I don't particularly find combat boots attractive."

"Chauvinist!"

"Don't let my grandmother hear you accuse me of that. She'd tan my hide if she thought I or any of my brothers were ever the least bit sexist."

"How many siblings do you have?"

"Two older brothers and two younger sisters."

"Ugh. You're the middle child, huh?"

He shrugged. "I don't pay much attention to all that psychology stuff."

Silence fell as they drove farther up into the mountains, and her thoughts turned back to the rumors Tyrone had shared earlier. "So, tell me, Archer. How close did yesterday's film shoot come to real combat?"

Archer's body went tense and his knuckles whitened around the steering wheel. He looked like he was waging some terrible internal fight with himself. Cripes! What had she said? "Are you all right?" she asked in quick concern.

His jaw rippled like he was clenching it, but he managed a terse nod.

"What did I say?"

He shook his head and stared fiercely at the road ahead. She subsided, alarmed. He drove for a good fifteen minutes in harsh silence before his hands began to relax and the terrible tension across his shoulders began to subside.

Without looking at her, he muttered, "Are you always so observant?"

What the hell had she observed that had made him so tight? She frowned across the cab of the truck at him. "Um, I guess so."

Thankfully, the road came down out of the mountains and into a small western town with a traditional main street lined with restored storefronts. Archer pulled the truck into a parking space and escorted her into a mom-and-pop joint that looked like the kind of place that would serve killer ribs. The smell of a mesquite smoker filled the space as they stepped inside.

The entire menu consisted of beef ribs, pork ribs, chicken or all of the above. They opted for all of the above and platters of barbecued meat, biscuits, mashed potatoes and gravy, corn on the cob and baked beans were set before them.

Archer smiled beatifically at the spread, and she couldn't help but laugh at him. "Getting your carnivore on, are you?"

"Talk to me in a half hour. I'll be busy until then."

"Just don't choke on a bone, okay?"

"I'm not going to keel over dead just because I took you out on a date. I promise."

Lord, she hoped not. She grabbed a rib and dug in with him. The meal seemed to break whatever tension she'd inadvertently provoked, and in a few minutes, he was chatting companionably with her once more.

He lifted a cold beer to her and announced, "Here's to beautiful camerawomen who save their pilots' butts."

"Steve Prescott seems like a reasonable guy."

"He is. And a reasonable man would have fired me."

"I'm glad he didn't."

"Me, too," Archer replied candidly.

"Tell me about yourself, Archer Archer." She worded the comment in general enough terms that he could take the conversation wherever he was comfortable having it go.

He grinned and picked up another rib off the pile. "I grew up not too far from here actually. Serendipity, California. Same place the movie studio is named after. I hurt my throwing elbow and lost a baseball scholarship partway through college, but I picked up a chopper slot in the Army. Moved around a lot in the job. Flew in Afghanistan for a while. Given my skill set, I hopped from war zone to war zone. But then I got a call from Steve Prescott asking me if I'd like to fly for him. And here I am."

Funny how a person could say so much and yet say so little. Like why he got that regretful look in his eyes earlier today when he'd mentioned his mother. Like how bad giving up his dream of playing baseball must have hurt—or not. Like what it was like to fly in combat. And after his earlier reaction to her question about how realistic the filming of combat had been, she had a feeling that one was key to understanding this man.

"Okay, Marley. Your turn to tell your life story."

"Born and raised outside Chicago. One sister. My twin."

"Identical or fraternal?" he interrupted.

"Identical. At least in looks. Other than that, we're about as different as two people can be."

She resumed her abbreviated life history. "I've been interested in photography for as long as I can remember. Came west to go to film school. Got a job filming early morning news in a small town. Out of the blue, I got a call inviting me to work on this film. One of the camera operators was in a car accident just as shooting was getting ready to start, and the studio asked me to fill in. And here I am."

"What's Chicago like?"

"Cold. And yes, it really is windy. Great museums. Great restaurants. Nice people. Hardy."

"Is that how you'd describe yourself? Hardy?"

She frowned. "I've never thought about how I'd describe myself."

"How about I try?" He studied her closely enough that she had to restrain an urge to squirm. "You're prettier than you know. Smart. Observant. Uncomfortable in crowds. You prefer to see and not be seen. How am I doing so far?"

"Not bad."

"And you're trying like hell to figure out what a guy like me sees in a girl like you."

Her gaze snapped to his over her rib. His gaze was hooded. Inscrutable. "And?" she asked cautiously.

"I won't pretend that I'm not decent looking. It's a fortunate accident of genetics that I had no control over. And yes, I've used it shamelessly over the years to pick up women. People always expected me to pick up the hot chicks, and I suppose I expected to bed the hot ones, too. But I've learned recently that there is more to a woman than how she looks." He waved a naked rib bone at her. "But even if I still rolled that way, you'd be at the top of my list of TBF women."

"TBF?"

"To be, um, bedded."

She started to shake her head, but he talked over her bubbling objections.

"Honestly, Marley, you're a bit of a mystery to me," he admitted. "I'm not exactly sure why I find you so intriguing. But there's no question that I do. I'll let you know when I figure it out."

Not a reassuring answer. But at least he'd been straight with her. She finished her rib in silence and reached for an ear of corn. The waitress asked if they'd like refills on their beers and Archer shook his head. When she raised a questioning brow at him, he replied, "I'm driving. And I'm flying tomorrow."

"So, I'm supposed to drink by myself?"

He grinned. "Next time, I'll take you somewhere we can both get plastered and dance naked on the tables."

"Sounds fun," she replied gamely. No way would she ever get naked in public, and it wasn't her style to make a spectacle of herself. But that was the whole point of a fling, wasn't it? To do things you never normally would and then walk away from them.

"Have another beer, Marley. You look like you could use it."

*What? Was he a mind reader, too?* She took the proffered beer and downed it in about three gulps. Laughing quietly, he reached for another rib.

They finished the meal with small talk, and he pointed his truck back in the general direction of the movie set. "I've got a surprise for you," he announced.

"What kind of surprise?"

"It wouldn't be a surprise if I told you, now would it?"

His smile stole her breath away. She breathed, "Man, you're beautiful."

"How 'bout we go with handsome instead? Or hot, or studly. But not beautiful."

"How about all of the above?"

He smiled. "Right back atchya, baby."

"Have you ever considered modeling?" she asked as he turned the truck onto a dark dirt road high in the mountains.

"I had a few offers to make porn movies in college."

She didn't know if he was teasing and to laugh or if he was being serious and to be appalled. She could totally believe porn producers would recruit him.

He turned off the main highway onto a one-lane road that was more trail than actual road. "Where are we going?" she inquired.

"You'll see."

Going secretive on her again, was he?

He stopped the truck in a few minutes and came around to help her out. "The view will be better in the back of my truck."

*Huh?*

She let him help her up into the high truck bed, and she was shocked to land on a thick foam pad. He pulled pillows from the hotel from behind his seat and unfolded a blanket over her. Was he...? Did he plan to...?

Holy crap!

He stretched out beside her on the makeshift bed, and the heat of his body reached out to wrap around her seductively. "There's a big meteor shower tonight. I thought you might enjoy seeing a little of it."

Okay, she would never have guessed his idea of a fun date was to lie under the stars and watch meteors. Personally, she loved the idea. Was he seriously signaling that he was prepared to take his time wooing her? To let her set the pace and be patient until she was ready for more. The king of the one-night stand? Not in a million years would she have seen that one coming. Indeed, meteors were streaking across the sky at a steady clip. The night was chilly with the promise of coming winter, but Archer and the quilt were toasty warm. Her mind was a whirl, though. If he was waiting for her to set the pace, how was she supposed to show him she wanted more?

"Do you do this sort of thing often with women?" she queried.

"Not many women like this sort of thing."

"Their loss."

"Yup."

Truth be told, she hadn't done all that much outdoors stuff. She tended to stream shows about it onto her computer. Like most adventurous things she was interested in. She watched. She didn't do.

They commenced a meteor-counting contest, which remained neck and neck as streaks flashed across the night sky. After a while, the peace and silence of the night emboldened her. "Can you tell me why you reacted so strongly to my question about yesterday's filming?"

"Can't."

"Why not?"

"Classified."

"Can you give me some generalities?"

"Nope."

*Well, shoot.* Maybe if she came at it from another angle, he'd talk a little and she could catch an inkling of what nerve she'd touched. "What's Afghanistan like?"

He answered emotionlessly, "Hot as hell in summer and cold as hell in winter. It has mountains, but not like these. Over there, the mountains are barren. Nothing grows on them. Huge stretches of country are nothing but gray rocks and dirt. Mile after mile of the stuff. It looks like the surface of the moon. The people are hard. Gotta be to live there, I suppose."

He pointed out a meteor streaking across the sky. "Mine. I'm ahead, twelve to ten." She groaned, and he continued. "Being in central Asia is like traveling back in time. Natives live like they did a thousand years ago. It's hard to believe they exist on the same planet we do at the same time."

"What can you tell me about your military flying?"

"I already told you, I come from the search-and-rescue community. Although it's more rescue than searching. With today's technology, the troops we pull out either have GPSs squawking their positions, or they have radios and can tell us where they are. My job is twofold. I have to get to the ground and get them on my bird. And I have to provide air cover to back off whatever hostiles are trying to prevent them from boarding my bird."

"Wouldn't hostile forces try to shoot at you, too?"

"Oh, they do more than try. We get shot at all the time."

She was aghast. "How do you not get hurt?"

His shoulder lifted in a shrug against hers. "Luck. A good door-gunner. And we tend to light up the hostiles pretty hard before we move in for the pickup. They're not usually feeling much like shooting at us by the time we land."

She shuddered. "How do you know Steve Prescott?"

"We go way back," Archer mumbled.

"How far back?" she prodded when he didn't say more.

"He was a Marine before he got into doing movie

stunt work. We crossed paths from time to time in the military. We've known each other forever."

"What's he like?"

"Good man. Honorable. Takes care of his own. Fair boss. Born-again bastard in a bar fight."

"You always were on his side in bar fights?"

Archer grunted. "Hell, yeah. I didn't want to lose. He saved my hide a few times, and I saved his a few. I lifted him and his guys into and out of some hot messes."

"What kind of hot messes?"

"Classified hot messes."

"As in combat?"

"As in I can't talk about it."

"Was it scary?"

He shrugged.

Scary enough to make him tense up like she had just hit him with a high-powered Taser gun apparently. "Do you look forward to going back overseas and doing more search-and-rescue flying?"

Another totally uncommunicative shrug from him. *Not helpful.*

"How'd you get from Chicago to California?" he asked in an abrupt and obvious attempt to change the subject.

So. He'd been thinking about her life story, too, had he? Or was he just trying to distract her from poking into his military career? "Greyhound bus," she replied lightly.

"No ducking the question. I was square with you," he declared. "Why the cross-country move to the West Coast?"

It was her turn to shrug. "Not enough happening in the Midwest. I wanted to be where the action was."

He frowned. "And yet, you don't partake of much action as far as I can tell. I don't get it."

*Drat.* He'd pegged her spot-on. She answered cagily, "I wanted the possibility of more."

"What's holding you back, then? Why not go for the gusto?"

Were they talking about sex? Or life in general? "I'd call giving up a steady job—in a tough field to get a job in at all—and trying to break into the movie business going for the gusto," she answered a shade defensively.

"Many men in your life?" he asked lightly.

She snorted with laughter before she could recall the sound back into her throat. He pushed up on one elbow to stare down at her. "You're an attractive woman. Enjoyable to talk with. Fun to be around. Has something bad happened in your past that's put you off men?"

She jolted. "Good Lord, no. Nothing like that." *Just the tiny fact that she was a hazard to their health. Mina was the one who got all the boys, while she was the nervous sister. The one who never knew what to say to a boy. The self-conscious Stringer girl.*

"Why are you so standoffish with guys?"

She was standoffish? Was *that* why men didn't date her? "Explain how I'm standoffish."

"It's a vibe you put out. Like you're not interested."

God, this was embarrassing. "But I *am* interested. Thing is, I've always been that girl next door who kind of fades into the woodwork or ends up being the friend-zoned, little sister to my male acquaintances. My sister, Mina, was the one all the boys wanted to date."

Propping himself up on one elbow, he laid a hand on her cheek and prevented her from looking away when she would have. His voice was low and intense. "Stop putting yourself down."

"But..."

His mouth closed over hers, cutting off any further conversation in no uncertain terms. His kiss was firm at first, firm enough to make it clear he didn't want to hear any more self-denigration out of her. But then his lips gentled. She registered how warm he was. How he tasted like barbecue. How he intentionally slowed this kiss down for her. His hand crept into her hair and he angled her head slightly to fit better with his.

His tongue licked across her lips and she gasped, surprised. He took advantage of it to taste her more deeply and the stars started to dance and spin overhead. All of a sudden, she was clinging to him as his hands roamed over her back and he kissed his way across her jaw and down her neck. He nibbled at her ear, and a strange sound she identified in shock as a moan escaped her throat. Funny things were happening in her nether regions and she pressed her thighs together, startled.

"Relax, Marley," he murmured against her earlobe. His hand roamed from the back of her knee up her thigh, and darned if her legs didn't obey him and fall apart. His hand slid by inches down her belly and cupped her intimately through her jeans. She about came undone right there.

"What are you doing?" she breathed as her fingers plunged of their own volition into his thick, dark hair.

"I'm establishing that all the guys who failed to ask you out in the past are complete idiots. Jinx be damned."

She smiled reluctantly against his delicious mouth.

"Are you okay with this?" he mumbled against her neck.

"No. I want more," she panted.

He laughed against her temple. "*Ahh*, Marley. You are some kind of wonderful."

The zipper of her jeans gave way slowly to his fingers and his hand dipped inside the back of the warm denim. One of his fingers lightly traced her tush and she gasped at how sexy it felt. Her hips lurched forward into him, and she abruptly became aware of the hard bulge behind his jeans.

"Is this really happening, or is it a dream?" she whispered as much to herself as to him. Her hands roamed through his hair, mussing it all up. She leaned up to kiss his jaw, savoring the rough stubble there. What would that feel like scraping across her naked body? Her hands wandered across his chest and down to his narrow, hard waist. She tugged at his shirt and it slipped free of his jeans. Her palms pressed against skin. Hot, hard, satin skin. Over washboard abs contracted into hard ridges beneath her hands.

"If this is a dream, let's not wake up," he murmured back.

Her shirt gave way to his hands, lifting over her head and drifting to the truck bed.

"We're good?" he checked.

*No imminent disasters looming. Check.* "Mmm. Better than good." And then she got to find out exactly what that whisker stubble felt like scraping lightly over her skin. Like sex. And man. And delicious temptation.

Her bra hooks gave way to his nimble fingers and the boring white cotton fell away from her body. Archer paused to stare down at her in the scant starlight. "How in hell didn't every guy in Chicago try to date you, Marley?"

Mentally, she frowned. Because she was awkward. *And a geek. Not to mention jinxed. And...and...still a virgin at twenty-five,* her mind whispered painfully. Her hands crept up to cover herself in spite of her resolve to go through with this.

Gently, he twined his fingers in hers and lifted her hands away from her embarrassed body. "You've got nothing to hide. I'm not kidding. I could look at you all night long."

"I'd rather you didn't," she said in a small voice. God knew, she'd imagined this moment a thousand times, but the reality was a whole lot more intimidating than her late-night imaginings of her first sexual encounter. And what if…

Lord. A thousand humiliating possibilities scrolled through her mind, totally paralyzing her.

Archer paused long enough to strip off his shirt, which was good, since she was too big a coward to do such a thing herself. His body was as perfect as his face, and in spite of her misgivings, she drank in the sight of him hungrily. His abs rippled with muscle, and a sprinkling of dark hair across his tanned chest was the perfect accompaniment to that six-pack.

She reached out tentatively to trace a scar under his right rib cage. Or maybe she was just delaying because she was scared silly. It was about the length of her index finger. "How'd you get this?"

"Bullet grazed me." His hands closed on her breasts then, and she totally forgot to ask when and where he got shot. *Oh, my.* His hands were scorching as they tested the heft and resilience of her flesh. She supposed that, compared to most women, she was pretty well endowed. But it had never been important. Until now. She was glad when his eyes lit up as he gazed at her generous breasts. His thumbs flicked across her nipples lightly and she cried out, equal parts shocked and aroused.

"Like that?" he murmured.

She nodded shyly.

He smiled and asked, "Want me to do it again?"

"Yes, please."

He laughed lightly. "Promise you'll tell me anytime you want me to do something specific."

"Um, okay."

He flicked her nipples again and her back arched by itself, offering her breasts up to him, begging for more attention. He leaned forward and sucked her left nipple, his tongue rolling around the nub as he tugged at it.

"Oh, my!"

She felt him grin against her skin just before he did it again to the other side. Her jeans peeled down her legs and went away like magic. Her panties followed suit and she did her damnedest to ignore the fact that she was now naked with this man. Thankfully, he didn't give her any time to think about it as he half covered her with his warm, wonderful body.

She managed to get his zipper undone and to brush her fingertips briefly against the iron hardness of his erection before he kissed his way across her shoulder and his mouth headed south, effectively removing his male parts from her reach. Dammit! She wanted to explore her first in-person erection more thoroughly.

"Tonight's all about your pleasure. No sex. Just enjoyment and relaxation."

No sex? *Well, hell.* She just wanted to get it over with. At the same time, though, she registered with abject gratitude that he was gentleman enough not to make this all about him getting in her pants and nothing else.

"Tell me if I'm going too fast for you," he murmured.

If anything, he wasn't going fast enough. Now that the moment had finally arrived, she was in a hurry to get on with it. She wrapped her legs around his waist to urge him onward and he laughed against her belly.

"If the lady's so insistent, maybe we'll have to put sex back on the table as an option. But first, I want you to enjoy yourself."

"I *am* enjoying myself," she groused. She half sat up beneath him and could barely reach around to the back of his jeans. She only managed to skinny them down around the tops of his thighs. But then, frustratingly, he moved away from her again.

His voice drifted up to her from the vicinity of her belly button, where his tongue was swirling around and driving her out of her mind. It was half a tickle and half a turn-on unlike anything she'd ever experienced. "Have you ever had a screaming orgasm?"

"I, uh, well..." she stammered.

"That's all the answer I need. If you didn't reply with an immediate and resounding yes, then you haven't. You'll know one when you have it. Trust me."

How did he know she'd never had an orgasm?

"Later," he continued against the flat plane of her stomach, "I'll show you how to give them to yourself. Then you can figure out what you like best and show me."

The idea of doing herself in front of him shocked her speechless and turned her on. Hard. But then his mouth slid lower, leaving a trail of hot destruction in its wake. Gently, he pushed her thighs wider as he shifted his body farther down the foam pad.

Panic and curiosity warred in her gut, effectively freezing her in place. His mouth closed on her...down there...and then she couldn't think of anything at all. If he weren't being so matter-of-fact about all of this, she'd be so embarrassed she could curl up in a ball and die. But as it was, it was hard to get too tense with him being so relaxed and casual…and with his tongue stroking…*holy crap*!

Something intense slammed into her as her body reacted powerfully to his mouth. Things were aching deliciously and getting hot and hungry, and wanting roared through her. She felt empty all of a sudden, and a desperate need to have him fill her, to turn loose that bulge behind his zipper and impale herself on it, about knocked her out of the truck bed.

Sure, she'd experimented around a little over the years with her body, but nothing had prepared her for the lightning bolts of lust zinging through her when his hot tongue swirled around like that. His teeth grazed flesh that was so sensitive she nearly howled with need, and her hips lunged upward in response. He laughed and his tongue swirled a little harder.

"Oh, my gosh," she cried.

Swirl and lick. Swirl and suck. He repeated it over and over until she was thrashing beneath him, swearing up a blue storm, demanding him to stop in one breath and never to stop in the next. Inhibition went right out the window as wave after wave of pleasure washed over her.

He murmured against her throbbing flesh, "You taste like peaches, baby. All sweet and slippery and juicy. I can't get enough of you. I may have to do this all night long."

She was going to pass out if he did it too much longer. She'd never survive an entire night of this madness.

"Come for me, Marley. I want to hear your first screaming orgasm." He paused, his breath warm against her flesh, and she hovered on the precipice of something spectacular. One of his clever fingers rubbed down the swollen length of her, easing just inside her tight passage and she shattered, climaxing with a long, keening cry as fireworks exploded all around her and through her.

Colored lights blasted behind her eyelids and it was as if the stars rained down around her. Pleasure shimmered all the way through her and right out her fingertips. Disoriented, she came back to earth gradually. Her entire body felt energized. Electrified.

It dawned on her that actual explosions were happening overhead. The movie. She recalled hearing something at this morning's briefing about night shooting some pyrotechnic scenes. A huge boom rocked the night and Archer flung himself up and forward, covering her body completely with his.

"Archer?" she asked tentatively.

*Nothing.* He was frozen on top of her. And he was heavy.

"That was amazing," she tried. He didn't answer and she felt him breathing heavily. "Are you okay?"

"Stay down. Keep quiet," he bit out. "New bird's on the way. Just have to stay alive till it gets here."

Huh? He must be having a flashback or something. So much for hot romance. Although it figured. That stupid jinx was going to be the death of her! Did she play along with whatever he was reliving or try to talk him down from his mental bridge?

"Archer, we're in California. On a movie set," she whispered.

"I'm out of ammo. Pass the med kit," he mumbled under his breath.

She pushed at his shoulders, but he didn't budge. The man might not be as big as Gordon Trapowski, but he was all muscle.

Another round of explosives went off overhead and his entire body flinched against hers. She wrapped her arms around him in an instinctive effort to protect him from whatever memory had him so freaked out. In the light of the explosions, his eyes were glazed and he looked a million miles away. Agonized. Lost.

"Hey, Archer. Are you okay?"

Worry flooded through her, washing away all thoughts of sex, as he flinched in time with the explosions.

"Archer!" she said sharply. "Talk to me." She pushed at his shoulders awkwardly, but it had no effect on him at all. His eyes were open, but whatever he was seeing was half a world away.

Desperate, she grabbed his face in her hands and kissed him. Hard. This was about getting his attention, not romancing him. She took his lower lip between her teeth and bit down.

*"Oww!"* he exclaimed.

She let go of his lip with her teeth and licked it apologetically. His mouth opened against hers, and he kissed her voraciously, desperately, even. He sucked her tongue, shocking her with the bolts of lust that shot straight to her girl parts. She moaned and her hips rocked against his.

Relieved that he'd come back from wherever his mind had gone off to there for a few seconds, her lust came roaring back. "Again," she demanded, desperate for another orgasm to tear her apart and put her back together.

Archer froze against her. His eyes opened wide. Oh, he was back with her, all right.

He stared down at her in horror. "What happened here?" he rasped.

# Chapter 5

Archer registered pain in his lip first. And then some of the softest, sexiest breasts he'd ever had the pleasure of lying on. Warm, soft lips soothed his mouth, and female thighs cradled his body sweetly.

And then the rest of it hit him all at once. *Marley. Naked.* Wrapped around him like he'd just flown her to the moon and back. Begging to do it again.

But that memory was interspersed with vivid images of his last mission in a classified valley a thousand miles from anywhere. His bird getting hit. Going down. Ending up stranded on the ground with the very men he was supposed to be rescuing. Radioing frantically for another rescue bird to come for them. Yelling for close air support.

*Ho. Lee. Cow. Had he just had sex with her?* Taken her virginity, if he wasn't mistaken. How long had he been mentally checked out, reliving the mission that had gotten him sent home? Remembering the way rockets had been coming in at them from every direction, the injured soldiers he'd been sent in to rescue moaning around him, Yelling on the radios for that back bird to hurry...

He rolled off Marley fast. What the hell had happened with her while he was in la-la land? He was still as hard as a rock. But just because he hadn't had an orgasm didn't mean the damage hadn't been done. He searched frantically for memory of what had gone on between the two of them and came up with a single sound. Marley keening in pleasure. That and explosions. He flung an arm across his face in distress while he pleaded with his brain for details.

Nothing. The past few seconds or minutes or however the hell long he'd been out of it were a complete blank. Except for the part where he became aware of her plastered against him begging for more. He sat up, propping an arm on his upraised knee while he shoved his free hand through his hair. He couldn't exactly blurt out, "Hey, baby. Did we just have sex?"

What the hell was a guy supposed to do in this situation? It was the most important sexual encounter of her life. It would set the tone for her entire attitude toward sex going forward, and he'd completely forgotten it. What kind of schmuck *forgot* that?

She leaned against his side trustingly and murmured, "That was amazing. You were amazing."

Damn, damn, damn, *damn*. They *did* have sex.

She said playfully, "It's safe to say we've established that screaming orgasms rock. And you were right. I definitely want more of that." And then she changed subjects abruptly. "How are you feeling?"

*Like gum on the bottom of a shoe.* "Aww, hell, Marley. I'm sorry…"

She slid around in front of him and wrapped her sleek arms around him. Her lush breasts pressed against his chest until he was so distracted he could hardly focus on what he was saying. "Hush," she murmured. "There's nothing to apologize for."

Panic clawed at him. There bloody well was something to apologize for! But if he admitted it to her, he would ruin her first sexual experience. He didn't have the heart to do that to her. *Jeez. Maybe there was something to her insistence that she was jinxed.* Surely, getting so freaked out by some fireworks that he blacked out on sex with her counted.

"What were you thinking about just now?" she asked curiously.

He owed her at least a little explanation, he supposed. "I had a really rough mission right before I got sent home on leave. Haven't had much time to think about it. I'll replay it in my head a few hundred times, figure out where things went wrong and then I'll be fine." *He hoped.* It had worked in the past. Nightmares and reliving missions were not uncommon in his profession, and all the guys knew to just ride through them, and they would subside over time. He only prayed it worked for this mission gone bad, too.

He just wished all to hell that he hadn't had to relive the damned mission when he was in the middle of making love to a beautiful woman he was genuinely interested in. She was so sexy even now, all worried about him and acting protective, that he was struggling to keep his mind on the problem at hand of figuring out what had happened in the past few minutes.

She shivered lightly against him, and he dived on

the excuse to get her dressed and safe from the lust still pounding through him like a jackhammer. "You're getting cold. Let's get you warmed up." He searched the truck bed, snatching up her clothes and practically throwing them at her. "Put these on," he ordered.

It dawned on him that it might look to her like, now that he'd gotten in her pants, he was in a giant hurry to get rid of her. God, could he screw this up any worse? "Take your time," he added belatedly.

He folded the blanket and stowed the pillows behind the seats in the truck, mentally cursing himself out all the while. Right now, all that mattered was damage control with Marley. "Are you okay?" he asked her gently as he opened the door for her. He kissed her sweetly before handing her inside.

She nodded as she climbed into the vehicle. Not helpful. In his experience, silent women were usually brooding women or scheming women. Neither ever boded well for the nearest male target. In this case, him. Of course, he deserved every angry word she could launch at him and more for the crappy stunt he'd just inadvertently pulled on her.

About the third time during the drive down the mountain that he asked if she was okay, she finally got a little short with him. "Will you stop, Archer? I'm fine. How are *you*? Can you talk at all about what you were remembering back there?"

There wasn't a lot to say. That last mission downrange had been a nightmare. Bar none the worst disaster in his entire career. But what would banish the nightmare—he had no idea. To top it all off, he'd possibly had sex with Marley and couldn't remember it.

*Damn, damn, damn.*

Marley fidgeted in her seat as the production meeting got under way and pensively watched the dancing of dust motes in the sunshine streaming in the window. Archer had been thoughtful and considerate upon their return to town last night. He'd kissed her long and romantically in the truck, murmuring about how great she was and how much he enjoyed being with her.

But he'd made a point of leaving her at her door and not inviting himself into her room or her into his, either. Had that momentary flashback, or whatever it was, upset him more than he was letting on? She chewed her lip anxiously. Was something serious going on in his head? Had the pyrotechnics being filmed in the valley just reminded him of a particularly rough mission, or was there more to it? Based on the things he'd mumbled in the thick of reliving it, there was no question something awful had happened on one of his flights, clearly involving explosions and his helicopter being hit.

She sighed. He'd zoned out at the worst possible moment. She'd been right on the verge of asking him outright to make love to her. Not that she could blame him for the rockets making him remember a bad mission, of course. But Lord, the timing of it was frustrating. She'd gotten *so close* to finally going all the way. The gods of love had a really awful sense of humor.

The production meeting adjourned, and she headed for her afternoon's assignment: shooting still shots of the quarter-scale city the set construction crew had spent the past several days building. It felt weird walking around the waist-high buildings. Like she was a giant stomping around among Lilliputians. The detail was meticulous, and she crawled around on her hands and knees with a shoulder-held camera, shooting the town from every conceivable angle.

A couple of times she thought she caught sight of

movement between the buildings. But she was the only camera operator scheduled to be out here today. It must be one of the other explosives techs getting ready for tomorrow's destruction of this set. Airplanes would fly over to simulate dropping bombs on the city, but pyrotechnics set inside the shells of the fake buildings would do the work of actually destroying the town. It should be pretty spectacular, if the big combat scenes to date were any indication.

The sun began to set, and Marley captured a few last shots of the buildings in silhouette. She was squinting into the setting sun when she thought she saw a person momentarily rise up from behind the spire of the central church in the "town."

She raised her eye away from the viewfinder quickly, and was promptly blinded by the actual setting sun, unfiltered by her camera lens. Darn it. She thought she'd recognized that profile. Surely not. Why on earth would *Mina* be here, across the country from home, where she didn't belong?

Marley shook her head. She was imagining things. It was just the talk about her last night that triggered her thinking she'd seen Mina today.

She packed her camera and headed to the bus stop for crew members. In a few minutes, a van came along and she hopped into the vehicle. She let the chatter of the other crew members flow past her, surrounding her in a web of human companionship that spelled safety.

She'd escaped her past and her sister's shadow, and she wasn't looking back. That part of her life was over. Done. Finished. She was her own person now.

But the incident disturbed her nonetheless. She grabbed a quick supper at the crew buffet and headed upstairs to her room early. The stunt pilots were all at some kind of briefing to go over tomorrow's flying sequences and would be tied up with it all evening, so there was no chance she could hook up with Archer tonight.

She crawled into bed, and as her thoughts turned to him, desire built of its own volition low in her belly. She imagined what would have happened last night if those explosions hadn't gone off overhead, hadn't thrown Archer back into combat inside his mind. The more she thought about it, the more turned on she got. Amazement that just thinking about the man could have this effect on her rolled through her. She had it *bad* for that guy.

An orgasm built deep within her, growing from an electric tingle into a massive storm of pounding lust. But thinking about Archer didn't quite push her over the edge. She hovered on the edge, desperate for the man himself. She needed his hands and mouth on her. His body moving inside hers. To feel his strength and possession filling her arms.

And then she remembered what Archer had said. He wanted her to show him what she liked. An image of him watching her wantonly exploring her own body exploded across her brain and her body arched up off the bed violently as an orgasm broke over her without warning, all the more violent for its surprise explosion. Her entire body clenched in a shuddering spasm of release.

She collapsed against the mattress, breathing hard while aftershocks rippled through her. Holy cow. What kind of wanton had he turned her into?

Whatever it was, she liked it. A lot.

Archer arrived at the airport barely after dawn to prep for the day's flying. He hadn't slept for squat, anyway, and had given up on sleep when the continuous hard-on he'd had ever since being with Marley drove him to the shower in desperation.

He preflighted Minerva and asked a mechanic to put a couple quarts of oil into her, but all the while, pressure was building in his gut. Finally, it bubbled over into conscious thought: he didn't want Marley to fly with him again.

He and Steve had argued about it last night. Steve thought there was no way Marley would sabotage a helicopter she was scheduled to ride in given how close she had come to dying the last time her ride had been messed with. Unfortunately, the crew was short on pilots and Archer was really needed for today's shoot, as was Marley's camera. The fake city could only be blown up once, so it was every camera on deck to shoot the scene from every possible angle that might conceivably be required in the final cut of the movie.

Steve had confessed that in a perfect world he would pull both Marley and Archer off the movie crew entirely, for Archer's safety and to get Marley away from the set where she couldn't cause any more trouble.

Steve had also reported that a background check on Adrian Turnow's finances showed the director had thrown most of his personal wealth into buying his share of Serendipity Studios. Steve still wasn't ready to admit that Adrian might be sabotaging his own film to collect the insurance on it. Of course, Steve had also declared that the director was innocent until proven guilty.

Archer had replied hotly that Marley was innocent until proven guilty, too. Steve's equally hot reply that all the facts pointed at her devolved into an argument that went nowhere. The upshot was an uncomfortable stalemate between him and his brother.

Archer got the distinct impression that Marley was on tight probation with Steve, though. One more incident in her wake, and she was out of here.

He'd lain awake for long hours, asking himself if he was missing some sign from her that she was pulling a con on him or that she was behind the string of accidents around the movie lot.

Cars were having violent tire blowouts, equipment was failing and a set had collapsed inexplicably. A heavy light bar had even fallen and narrowly avoided crushing several crew members, the power to the soundstage had failed for no apparent reason, costing an entire lost day of shooting...the list went on. And recently, the accidents had gotten more serious, as if the saboteur was getting more bold...or more crazy.

Rumors were starting to circulate around the set, and the crew was getting nervous.

When Archer had seen the full list of incidents, he'd understood why Steve was convinced a saboteur was at work. Even the worst run of luck ever couldn't explain the continuous stream of problems, particularly given the experience and professionalism of this crew. Most of them were longtime movie veterans with excellent reputations.

When he hadn't been fretting over her guilt or innocence, he'd spent much of last night imagining how fantastic sex with Marley—that he remembered the next time—would be. Of course, he'd spent the remainder of the night worrying about his own screwed-up head.

Intellectually, he knew he hadn't even begun to process what had happened on that last, disastrous mission. He also knew it hadn't been his fault that the rescue had turned out to be an ambush. It wasn't the first time he'd been ambushed moving in to extract a patrol in enemy territory. It came with the job.

But men had died out there. Men who'd been counting on him to pull them out. To get them to hospitals. He'd lost troops before. Been through the ringer of dealing with guilt and grief. They were kids, mostly. With their whole lives ahead of him. Sure, he knew they'd volunteered to be out there. He knew that his government, not he, had sent them into that war zone. That he, too, was just a schmuck doing a job. If not him, some other warm body would have been out there that night and gotten shot down.

In some ways, he was glad it had been him who'd taken that rocket through his engine and not one of his less experienced fellow pilots. At least he hadn't panicked under fire. Had gotten off those last, critical radio calls as he fell out of the sky that had brought help, and lots of it, when it had finally shown up.

But still. The guilt would have its due.

The flight surgeon had been right to send him home for a while. To give him time to work through the inevitable aftereffects of a mission gone south. *Way* south. South Pole south.

At least he'd met Marley out of this rotation stateside.

To say he gave Minerva a detailed preflight would be the understatement of the century. If his life and Marley's were on the line today, he was going to make damned sure both of them came home from this flight in one piece. He examined every square inch of the helicopter, opened every panel, looked in every nook and cranny where anyone could possibly stick a device, cut a wire, fray a connector or otherwise set up his bird for a problem of any kind.

He was conflicted about today's flight. On the one

hand, he was desperate for any excuse to be with Marley. And tucked together in the close quarters of his aircraft, where he got to display the other thing he was really, really good at doing, was very appealing.

But on the other hand, he was terrified that she would reveal herself to be the saboteur in some way. It wasn't so much that he was worried for his own safety. He just desperately wanted her to be as innocent as she seemed, to be every bit as sweet and naive for real as his gut shouted at him that she was.

He sighed and climbed into Minerva to wait for Marley to arrive. Until they took off, he would not leave the helicopter again. He wasn't taking any chances with someone messing with his aircraft.

He spotted her the second she emerged from behind the hangar. She was wearing tight jeans and a pale pink oxford shirt, with a jaunty red scarf tied around her neck. Those oversize sunglasses made her look like a movie starlet straight out of the 1950s. A bunch of the guys had commented on how much she looked like Marilyn Monroe, and he saw the resemblance. She had the same sex-kitten vibe, too.

He jumped out of Minerva to go around and open the passenger door for her. "Hey, beautiful," he murmured as he helped her climb up into the seat. He reached for the seat belts and buckled her in like he had the first time they flew together. And this time he had no compunction about overtly stroking her breasts with the backs of his knuckles. Her inhaled breath was even sharper this time, the dilation of her eyes wider.

"You ready to fly with me?" he murmured, smiling a little.

"You have no idea," she muttered back.

His grin widened as he tugged her lap belt tight. He

knew precisely how turned on she was. He was in the exact same state of anticipation. The good news was that she didn't seem at all scarred by their first sexual encounter. He'd successfully hidden the fact that he didn't remember how it had ended. Thank God. The last thing he would ever want to do was hurt her in any way.

She sat quietly through the preflight sequence and checked over her camera as he got clearance to lift off.

"Here we go," he announced to her as he eased back on the stick. There was something magical about taking off. About leaving behind the earth and gravity to enter the realm of birds and gods.

It was a beautiful morning. The sky was brilliant blue, the mountains shining gold as the aspens declared fall to be in full swing. He headed for the head of the valley, just like last time. Except today, they would approach the fake town and hover next to it, filming, as airplanes made mock bombing runs past it. His job was merely to park in position and hold a steady hover.

Truth be told, a decent hover was harder than it looked. Depending on wind and turbulence, hovering could be a bitch. But he was no amateur and would give Marley a perfectly still platform for her camera.

Steve counted down the various flying sequences over the radio, and fighter jets hired from a reserve military base not far away came streaking down the valley toward them.

"Whoa," Marley breathed as her lens caught the incoming birds. "They're really moving."

He snorted. "They're only going a few hundred miles per hour. You ought to see them when they come in supersonic. They streak past so fast you barely register them before they're gone."

She went silent, face plastered to her viewfinder, her

concentration complete. He glanced over from time to time at her as she panned her camera across the town. A little frown puckered her brow, and even that was sexy. The helicopter floated a little and Marley made a small sound of protest.

*Focus, idiot.* He settled Minerva and glued his gaze to his controls and to the line of mountains outside that he was using as a horizontal reference point.

Steve's voice came over his headset. "Trigger the first explosion in three…two…one…"

An almighty blast exploded practically beneath them. The windshield filled with a wall of flames and smoke as the flight controls ripped out of his hands. This was not good. Not good at all.

# *Chapter 6*

Marley screamed as the entire mock city blew up all at once in a spectacular fireball in her face that slammed the helicopter on its side and blew it back violently from its previous position.

Archer swore in a tense, continuous stream beside her as he fought to regain control of the helicopter. She sat still in frozen horror, doing everything in her power not to distract him while he tried to save them both from crashing into the midst of the fireball in front of them

"Report!" Steve was shouting into the radios. "By the numbers!"

The various aircraft parked around the burning set each reported their status tersely in numerical order. When his turn came, Archer bit out, "Heli Four unharmed."

"Are we really okay?" Marley asked in a voice that quavered in spite of her best efforts to control it.

"Yup." She didn't ask for any more information as

his hands raced over the controls and he flipped through the checklists strapped to his thigh. It looked as though he was running a series of diagnostic tests on the aircraft's systems to make sure Minerva was, in fact, okay. The good news was they were low and slow. If they crashed from this height, she suspected they might actually stand a chance of walking away, if not unharmed, at least alive.

"Everybody return to base," Steve Prescott ordered tersely.

With a dozen aircraft to recover to one runway, it took a while for the air traffic controller to sequence the faster fixed-wing planes first for landing, and then the slower ones. The helicopters were brought in last. But finally, Archer set Minerva down in her assigned parking space and shut her down.

He looked over at Marley and she stared back at him. He was as white as a sheet. She would bet it was not often that he was so overtly shook up. "Why the pale face?" she asked in a small voice. "We're fine. Right?"

"Yeah. We're good," he answered gruffly. "That was just a flipping close call. I've never come that close to getting sucked into a fireball before. We nearly didn't make it clear of the blast."

*Oh. Gulp.* It took a few seconds for her pucker factor to subside enough to ask him, "What happened back there?"

"My guess is something went wrong with the wiring of the explosions. There were supposed to be about forty separate, small blasts, but it appeared that they all detonated at once."

"It sure was spectacular."

He snorted. "That's a word for it. Let's hope you camera folks got usable footage out of it."

Startled, she glanced down at her camera. It was still running, in spite of nearly being incinerated back there. She hadn't even thought about shooting the explosion; frankly, she'd been much more concerned with the whole concept of not dying.

"I have no idea what my lens captured. Whatever it was pointed at, I guess."

Archer commented, "Rebuilding that city and blowing it up again would cost an arm and a leg. And this film's in trouble already."

She looked over at him sharply. "How's that?"

He winced. "I'm just saying. There've been a lot of accidents on this film. And each one costs money."

She'd heard a few rumors that Serendipity Studios had invested every cent it had in the making of this film. If that was true, the failure of this film could spell disaster for the young studio.

Archer glanced over at her with casual relaxation that could not possibly look more fake if he tried.

"They wouldn't shut the movie down, would they?" she asked in alarm.

"Nah. Adrian Turnow believes in this film, and I'm sure his investors do, too. They'll get it made regardless of any obstacles thrown in their path."

"I sure hope so. He's a nice man. Talented director. And on a purely personal note, it's my first movie. I'd hate to have my entrée to cinematography fail so spectacularly that I can't even use it on my résumé. I need this film if I'm to get other jobs in the business."

Archer looked thoughtful in response to her comment. "We'd better head inside. Steve's going to want to see your footage right away."

"Why?"

"To see if he can spot exactly what happened out there."

Of course. It made perfect sense. She was still too rattled by the experience to be thinking on all cylinders. "I'm sure all he's going to see is a giant explosion. Although maybe a frame-by-frame playback will show him a daisy chain of the charges setting one another off or something."

The other camera operators had all had the same idea and congregated in Steve's office to share their playbacks with him directly. Ultimately, the super-slow-motion playbacks from each camera showed the exact same thing. All the charges detonated simultaneously. Which meant something had definitely gone wrong with the wiring of the various triggers or their sequencers.

She caught Steve Prescott trading grim looks with Archer, but then the head stunt coordinator thanked everyone quietly and asked them to leave. She was shuffled out of the office along with the herd of other cinematographers and pilots and lost sight of Archer.

Stunned and appalled, she wandered around the airplane hangars, waiting for Archer to leave his boss's office.

Why did stuff like this happen to her all the time? Even as a kid, she'd had terrible luck. Any time a boy showed an interest in her, something bad inevitably happened to him. Any time she tried a new hobby or sport, same deal. Disaster struck. Only when she was with Mina did things seem to go all right.

The two of them had been inseparable as kids. They'd been lucky that the foster-care system had found them a long-term family that would take in both girls as a pair. Their foster parents had been an older couple of modest means, but with giant hearts and plenty of love.

Marley still considered them her parents and spent holidays with them and stayed in close touch. She doubted that Mina stayed in touch with them. She'd been a rebellious teen to say the least and there'd been a ton of friction between them and Mina.

She'd really hoped when she left Chicago that the curse would not follow her, but it most definitely had found her in California.

Maybe she should quit this job. Take herself and her jinx as far away from here as she could. Although her heart rebelled at the idea of leaving Archer when the two of them were just finding each other. She wasn't delusional, was she, to think that something special was developing between them?

She might not be the queen of relationship experience, but he seemed as attracted to her as she was to him. Not that she had any idea what he saw in her. Sure, she cleaned up pretty well and even did a credible Marilyn Monroe–throwback look. But there was more to it than that. Archer seemed to genuinely like her and be concerned about her.

For her part, she didn't know if she was more fascinated by his attractiveness and sex appeal or his intelligence and humor. He completely filled her senses. He was all she could think about in her waking hours, and he was the beautiful specter she dreamed of in her sleeping hours.

And if she really cared about him, she would go far, far away from him and take her bad luck with her.

Steve dismissed the rest of the crew, but met Archer's gaze and silently indicated that he should stick around. The room cleared until it was just the two of them. They might have had their issues as kids, but they were family, and family stuck together in a crisis.

"Take a ride with me, little brother."

They jumped in Steve's Jeep and went out to the site of the explosion, which firemen were just finishing extinguishing. They were spraying a few desultory hot spots here and there that still smoked.

Steve had a word with the fire marshal, who pointed them toward a man in a jacket, standing off to one side. Jacket Guy introduced himself as the arson specialist for the local fire department.

"What have we got?" Steve asked. "Is it arson?"

The guy grinned. "Well, yeah. This set was definitely blown up intentionally. The question is, did it blow up the way you meant for it to, or did someone tamper with the manner in which it was exploded?"

Steve huffed and Archer grinned behind his brother's back.

"And?" Steve demanded.

"Come with me," the investigator said. They picked their way around smoking debris to the western edge of the mock-up. "Take a look at this wiring and tell me if this is how your guys wired the charges."

Steve crouched to look at a jumble of wires tangled on the ground at his feet. "Here. And here. These splices aren't ours."

The arson investigator knelt beside Steve, pulled out a digital camera and started snapping pictures. The guy eventually announced, "There's your answer, then. Someone came in and redid your wiring prior to detonation."

"Sonofabitch," Steve swore quietly. He glanced up at Archer. "Marley was out here yesterday afternoon for several hours, shooting stills."

His stomach plummeted to the vicinity of his shoe-laces. It couldn't be her. It just couldn't! "So were a couple of other cameramen," Archer snapped back.

The arson investigator moved away, which was just as well, for Steve muttered, "I'm gonna have to let her go. I'm sorry, bro."

"You have no proof!" Desperate, he added, "She's a union worker. You fire her without cause, and the Cinematographer's Guild will be all over you."

Steve scowled at him. "We both know why you're defending her. You want in her panties. Quit thinking with your crotch for just one minute, will you?"

"You've convicted her in your mind because you're so desperate to find a culprit you'll latch on to the first convenient suspect to come along. Get your head out of your ass, bro. I know you're under huge pressure to stop the accidents, but don't throw Marley under the bus while the real saboteur gets away."

Steve exhaled hard. "Let's pretend for a moment that you're right. Who in the hell would do all this crap to us?"

"Look to the studio's enemies. To Adrian Turnow's enemies." Even to his own ears, he sounded desperate, like he was reaching for straws.

"This studio is under brand-new ownership. They haven't had time to piss off anyone. This is only their second film."

"This is Hollywood. Everyone has haters. Jealousy runs rampant in this town, in case you hadn't noticed."

Steve sighed. "My fiancée's a famous actress, in case you forgot. I'm well aware of the jealousy and the nut balls this town attracts."

"Do me a favor. Dig hard into Marley's past. Drill down all the way. Financials, past employers, hell, check out her love life. Intrude into every corner of her life. If you still believe she's the saboteur after you're done investigating her, I won't argue if you want to fire her."

"First, I've got to go talk to Adrian and Jackson. Explain to them what happened." He shoved a distracted hand through his hair. "God, I hope the camera crew got some usable footage out of this disaster."

"It looked pretty spectacular from up close to the blast. Hell, we were practically inside the fireball."

Steve just shook his head as they climbed in the Jeep and headed back to his office. To his credit, he did call his private investigator and quietly instruct the guy to find out *everything* about Marley Stringer by whatever means necessary. Archer felt bad asking his brother to invade her privacy like this, but he had to do *something* to clear her name.

When they got back to the airport that was the stunt crew's base of operations, Archer prowled the hangars restlessly. There had to be some way to prove she was innocent. Some piece of overlooked evidence that would point at the real saboteur...

He felt her presence before he saw her. All of a sudden, awareness skittered across the back of his neck. He whipped around, and there was Marley, silhouetted in the big hangar door, watching him, all soft, sexy curves and lush red lips and sassy blond curls. He smiled intimately at her, and she smiled shyly back. No way in hell was she that good an actress. No way.

"You ready to head back to the motel?" he asked her.

"Yes. Are you perchance offering a girl a ride?"

"Perchance I am."

"Then I accept." Her smile was more flirtatious this time, and his stomach clenched in a tight knot of pleasure at the idea of getting to spend more time with her. Man, he had it bad for this girl.

*Bad enough that she had blinded him to her true nature?*

Sobered, he installed her in the passenger seat of his truck and started down out of the mountains. The drive back to the motel was pretty, with winding roads that occasionally opened up into breathtaking vistas out across the coastal plain.

They were approaching one such stretch of open road, going around a tight hairpin turn that a fast-moving SUV pulled up right on his tail. The road straightened out, the trees thinned and the mountainside dropped away precipitously beyond the low guard rail. The SUV pulled out to pass him, and Archer shook his head, touching his brakes. *Crazy California driver.*

Without warning, the SUV swerved hard toward his truck. His quick reflexes were probably all that saved him and Marley from going over the cliff. He steered hard into the SUV with his truck, meeting the collision with momentum of his own. The truck and the SUV weighed close to the same amount, so although the crunch of metal on metal was sickening, the SUV didn't succeed at driving him off the road.

"Oh, my God!" Marley cried out. He ignored her, grimly concentrating on the crazy bastard in the other vehicle.

The SUV swerved away and then slammed back into him again, but he was ready for it this time. He slammed on his brakes just as the SUV came toward him. The other vehicle shot ahead of his truck and nearly went over the guardrail itself as the driver's hard swerve toward the precipice was no longer impeded by his truck. With a screech of tires as the vehicle fishtailed violently, the other driver managed to save the SUV, straighten out the vehicle and accelerate away from them. Archer tried to catch the license-plate number, but it was covered in a layer of mud and impossible to read as the car sped away.

He briefly considered giving chase, but one glance at Marley's white-faced horror was enough to dissuade him from pursuing his attacker. Slowing to a stop, he pulled over at the side of the road to have a look at the damage to his truck.

The left headlight was smashed and the left front side panel dented. The bumper appeared a little bent, but it had done its job today and absorbed much of the initial impact.

Marley joined him on the side of the road. He held his arms out silently, and she stepped into them, hugging his waist painfully tight as he wrapped her in his embrace. She was shaking like a leaf. He held her for a long time, offering wordless comfort in the form of his strong, solid body.

Gradually, her trembling lessened, and finally it disappeared. At length, she mumbled against his chest, "I told you I'm jinxed. I wasn't kidding."

Something dawned on him with the force of a revelation. If this was another one of the movie's many "accidents," Marley had been in his truck with him when it happened. No way could she have been the driver of that other vehicle who'd caused the incident. This was proof positive that she was not the saboteur. Impatience to get back to town and tell Steve rushed through him.

He asked her gently, "Did you get a look at the driver?" God knew, he hadn't. He'd been doing his damnedest not to get knocked off the side of the mountain and roll hundreds of feet to a fiery death.

"He was wearing a baseball cap. And a dark sweater or sweatshirt pulled up around his ears." She frowned, thinking hard. "I don't think he was a real big guy. My impression was of someone fairly slight."

Wow. That was more than he'd hoped for. It still wasn't enough to go on to find the bastard. But it was better than nothing.

He pulled out his cell phone to report the incident to the police and then call Steve, but partway down this valley, they had no cell coverage. "Is your phone working, baby?"

Marley fished hers out of a pocket to have a look. "Sorry. No signal."

He swore under his breath. "We need to get to a spot where our phones work ASAP."

He drove as quickly as was safe down the mountain and pulled into the parking lot of the motel about the same time Marley reported that she had a cell phone signal back. He called the police and an officer agreed to come out and take a report from him. While Archer waited for the cop to show up, he called his brother.

"Steve. An SUV just tried to run Marley and me off the road up in the mountains."

"Where?"

"That stretch of road in San Angelo Pass with the big drop-off."

Steve swore quietly. "Was it our saboteur? Did you get a look at him?"

"More to the point, Marley was in the truck with me."

His brother fell silent at that bit of news.

"I'm right. I'm tellin' ya," Archer added.

"Did you get a look at the guy?"

"Marley did. Slight in stature, wearing a sweatshirt and baseball cap."

"And you're sure this sideswiping was intentional?"

Archer answered firmly, "Absolutely. He hit me once, bounced, then came back for a second hit. I jammed on my brakes and he nearly went over the edge himself. Then he sped away."

"You call the cops yet?"

"On their way."

"Okay. Make your report and then come up to my room."

A deputy from the county sheriff's office showed up quickly and took both his and Marley's statements. Archer gritted his teeth as the guy flirted with Marley, but she was too shaken up to notice as far as Archer could tell. Or maybe she was just that naive. Either way, he was pleased when she didn't rise to the broad hints the cop dangled in front of her.

Finally, the squad car pulled out of the parking lot. He would deal with getting his truck fixed later. Right now, he needed to get Marley to her room. She still looked totally freaked out.

He led her upstairs, took her key card from her unsteady fingers and unlocked her door. As tempting as it was to strip her down and climb into bed with her, she was upset. And he was not heartless enough to take advantage of her emotionally fragile state.

He did close the curtains and tuck her into her bed, though, insisting that she try to take a nap. She huddled under the covers while he sat on the edge of the bed beside her, stroking her silky soft hair. Slowly, she grew drowsy and relaxed, curled up against his hip. Her big blue eyes drifted closed. He sat there a few minutes more just watching her sleep. It was intimate and deeply soothing just being with her like this.

Unbelievable. He'd never imagined any woman could have this kind of a domesticating effect on him. He was a combat pilot, for goodness' sake. He wasn't the type of man to be tamed by a woman. He chased skirts, laid groupie chicks and walked away without a regret or a backward glance.

But Marley was different. With her, he dared to think of finding something…more. More personal. More lasting.

As her breathing settled into a slow, steady rhythm of sleep, he eased away from her and moved silently to the door. He shut it quietly behind him and was shocked to realize he was smiling as he turned away from her room.

Mentally shaking himself, he hurried upstairs to his brother's room. Relief that he had proof Marley wasn't the saboteur made his steps light and quick. He knocked on Steve's door.

"There you are. Come in, bro. I've got something to show you." His brother's voice was heavy. Laced with regret.

"Did you find the bastard who tried to kill us?"

"No. My private investigator just sent me something you need to see, though."

"What is it?"

"Marley's police file."

# Chapter 7

Archer poured himself another cup of coffee out of the pot in his brother's office. Cripes, he felt like crap on a cracker. He'd barely slept a wink last night. Visions of the computer printout of a mile-long rap sheet had him tossing and turning for hours.

Loitering. Vandalism. Breaking and entering. Petty theft. And then later...possession of controlled substances. Solicitation. Even extortion. How in the hell did a juvenile girl extort anything from anyone? And *what* had she extorted?

He simply could not reconcile the profile of a classic troubled, angry kid with sweet, naive Marley. Was she schizophrenic or something? He couldn't come up with any other explanation for the violent shift of personality. Even Steve had been confused by the rap sheet.

"Why didn't any of this stuff show up when I did a routine security check on her before she was hired? None of it is associated with her social security number."

The private investigator—on Steve's speakerphone—had no answer.

But Archer did. "She has a twin sister. What if all this stuff belongs to her?"

"What if it doesn't?"

The investigator interrupted. "I specifically asked for the file on Marley Stringer. This is what I got."

When he got off the call, Steve had turned to him heavily. "Give me one good reason why I shouldn't fire her and escort her off the set right now."

Archer would never forget the knife twisting in his gut as he'd stared back at Steve. Finally, he'd confessed, "I've got nothing."

"I'm sorry, man."

"Can I be there when you do it?"

Steve had frowned. "I usually prefer to fire people in private. Why do you ask?"

"I need to see her face when you show her that rap sheet. I need the closure of seeing the real Marley Stringer just once."

"Yeah, I get that. I guess I can make an exception and let you sit in on this one."

Archer had spent the rest of the night trying to envision what he was going to see this morning when her true stripes were revealed, and he just couldn't wrap his head around it. Hence the chain coffee drinking and continual pacing this morning.

He heard the crew van pull up outside, its brakes squealing a little. He slugged down the remainder of the coffee and took a deep breath, steeling himself. He'd tried, really tried, to get pissed off at her. But the best he could manage was tired disappointment. He'd really thought they had something special going.

"You ready for this?" Steve asked heavily from the doorway.

"Hell, no. But let's get it over with."

"You wanna go get her or should I?"

"I'll do it. I'm the one who wouldn't let you fire her days ago." Archer stepped out into the hangar and watched as various mechanics and pilots dispersed to their various tasks.

He spied the bright blond curls across the hangar at the scheduling board and dread pounded through him. God, he hated this. If only he could work up a little hate toward her.

She turned just then and spied him across the big, open space. Even from here, her smile was so dazzling it hurt to look at. How could such a hardened criminal be so unaware of her effect on men? Or maybe not so unaware. The extortion and solicitation charges danced through his awareness.

Dammit.

She sashayed over to him, her hips swinging with a promise of sex that made him hard in spite of his resolve to feel nothing for her, to have no reaction to her at all. Apparently, his man parts hadn't gotten the memo yet.

"Hey, handsome," she murmured. "I'd throw my arms around you and kiss you if there weren't so many people around."

His pulse leaped in spite of itself. Nope. Not over her by any stretch. "You got a minute?" he asked her.

"Yes, of course. I'm flying with you later this morning, so I'm all yours until it's time to check my camera."

Adrian was determined to keep the movie shoot on schedule in spite of yesterday's disastrous explosion. Archer had heard a few rumbles in the breakfast line this morning that the film footage from yesterday had been dramatic enough that it might be usable in the film, after all.

He turned silently and led the way to Steve's office. She followed him inside and he closed the door. Her hands started to come up, reaching for him. He winced as he stepped back. She thought he'd brought her in here for a little hanky-panky. He felt like a schmuck for luring her to her unwitting doom like this.

"Hi, Marley. Can I get you something to drink?" Steve asked quietly.

She started and her hands dropped to her sides. She looked back and forth between Archer and his brother, frowning a little. "No. I'm fine. What's this about?"

"I need you to look at something," Steve said without preamble. He pushed the sheaf of printed papers across his desk that had given Archer so much pain last night.

She picked it up. Took one look at it. Sank into the chair in front of Steve's desk. And said the last thing Archer ever expected to hear from her. "What has she done now?"

The resignation in her voice had nothing whatsoever to do with guilt.

"What do you mean?" Steve asked.

Marley looked up at him, frowning.

"Do you know what that is?" Archer tried.

Her blue gaze swung to him. "Yes. It's a rap sheet. A list of criminal charges and convictions."

Archer's gut twisted painfully. "So you admit to being responsible for those crimes?"

Guilt and shame flashed in her oh-so-open and readable face. "I tried to stop her. I really did. But she never did listen to me."

"Who's she?" Steve asked.

"My sister. Mina. This is her rap sheet."

Relief so intense it nearly drove him to his knees broke over him.

Marley looked back and forth between the two of them in confusion that quickly turned to horror. "You thought this was me? You thought I was capable of doing all this stuff?"

She stood up indignantly. "In the first place, my sister's juvenile record is sealed. How did you get hold of it? And in the second place, how dare you think I could do all those things!"

She spun to face Archer and he flinched a little in the face of her rage. "You of all people should know me well enough to know that I would never break the law or hurt people like Mina does. I am *nothing* like my sister!"

He didn't know what to say.

He looked over at his brother in distress.

Steve asked her gently, "When's the last time you spoke with your sister?"

Marley's expression became pained. "Six years ago. When I left home to come to California."

"You're not in touch at all?" Archer blurted.

She shook her head. "She was furious at me for leaving her. She accused me of abandoning her. Told me she never wanted to see me again."

"And you've never reached out to her?" Archer asked.

"I've tried to contact her. But she disappeared a few months after I left home. No one in the family has a phone number or even an email address for her."

Steve spoke heavily. "I'm sorry, Marley. It's just that we've been having an inordinate number of accidents on the set and we're checking out everybody in the crew more closely. When we ran into this rap sheet, we were concerned. I'm sorry for the invasion of your sister's privacy."

Marley nodded stiffly at Steve's apology. But in his direction, she merely glared.

Steve must have caught her acidic look because he added, "Archer's been your most forceful advocate. He was the one who was convinced you couldn't be involved with any of the accidents. He has been arguing stridently in your defense."

Although her scowl flickered momentarily, it didn't go away entirely.

Steve threw him an apologetic shrug. Hey, he had to give his brother props for trying to patch things up between them.

"Can I go now?" Marley asked abruptly.

"Yes. Of course. Thanks for your cooperation."

She spun and marched out of the office in high indignation, her tush twitching angrily. It was so sexy Archer had trouble standing upright as he watched it.

"She's a spitfire, all right," Steve commented behind him.

Archer winced. "I think our next several conversations are going to involve her throwing heavy objects at my head and me dodging while I apologize over and over."

Steve shook his head. "Hell hath no fury like a pissed-off woman."

"I don't think that's how the saying goes."

"Scorned women just get revenge. Pissed-off women hurt anyone who gets in their way *and* get revenge. I know what I'm talking about, bro. Passionate women can get a hell of a mad on. It's a take-the-bad-with-the-good thing. And right now, your woman's hella pissed."

"Yeah. I noticed."

"Don't let it sit. Work it out with her. The sooner, the

better. Women like that just get more ticked off if you let them simmer."

"Thank you, Oprah."

"Screw you, Archer."

One thing Marley hated about movie sets was the complete lack of privacy. There were people everywhere. She looked and looked for a quiet spot where she could have a good, hard cry, and it took her so long to find an equipment storage room to hide in that she thought she was going to explode by the time she finally let down her guard and the tears came.

Holding in her hurt was a skill she'd perfected over the years of growing up with Mina. People mistook her for her sister and said terrible things to her, or they subscribed to guilt by association and blamed her for her sister's transgressions. Just like Archer had.

Unlike Mina, she had a highly developed sense of shame. She couldn't count how many times she had just wanted to crawl under a rock and never come out after one of Mina's more outrageous acts of defiance.

Steve, she could forgive. He had a movie to protect, and she was as aware as everyone else that something was wrong on the set. That far too many mishaps and accidents were happening.

But Archer had no excuse. She'd been nothing but honest and decent and open with him, and he had to go and believe that she was a horrible, mean, destructive human being. Thank God she'd never managed to sleep with him, after all.

Recollection of her failure to divest herself of her stupid virginity sent her off on a whole new wave of tears in the cramped storeroom. Damn him, anyway. If only Mina were here. At least there would be a logical explanation for the mayhem on set. That girl was a hurricane who left a trail of destruction in her wake everywhere she went. Marley had long believed her sister was mentally ill and in need of medical help.

The storeroom door opened without warning and she squinted up into the glare of bright light streaming in.

"There you are," Archer declared. He strode forward to sweep her in his arms. "I was worried about you."

She stiffened against him, having no part of his hug. He ignored her silent rejection, though, and gave her a thorough hug before finally turning her loose.

She took a step back and glared at him. "I'm still furious with you."

"Fair enough. But I was still worried about you. We have to fly in an hour. I thought you might want to check over your camera after yesterday's explosion. You know. Make sure it wasn't damaged."

Crap. She hadn't even thought about that possibility. Scowling, she moved past him—or tried to move past him. But his arm shot out and blocked her way. "I never thought you were behind the attacks. I really did argue with Steve about it. My gut said all along that there was no way you could hurt other people."

Her stare narrowed menacingly. "Don't be so sure about that. I could hurt you pretty easily right about now."

He grinned down at her. "I know it'll piss you off, but I can't help saying it. You look like a kitten with her claws out. And it's adorable."

He was right. She was in no mood to be compared to harmless, helpless kittens.

He added hastily, "And this is exactly why I couldn't believe you were the saboteur."

"Someone's trying to ruin the set?" she exclaimed.

Archer winced and then swore. "Look. I really need

you not to repeat that. So far, everyone thinks there've just been a bunch of accidents. We need to keep it that way so people don't panic and quit in droves. The studio has a lot riding on this film and needs everyone here, doing their jobs."

Yikes. No wonder Steve was poking around into everyone's extremely personal lives. Poor Adrian. She really liked the director. He had a great eye and seemed like a genuinely nice man.

"If you would please move your arm, I need to go check out my camera now."

Archer's arm blocked her for a moment more, and then fell away. Okay, that made her feel like a bit of a heel. He'd offered her a sincere apology, and she'd been bitchy and refused to accept it.

He followed her out to Minerva in silence and pre-flighted the helicopter while she partially tore down her camera to make sure nothing had been damaged or dislodged. Finally, she turned it on and tried filming the airfield, panning across it with her remote control inside the cockpit.

Abruptly, a male crotch completely filled her view-finder. She jerked back, and lifted her face away from the blatantly sexual display, embarrassed. The sad thing was, she knew that crotch. She'd actually studied the damned thing in enough detail to know that telltale bulge behind the zipper. What kind of a pervert did that make her?

"Like what you see?" Archer asked, dry as dust.

"My camera's working," she retorted, refusing to give in to his flirting.

"You're a stubborn, hard-hearted woman, Marley Stringer," he sighed.

Was he right? She was more stung by the comment

than she let on. She broke down and asked stiffly, "How's Minerva today?"

He grinned at her. "Getting lubed up for me as we speak."

Her jaw dropped. She couldn't think of a single comeback to that outrageous remark.

He continued blithely, "Once the mechanic tops off the oil, we'll be good to go."

Something inside her uncoiled a little. If only. She really had been hoping for a different outcome with him.

Archer finished up outside and then joined her in the tight confines of the cockpit, strapping in as he spoke. "I thought about you all night last night. Did you dream about me?"

In point of fact she had. And the dream had bordered on mental porn. Even now, her body responded a little in recollection of the things her unconscious had imagined the two of them doing.

"Why, Miss Stringer. Is that a blush I spy blooming upon those rosy cheeks?"

She swatted his arm. "Hush up. It's not nice to embarrass a lady."

"I almost came to your room," he confessed.

The notion galvanized her. All of a sudden, her body was languid in the seat. Hungry. Restless.

Archer's nostrils flared and his voice dropped into a husky timbre. "Would you have let me in?"

Honesty forced her to mumble, "Uh-huh."

He sucked in a sharp breath between his teeth. She knew the feeling. All of a sudden, the air in the cockpit was crackling, charged with sexual energy that all but fried everything and everyone in its path. If the helicopter had a problem today, it was on Archer's head. He was the one who'd generated this crazy energy field between them. She'd been perfectly prepared to sulk at him through the whole flight. But now she was going to struggle to keep her hands off him and her eyes on her work.

The mechanic stuck his head in Archer's door without warning, and she jumped about a foot in the air. "Your girl's ready and waiting to fly for you, Archer."

The guy backed out and Archer shut the door, laughing a little under his breath. A quick glance at Archer's crotch showed that he was every bit as turned on as she was. Well. This was going to be an interesting flight.

"Are you safe to fly right now?" she asked him cautiously.

He made a strangled sound somewhere between laughter and a groan. He ground out, "Yeah. I'm good."

She couldn't resist getting a little payback and muttered, "I hear you're better than good."

"Do tell," he murmured as he opened his checklist. She smirked as he squeezed his eyes tightly shut for a second and shifted uncomfortably in his seat before starting running his various checklists. Yup. This flight was going to be very interesting indeed.

Archer closed his eyes against the lust surging through his groin. He could smell the sweet, needy musk of Marley's body. *Ready and waiting indeed.*

This was madness. He should back away from her. Give some decent guy an opportunity to catch her eye. To make her happy. To treat her the way she ought to be treated. He did not deserve her. His mother and all the other women in his life had seen what a mess he was. Had dropped him like a hot potato. But damned if he didn't want Marley worse than life.

Sure, he'd been horny and chased after skirts for the

easy sex as much as the next guy, but nothing he'd ever felt had prepared him for the way he wanted her all the damned time. This wasn't simple lust. Every cell in his body hungered for her. It consumed him. Completely.

And he'd *blown* it with her. She had every right to be chippy with him. Sure, he was doing his best to charm her out of her snit. But it was a well-deserved snit nonetheless.

Prescott called out across the ramp on a megaphone, "Ten minutes to countdown."

Work called. "We'll…talk…later. I have to do a little flying now, sweetheart. I have no intention of crashing and burning until I've made things right between us."

Swear to God, the temperature went up in the cockpit a few degrees as her libido ratcheted up even more. The woman was a sexual volcano waiting to blow.

She nodded and looked for all the word like speech had deserted her.

"Work first, baby. Then play."

"Promise?"

"Oh, hell, yes." But the little voice in the back of his head taunted him that he wasn't the guy for her. And it refused to shut up for even a second, telling him over and over that she wasn't his sandbox to play in.

She let out a hard, relieved breath that made him laugh reluctantly. He knew the feeling. How in the hell was he going to break it to her—that they couldn't be lovers—without breaking her heart?

But first, he had to get through this flight.

Without killing them both.

Marley went through checking out her camera by rote. She was so intoxicated by being close to Archer that she could hardly remember her own name, let alone what she was supposed to do to prep her equipment. He looked as distracted as she was. Of course, he had a flight over another fake combat zone looming before him. A brief vision of that mountainside racing toward them flashed through her head. He'd be all right, wouldn't he? There wouldn't be another episode like the last one, would there?

"Archer, the calibration on my camera is off a little. Do I have a minute to jump outside and adjust it before we have to go?"

"Yes. But be quick about it."

She went outside and knelt in front of the helicopter, adjusting the mount, which must have bent a little in yesterday's explosion. A movement out of the corner of her eye made her look up. She scowled to see a familiar, hulking form strolling toward her.

"Hey, Gordon," she said reluctantly.

"You're not going up with him again, are you?"

"Well, yeah. It's my job."

"Can't you set up your camera to be remote controlled or something?"

She frowned at the big man. "Not really."

He swore colorfully. "Look. Archer's a head case. I saw what he did the other day. You shouldn't fly with him again. He's gonna get both of you killed."

Gordon's warning was a dagger of doubt to her gut, but she still said stoutly, "It'll be okay. Archer's a fine pilot. I trust him."

"With your life?" he asked skeptically. He shrugged. "I tried to warn you. Sorry, babe. Let me know when you're ready to date a real man."

"I am dating a real man, thanks." Lord, it felt good to say that. And even better, it made Gordon scowl and stomp away from her. She might still be furious with Archer, but they were by no means over.

She climbed into the seat beside Archer, feeling a fair bit more charitable toward him after their earlier clash.

He asked tersely, "Was Gordon respectful toward you, or do I have to kick his ass when we land?"

"He was fine. He asked me out on a date—reasonably nicely for him, I might add—and I said no."

"Persistent bastard."

She had to give Gordon credit, though. At least he'd been a little concerned about her safety. She had to give Archer credit, too, for making her feel safe and protected, neither of which were sensations she was in the least bit accustomed to. They were nice. Very nice. Most of her remaining irritation at Archer for doubting her drained away. God, she was such a pushover where he was concerned. Either that, or she had fallen a lot harder for him already than she'd realized.

Archer smiled over at her a little as he asked for takeoff clearance, and her heart melted at the gesture. He was trying to act nonchalant about this flight, but his forehead was tight, and lines of stress pulled at the corners of his eyes. And still, he went out of his way to reassure her. He really was a decent guy. Who was she kidding? She'd totally fallen for him. It was a done deal.

As the engine cranked up and the rotor started to turn, she murmured, "Are you okay?"

"Right as rain, darlin'."

"I'll be more concerned if you aren't at least a little tense about this flight, Archer."

"Okay, fine. I'm a little tense. Happy?"

"Relieved. Just tell me what I can do to help."

"You get the best camera shots you can. Impress the hell out of Adrian Turnow."

She reached out to touch his arm and his muscles went rock hard. "We'll get through this together."

"It'll be a low-speed pass down into the valley today," Archer said a little too calmly. "I'll slow to a hover beside the Sikorsky and the stunt guys will do their thing. Just so you know, a hover isn't an easy maneuver. Of course, I happen to be a magnificent pilot and will give you a steady platform for your shot. But if it's windy or turbulent, we could move around a little."

"Of course you're magnificent." She grinned. "But the inertial stabilizers in my camera mount will compensate for small movements, anyway," she replied as she glued her face to her viewfinder.

Adrian Turnow handed the conn over to Steve Prescott, and the countdown to special effects commenced. Everybody sounded a little tense over the radios after yesterday's explosion.

She reported in and duly started filming as the narrow valley came into view in her lens.

"Talk to me, baby," Archer murmured.

Without lifting her face from her camera, she said, "Could you speed up a little as we head down the head of the valley? It'll give us a sense of rushing headlong into the battle."

"Coming up."

The view moved past a little faster outside. "Perfect."

"There's Gordon's chopper. Big green blob at our eleven o'clock. See it?" he asked.

"Uh-huh," she replied, bringing the Huey into focus.

"Do me a favor and flip him the bird when we get close. My hands will be busy on the controls."

She snorted with laughter. "You got it."

She zoomed her lens in on Gordon's aircraft as it swept across her field of view, swooping down aggressively to a few feet off the ground. Stunt men and actors started jumping out of it and into her shot.

"Why doesn't the helicopter just land to offload the soldiers?" she asked curiously as her camera rolled.

"Land mines."

*Yikes.* "But the soldiers are jumping to the ground. If there's a mine, they're gonna trigger it, right?"

"They're expendable. Helicopters cost a lot of money and are finite resources. Even a few feet of separation above a land mine makes a significant difference in survivability. You saw yesterday how explosions throw helicopters aside without destroying them."

She shuddered. "That's pretty cold logic to save the machine but sacrifice the people."

"That's war."

He sounded bitter. But then, she supposed he had a right to. "It must suck being a little cog in a big war machine. Do you ever feel like just a number?"

"Pilots are expensive and finite resources, too. It costs millions to fully train us. Grunts, not so much."

"Wow. That's harsh."

"I never said I agree with that sort of thinking. That's just how it is."

The last soldier leaped off the other helicopter and the bird began to rise into the air as she completed her shot. A wash of turbulence slammed into their helicopter and Archer swore under his breath. Minerva rocked violently, and he fought the controls grimly. He'd no more regained control of her than an explosion erupted directly in front of them at a distance of not more than fifty feet. Clods of earth pelted them as a plume of smoke and flames spouted from the earth.

Marley jerked backward, startled badly, even though the explosion had been briefed in this morning's walk-through of the day's shoot. Archer lurched nearly as hard as she did. Both of them were jumpy today. Maybe it wasn't such a great idea having the two of them flying together like this after all the mishaps they'd had.

Right. Like it was a better alternative to spread the jinx around to all the other pilots, too. She really needed to seriously consider quitting this job. She would in a heartbeat if it wouldn't wreck her career and any chance of her ever breaking into film cinematography.

It wasn't like she had her overnight camera-operator job to go back to. She'd gone all in and resigned that position when she took this job. Stupid, stupid, stupid. But she was well and truly stuck now. She had to see this movie through no matter what accidents erupted around her. Besides, it wasn't like she was going to do anything that took her away from Archer. Even if it killed her.

Now all that remained to be seen was whether or not she would be fired because of the damned jinx… and whether or not Archer would survive the curse that clung to her regarding men.

Blessedly, the remainder of the flight went uneventfully. They returned to base and she left Archer to refuel the helicopter and put Minerva to bed while she headed back to the motel. Separate vehicles seemed to be a good idea at the moment, given yesterday's disastrous trip back to town and the SUV that had nearly run them off the mountain.

She strolled toward the bus stop where the crew bus would eventually arrive. But before it could show up, a big Jeep pulled up with two other guys in it. Gordon Trapowski was at the wheel.

"Heading back to the motel?" he asked civilly enough.

She nodded.

"Get in. We're headed back to the studio. I've got

time to make a quick run that way and make it over to the soundstage to rehearse my stunt sequence."

With the other guys in the vehicle, too, she was inclined to take him up on the offer. Sometimes the crew bus took up to an hour to make a single circuit of the sprawling movie set. Besides, maybe she could get some more out of him about Archer's last military mission.

The guy in the passenger seat hopped in the back and she took his place beside Gordon, who wasted no time demanding, "Archer flip out on you again?"

"Again?"

"He 'bout ran you into the side of a mountain a few days ago. He still pulling weird stuff like that on you? Just say the word and I'll get his ass grounded."

"No. He's fine," she blurted in alarm. "Just fine."

Trapowski looked over at her shrewdly. "You sure? Don't protect him if he needs to be put down. Not only will he get you killed, but it's bad for him not to take time off if he needs to."

Even if he did make Archer sound like a rabid dog, Gordon did make a valid point. Still, she felt deeply uncomfortable talking about Archer behind his back, particularly with a known enemy of Archer's.

"Do you know anything about the kind of flying Archer was doing right before he came home?" she asked Gordon.

He puffed up importantly. "Yeah. Sure. I know all about military flying."

"Can you tell me anything about his flying overseas?"

"Nah. That's classified."

She was half inclined to believe he didn't know anything and was using the whole classified bit as a cover-up.

"I can tell you one thing about that bastard, though.

He ain't all together up here." Gordon tapped on the side of his head.

"What does that mean exactly?"

"He's lost his marbles. Gonna get grounded for good any day now. Why else do you think Steve hired him? He's trying to save the guy's wings, but it looks like a lost cause to me."

*That* was why Prescott had offered Archer this job? Did Archer know that?

"The way I hear it, when Archer goes back to his unit in a few weeks, the flight surgeon's gonna take his wings away so fast his head spins."

"Wait. What?" she blurted.

"He's home on leave for sixty days of R and R to get himself together before he goes up in front of a psychological review board. He's going back to face the board in a few weeks."

And Archer hadn't seen fit to share this little detail with her? Stunned, she rode the rest of the way back to the hotel in silence, letting the banter of the other guys roll off her, mostly unheard.

She tuned back in, though, when the conversation devolved into war stories featuring Steve Prescott. She gathered soon enough that he'd been a Marine's Marine before he'd been sent away to do some embassy job and his military career had ended abruptly under mysterious circumstances. The guys in the Jeep agreed that he should have stayed in combat theaters and not gotten tangled up in politics that ruined his career. They also agreed that they were glad to be working for him and his brother, Jackson Prescott, now.

*Whoa.* "Jackson Prescott, the movie star? Star of this movie? He's Steve's brother?" she demanded.

The men laughed heartily at her shock. Although

now that she thought about it, the stunt coordinator did look quite a bit like the actor-turned-producer Jackson Prescott.

She hadn't met Jackson in person, but she'd seen him at a distance around the set. No wonder Steve Prescott was being so grouchy about the accidents around the filming. This was a family thing, and he was taking it personally. She could relate. If anyone had tried to mess with her sister, she would've leaped to Mina's defense.

The Jeep pulled up in front of the motel and she reached for the door handle. "Thanks for the ride, guys."

"Take my advice, Marley," Gordon said soberly. "Stay the hell away from Archer. He's trouble. Bastard like that is no good for you." The guys in the backseat nodded in agreement. What on earth did they all know about Archer that she didn't?

"I'll take that under advisement," she murmured.

She climbed out of the vehicle glumly. Why hadn't he been honest about the fact that he was leaving in a few weeks? It had been pretty crappy of him to lead her on, to make her think they could have a real relationship when, all along, he was about to ship back out to the end of the earth.

He'd kept his and Steve's suspicions from her and acted like he was falling for her when, in fact, he thought she was running around sabotaging the movie. He'd deceived her right from the very start.

She waited all afternoon in her room for Archer to show up so she could confront him about his future plans and about his dishonesty with her. Had anything he'd said to her been true at all? Or had it all been lies? Humiliation at the things she'd let him do to her roiled through her, slimy and sickening. God. To think she'd been so close to having sex with him.

She got in the shower and scoured her skin vigorously with a loofah sponge, but nothing would get rid of the filthy feeling clinging to her body. The longer she stood under the steaming water, the angrier she got. He'd taken gross advantage of her. He knew she didn't have much experience with men, but he'd romanced her and swept her off her feet, anyway, knowing full well he was going to love her and leave her. What. A. Jerk.

She'd been blind. A total fool to fall for his line. At least she had the consolation of knowing it had been a freaking slick line. But still. She could kick herself for believing anything he said. Her first instinct had been correct not to believe that a guy like him could fall for a girl like her.

Frantically, she scrubbed at her face, removing any lingering remnants of the makeup she'd been naively plastering on...as if anything she could do would make her genuinely attractive to a man like Archer. God, what a colossal fool she'd been.

Restless, she paced around her room. Although the movement eased the terrible tension across the back of her neck, no answers were forthcoming about what to do about Archer.

Should she break things off now and cut her emotional losses, or was she an idiot to walk away from a guy who was ready, willing and able to have a hot, utterly meaningless fling with her? Was this all her fault for expecting too much from him? Maybe she should start with a nice, simple, throwaway relationship like he could give her before she went looking for true love forever.

She called his phone and got kicked over to voice mail. "Hey, Archer. It's me. We need to talk."

She waited for *hours* for him to call back. But her

email and phone remained stubbornly silent. He didn't want to talk? Okay, fine. She wasn't going to beg. If he wanted to see her, he could damn well call her back. But it was hard to keep putting down her phone every single time she picked it up. Finally, in desperation, she headed down to the motel bar for happy hour.

Tyrone and a few of the other makeup artists waved her over to their table, and she joined them gratefully. She didn't need a drunken Gordon hitting on her and making a scene.

Tyrone shook his head when she sat down beside him. "I hate to say it, but I may have been wrong. That flyboy's trouble," he said direly. "I've been hearing the crew talk. They're saying he's lost the handle. Honey, I don't care how pretty he is. He's not worth getting hurt over."

She clenched her jaw on a terse reply. They meant well. And it was sweet of them to worry about her. Archer could hurt her, all right. But not in his helicopter, as it turned out. He had the power to hurt her a lot more deeply than merely physically injuring her.

"Earth to Marley, come in," Tyrone said in her ear.

Crap. Everyone at the table was staring at her. The last thing she wanted to do was pour out her heart to this gossipmongering bunch. Frantically weighing what she could say to distract them and get them off her case, she said lightly, "Sorry. I was just thinking about how great an ass Archer has."

The makeup artists hooted, and sure enough, the conversation turned to how hunkalicious he and his ass were. Before long, a consensus emerged that even if he was crazy, he might still be worth having gnarly sex with. Marley had to admit, their narcissistic logic made a certain sense. Grab some pleasure and run.

But the worried look lurking in Tyrone's eyes every time he glanced over at her didn't go away. She squeezed his hand both in thanks and reassurance. He was a good friend. But now that she knew the score on him, she wouldn't let Archer break her heart.

She hoped.

She passed most of the evening in the bar with the makeup artists, and Archer never showed. What the hell was going on with him?

She briefly considered asking Steve Prescott if he knew where Archer was, but she dared not draw any more of his boss's attention to her that was absolutely necessary. She might have cleared up the mystery of her sister's rap sheet, but that didn't necessarily mean she was off the hook as a suspect for the accidents around the set.

She had an early showtime in the morning and crawled into bed, angry and upset. What was she supposed to do now? Should she walk away from Archer? From this whole disastrous movie adventure? Go back home to Chicago with her tail between her legs and try to pick up some work there?

She woke up no closer to any answers than she had been before she fell asleep.

Two things became clear to her with the bright light of a new day. One: a long-term relationship—make that a real relationship of any kind—was off the table with Archer. No way could she be with a man who was dishonest with her. Two: she still wanted to sleep with him. She just needed to have sex and get it out of the way once and for all so she could get on with her life.

And who better to have cheap sex with than a gigolo-wannabe who was going to leave and go halfway around the world in a few weeks, never to see her again? It was actually kind of perfect as long as she didn't mind using him as coldly as he'd been planning to use her. For once, she should be more like Mina. Take what she wanted and run.

A plan. She needed a plan. There had to be a way to get him in the sack…and then kick him out of it after she got what she wanted.

A big storm was forecast to roll in overnight, and the remaining action sequences to be shot would require airplanes and helicopters. Bad weather meant no flying, and no flying meant no outdoor filming. Adrian pulled the actors into a soundstage to work on indoor shots, but only a handful of camera operators were required for that. The rest of the cinematographers and stunt crew were given the next three days off to wait out the storm.

Marley's motel-room walls closed in on her as the skies grew gray and heavy enough to match her mood. She would go nuts if she had to spend all weekend staring at her walls and watching bad reruns on television, or worse, hanging out in the bar with the crew while Archer assiduously avoided her. She had still not seen more than brief flashes of him in the distance since yesterday's revelations.

What. Ever.

She thumbed through the newspaper to see if there was anything local she could do to keep her from going stir-crazy, and she spied an advertisement that made her stop and read it through again. "Great cabin in the mountains, perfect getaway from it all. For rent by the day or the week." On impulse, she picked up the phone and dialed the number.

An elderly man answered the call. The cabin was available for the next three days, and in a few minutes, she'd given the man her credit card number and gotten directions to the cabin. He made some mention of the cabin being above the snow line, but thankfully there wasn't any snow in the forecast. Just rain, and lots of it.

She signed out one of the common-use cars that had been made available to the crew, threw an overnight bag in the backseat and headed up into the Sierra Nevada mountain range.

The drive was gorgeous. Towering pine trees crowded the road, their tops appearing to scratch the belly of the sky. The stress of the past few days fell away from her the farther she got from the movie set. This had been a great idea. Her soul expanded in relief with every mile and every magnificent pine tree she passed.

The cabin turned out to be a one-story log-and-stone affair. Classic Craftsman bungalow architecture. Neat and well kept, the key was exactly where the owner had said she would find it. She let herself in and shivered in the chill. She turned on the furnace and, after exploring both bedrooms and choosing the larger, front-facing room for herself, made her way back to the main living area.

Firewood and kindling were neatly stacked beside the fireplace, and a box of long matches stood on the mantel. Smiling, she knelt and built a fire her Girl Scout troop leader would be proud of. Soon, a blaze crackled cheerfully on the hearth. The silence of the place was so deep it soaked into her bones. She idly wished Archer were here. He could use a dose of the peace of this place. And then she remembered that he was a lying bastard and that she was furious at him.

The light coming in the windows dimmed a little. Or maybe that was just the storm rolling in from the coast and catching up with her.

The cabin's owner had said there were plenty of staple foods in the cupboards, and he had not been lying. She'd picked up a few perishables on her way up here—milk, bread, eggs, fruit and salad makings—and she stowed those in the fridge. Opening a can of chili, she poured it into a pot to heat, then popped some ready-made biscuits into the oven.

After the bracing meal, she settled down in a big armchair in front of the fire with her journal, which she had sadly neglected the past few days. The combination of full belly and soothing heat from the fire must have knocked her out because she jolted awake some time later. It was dark outside but oddly bright light came in through the big picture window. She got up and stared in shock at the thick blanket of white covering the ground. And more snow was falling in big, fat flakes that settled softly to earth.

It was only October, for crying out loud! Since when did it snow this early, especially in California, land of eternal sunshine? Apparently since she'd ventured above the freaking snow line. The little car she'd driven up here already looked like nothing more than a vaguely car-shaped mound of white. At least six inches of snow covered it.

She reached for the light switch beside the door and flipped it on. *Nothing.* She flipped the switch a few more times, which, if she stopped to think about it, was rather dumb. If it didn't work the first time, there was no reason for it to work the third time. She moved over to the kitchen and noticed the digital clock on the stove had gone dark.

*Damn.* The power was out? In a snowstorm? *Uh-oh.*

At least the fire was still going and the main room held leftover warmth from the furnace earlier. She stoked up the fire with plenty of wood as, over the next few hours, the snow piled up outside until it was a good twelve inches deep. The cabin cooled somewhat, but the stone walls and roaring fire held back the worst of the cold outside.

She jolted when a loud ringing noise exploded from the direction of the kitchen. An old-fashioned land-line telephone jangled away. Must be the cabin's owner checking in on her. What a sweet old guy.

She picked up the phone cheerfully. "Hello, this is Marley Stringer."

"Where the hell are you?" Archer's voice demanded.

He sounded way too calm. The kind of calm that meant he was really mad. Trepidation zinged through her. "How did you get this number?"

"You listed it on the checkout paperwork for the car you borrowed. Where are you? The mother of all rain-storms has cut loose and you need to stay off the roads."

She laughed. "I doubt I'll get on a road anytime soon. I think I'm pretty well snowed in."

"Snow? Where *are* you?"

"A cabin in the mountains. Um, above the snow line."

"Christ. How much snow is on the ground?"

"I don't know. Ten, twelve inches, maybe."

He swore some more. "Roads are flooding out all over the place, and the news is reporting mudslides and rockfall warnings. When are you due back in town?"

"Sunday evening."

"Negative. Don't drive anywhere until the roads clear up."

"I can't stay here forever. After all, the power's out," she added with a frown.

*"What?"*

"Hey, I was a Girl Scout. I've got this covered." If

nothing else, she could live on roasted marshmallows and s'mores.

"This isn't the Girl Scouts, Marley. This is goddamn serious."

"Excuse me? Are you insulting my Girl Scout training?"

"Damn straight I am. What's the address of the cabin?" he demanded.

She narrowed her eyes. "Why?"

"I'm coming up there to pull you out."

"Oh, for heaven's sake. That's not necessary. I've got a big stack of firewood and a cupboard full of food. I'm all cozy and warm, and I'll be fine."

"*Mmm-hmm.* Unlock the door for me and make a bed in front of the fire where you'll be warm."

That did not sound like a ringing endorsement of faith in her survival skills. And since when did he care, anyway? Besides, the last thing she wanted was for him to come barging up here like the damned Lone Ranger to rescue the damsel in distress. Annoyed, she said more forcefully, "Archer, I can take care of myself."

"Did it ever dawn on you that I don't want you to have to take care of yourself?"

She snorted. "Yeah, I've noticed that you like to have things exactly your way."

There was a moment's silence. "I would ask you what that means, but I'd rather hear your explanation in person."

"I don't want or need your help. Stay home."

"Not happening. I'll worry about you until I know you're safe."

"I'm safe already!"

"Gonna have to see that with my own eyes. Sorry."

She had to give him credit for sounding sincerely

worried about her. That was hard to argue with. But she did, anyway. "Look. I doubt the roads are any safer for you than they'd be for me."

"I've got a truck," he reminded her. "And chains. And I grew up driving around in these mountains."

She tried one last time. "It'll warm up in a day or two and the snow will melt off. I promise I won't try to drive out until I can see dirt. Does that make you happy?"

"Just don't go anywhere. Got it?"

# Chapter 8

She started to tell him she was from the Midwest, which didn't have the world's most gentle climate, thank you very much, but the line went dead. In her ear. Omigod. *Did he just hang up on her?* Or maybe the phone line cut off due to the snow continuing to pile up outside.

She looked out the front window dubiously. It really was snowing hard, even by Chicago standards. Surely, he wouldn't try to make it all the way up here in that mess.

She hunkered down in front of the fireplace once more and picked up her journal, pouring out her hurt, anger, frustration, and confusion. She had no idea what to do about him. She didn't trust him any further than she could throw him, but her unfulfilled lust seemed to think it was still okay to sleep with him. Did that make her no better than him if she succumbed to those urges? Her rational brain shouted that it totally did. But the beast gnawing at her belly still hungered for what Archer could give her.

Maybe if she got drunk, then she couldn't be held responsible for what happened between them. She doodled in her journal and decided that using alcohol as an excuse was no excuse at all. Rats. Like it or not, she couldn't have her cake and eat it, too. She either had to take the moral high ground and stay away from Archer or be no better than him. Reluctantly, she jotted down "No booze. And no fun. Dang it."

She could always take the direct route and tell Archer outright that she wanted sex with no strings attached and without any more of his seductive lies to sugarcoat what they were doing. She noticed with a start that she had written down, "Tell Archer I want sex." She crossed out the words hastily. "Bad idea. Very bad idea." Moral high ground, dammit.

If only she were Marilyn Monroe. She would use her sex appeal to snare the guy in her web, take what she wanted and walk away. She looked down at her page and laughed. She'd written down "Channel Marilyn Monroe." It wasn't a half-bad idea. Not that she could even dream of pulling that one off.

The hour grew late, and the quiet hissing of the fire lulled her nearly into unconsciousness. She headed for the bedroom whose door she'd prudently left open all evening. The room was cool, but habitable. She pulled on a big, sloppy T-shirt and slipped under the fluffy down comforter. *Flannel sheets.* Give the owner of this place a gold star. The bed warmed up quickly, and she hunkered down blissfully, well satisfied with her getaway so far. It was actually fun being snowed in like this, given that all of her survival and comfort needs were met.

*Soon.* If not with Archer, she would get rid of her virginity one way or another soon and get on with a normal social life. And then she would make an effort to go on dates and have interesting social interactions. Maybe even a boyfriend.

She couldn't wait. She ignored the little voice in the back of her head whispering insidiously that she'd already found the perfect guy for her. Hah. Lie. Archer was Trouble. Capital *T.*

Archer squinted through the driving snow as his truck crawled forward at barely ten miles per hour. His GPS said the turnoff to Marley's cabin should be somewhere along this stretch of road. Although the pine forest blocked the worst of the howling winds, it also made the falling snow swirl in his headlights in badly disorienting patterns. His four-wheel-drive truck and chains were barely managing to forge through the huge drifts of snow. When he'd left the valley where the movie was shooting, this had been a downpour of rain, which had been blinding enough. But in the form of snow, visibility was almost zero.

*There.* An opening in the trees that might be a driveway.

He stopped the truck and got out. The cold and snow slammed into him and he yanked his mountaineering shell up around his ears. He slogged over to what he thought might be the driveway and kicked his boots through the snow. Yup, there was gravel beneath. Firm ground. A road bed. He shook off the worst of the snow as he climbed back into the truck.

Downshifting, he eased the vehicle onto the narrow track. He had to stop twice to peer ahead in the beams of his headlights and find the driveway again.

But finally, a tidy log cabin came into view. A mound of snow that might once have been a car stood beside the structure, and a faint, orange glow came through the front window.

He stomped through knee-deep snow to the front porch and knocked on the door. Nobody answered. He moved over to the window to peer inside. That was definitely the glow of a fireplace. But there was no sign of Marley. Dammit, he'd told her to sleep in front of it!

Alarm erupted in his gut. She hadn't gone outside, had she? Or maybe succumbed to the insidious onset of hypothermia. Or gotten injured. Or worse…

She'd better at least have left the door unlocked as he'd told her to or there'd be hell to pay—and a broken door to fix. He reached for the doorknob and tried it. The thing turned, which was good given that he was absolutely prepared to kick it down. He stepped inside and quickly shut it behind him.

"Marley?" he called.

Nothing. *Dammit!* He'd *told* her at all costs not to leave. Where the hell was she? He spied an open door across the room and stormed toward it, panic clawing at him as it hadn't since his disastrous last mission.

He barged into the darkness, which turned out to be a bedroom, and spotted a long lump in the bed. God, he prayed that was Marley. He sagged in relief as he recognized the blond curls peeking out from under the top of the down comforter. *Thank goodness.* He didn't know what he would've done if something bad had happened to her…

The thought stopped him cold. *Jeez.* How far gone *was* he over this woman?

He stared down at her sleeping form. Nothing but her nose and the top of her head were visible on the pillow. The rest of her was snuggled down deep under a puffy down comforter. She must be sleeping hard not to have heard him pounding on the door or calling her name. He ought to wake her up, bundle her in the truck and get the hell out of here before the roads got any worse.

But he wasn't at all sure his truck would make it back down the driveway with the snow piling up as fast as it was and the winds picking up enough to push it into giant drifts. He'd barely made it up the drive, and by the time he packed up Marley and her things, he suspected they would get stuck, and then they would really be in a pickle. He probably shouldn't attempt the miserable roads at this late hour, anyway. It was nearly 2:00 a.m., and he'd had a long day with that rough drive up here. Better to ride out the storm here in relative warmth and safety.

And damned if the other side of the bed didn't look incredibly inviting.

The sensible side of his brain, the one that was determined to be honorable and not take advantage of Marley, warned him that this was a lousy idea. There appeared to be another bedroom next door. He should go in there to sleep.

But Lord, she looked all warm and soft and cozy. He could crawl in beside her, wrap his arms around her, lose himself in her sweet scent and fall asleep relishing the curves of her body against his. The exhausted warrior within him ached for rest beside her so bad he could hardly stand it.

Except the way his male parts had just leaped to attention, he sure as hell wouldn't be falling asleep any time soon. Silently swearing up a blue storm, he whirled and fled the bedroom before he had sex with Marley while *she* was unconscious this time.

He went back out to his truck to grab the bag of emergency supplies he'd hastily thrown together before heading up here. Although he had to give Marley credit. She did appear to have things well in hand. He hauled in several big armloads of wood and stacked them on the stone hearth, and added a bunch of wood to the mostly burned-down embers of the fire.

As it flared up, he spotted an open journal lying in the big chair in front of the fire. He glanced at it before he'd really registered what it was. He didn't mean to pry. But the word leaped up off the page at him. He couldn't help it that he'd spotted his own name like that. He picked up the journal to read what he'd seen again.

*"Tell Archer I want sex."*

What the heck?

He dropped down in the chair, propped his hiking boots on the hearth to dry and read through Marley's doodles with growing amazement. Apparently, she was really mad at him for lying to her about something. Although what, exactly, wasn't spelled out. But she still wanted to have sex with him and was conflicted about what to do.

He got to the part where she wondered if she would have become as low as him if she just used his body for sex. *Ouch.* Was that what she thought of him?

He had no illusions that most of the women he went to bed with used him purely for sex. Hell, he used them for sex, too. But he'd thought Marley was different. No, she *was* different. She was at least having an internal debate with herself over the rightness or wrongness of using him.

He supposed he shouldn't be too offended. It was what all women did: they took one look at him and saw an uncomplicated lay with a hot guy. And he had let them be correct over the years. But realizing that Marley wanted the exact same thing from him hurt a little. *Correction.* It hurt like hell.

Which shocked him to his core. What in the hell had she done to him?

She was absolutely not the wham-bam-thank-you-ma'am type. And he had just a few weeks left to build something that would withstand thousands of miles of separation and months apart. Yeah, right. Like that was possible. Not to mention, Marley needed wooing. Seduction. Emotional involvement, dammit. All the things he didn't even know how to *do* with a woman. It wasn't like any woman in his past had ever shown him how...

And it wasn't like he'd ever wanted to learn.

Until Marley.

Her sweetness and goodness—which were real no matter what Steve said, dammit—challenged him to be...more. To man up and engage with her intellectually and emotionally. Not just physically.

But he really shouldn't be looking for anything serious with any woman.

*Shouldn't.*

Wow. Did he just think that? He *wasn't* looking for anything serious!

His career made long-distance relationships necessary, and he knew from watching his buddies that they were flipping hard to sustain. They took a ton of work and commitment from both ends of the relationship. He wasn't up for anything like that.

And yet, here he was high in the mountains, in the

middle of the night, to rescue Marley from a damned snowstorm. Contemplating the unthinkable. Giving her the real relationship she craved. That *he* craved.

He stared into the fire a long time. Hell, he didn't even know if she would consider having one with him.

One thing he did know. He wasn't going to hook up with her, have a cheap one-night stand, and then dump her. She damn well deserved better than that.

Bleakly, he headed for the spare bedroom. It was freezing. That door hadn't been open to the living room through the evening apparently. He stripped off his damp clothes, hung them up to dry and crawled under the down comforter. It didn't take long for his thoughts to turn to the woman sleeping next door, and suddenly, staying warm was not an issue. Cooling off was going to be the problem tonight.

He woke abruptly to the piercing sound of woman screaming a few feet away, and he lurched upright. *Must protect Marley...*

"Archer! You scared me half to death!"

The woman in question stood over him, a fire poker raised high over her shoulder. And she looked jumpy as hell.

*Join the club.* Disorientation swirled around him. "Um, could you lower the poker, please? I'm in fear for my life here."

"Oh. Sure." She did so, then demanded, "When did you get here?"

"After midnight. You were asleep and I didn't want to disturb you." He glanced at the frosted-over window. Daylight came through it, but gray and dim. "The roads sucked. It took me hours to get here. Is it still snowing?"

"Yup. Still coming down thick and—" her voice stumbled "—uh, hard."

His gaze snapped to hers. The way she'd reacted to those words…and the way she was staring at his bare chest… *Damn*.

His arousal took up where it had left off last night. If anything, it was even more insistent than before. Gritting his teeth against the pounding lust, he swore under his breath. It didn't help that, beneath that sexy T-shirt, her legs were bare, all smooth and slender. He could already feel them wrapped around his hips, urging him deeper inside her…

He broke off the train of thought sharply, kicking himself mentally. Marley deserved a gentleman, not a jerk like him. That girl messed with his head.

"Could I have a minute to get dressed?" he asked carefully. "I'm a little bit, uh, naked."

Darned if her eyes didn't light up with unholy interest at that. Her gaze slid down to the fluffy comforter, which thankfully hid his epic erection. He was going to explode, though, if she looked at his lap much longer with that much heat in her eyes.

She turned and strolled out of the bedroom, her rear end twitching so pertly he groaned aloud at the pain watching it caused him. He pulled on jeans and a sweater and joined her in the main room. She'd already stoked up the fire and was rummaging in the cupboards.

"How do you feel about fruit pies over the fire for breakfast?" she asked in a muffled voice from inside a cupboard.

"Is that a Girl Scout thing?" he responded.

She emerged with a can of what looked like pie filling in hand and a loaf of bread. "I found one of those iron things where you open it up, put in two pieces of bread and filling, close it and toast it in the fire. We need something like butter to grease it up, though."

He'd love to grease her up and... *Stop that, dammit!*

"There's a freezer in the mudroom in the back. Could you check and see if there's butter in it?" she asked. "I found some frozen orange-juice concentrate earlier and will mix that up for us."

He passed by her, his hands itching to reach out and pull her into his arms. To cup her breasts and run his palms down her belly, to make her hot and needy for him, to have her writhing on his fingers and crying out her release...

*Butter. Must. Get. Butter.*

When he returned, she was bent over by the fire, her tush cupped in tight jeans and sticking up in the air as proud as you please. He could slip those jeans down, grab her hips and drive into her tight...

*Butter. Must. Give. Her. Butter.*

"I found some," he mumbled.

"Great! I've got everything we'll need right here. Is cherry okay?"

He mentally swore and narrowly avoided burying his head in his hands.

She buttered up the fire toaster, lined it with bread that she smashed flat and then she stopped, looking flummoxed.

"Need help?" he ground out from behind his clenched teeth and his raging lust.

"Can you open the cherries? I don't have the right tool."

He did groan aloud then. He actually had to turn away from her to hide his bulging flesh as he fished out his pocket knife and unfolded the can opener attachment. He passed the opened can over his shoulder to her and saw out of the corner of his eye when she stuck the toaster into the coals.

"Are you okay?" she asked. And, oh, God, she laid her hand on his back.

He wanted her hands all over him so bad he could hardly stand it. In desperation, he sank into the armchair beside the fire and propped up one knee to disguise his arousal at least a little.

"Yeah," he managed to choke out. "I'm fine. You?"

"Well, I think we're snowed in. It looks like another six or eight inches fell overnight. When do you suppose it'll stop?"

If it didn't stop snowing soon, he wasn't going to make it out of here alive. His lust was going to kill him.

He shrugged, blatantly faking casualness. "Weather forecast said it should taper off sometime today and start to warm up. Could be a day or two for this much snow to melt. Could be another day or two after that for the snowmelt to run off and finish flooding the local gullies.

"You really didn't have to come up here to rescue me. As you can see, I have things well in hand."

He could think of something he wanted in her hand…
*Stop. That.*

He forced out, "The good news is Adrian's going to have to wait for the valley to dry out enough to continue shooting. He can't drive tanks and Jeeps through too much mud, or equipment will get stuck and make filming impossible."

"Whew. I really can't afford to mess up this job. I don't have a backup gig like you do."

His backup gig wasn't looking all that appealing these days. The idea of leaving her behind and never looking back physically hurt to contemplate. Lord, what had she done to his head? Suddenly the cabin felt like a tiny, confining box, the walls collapsing in on him. Cursing, he grabbed his coat, threw it on and barged outside into the storm.

# Chapter 9

Marley still didn't forgive him for suspecting her and not telling her he was leaving in a few weeks, but it had been nice of him to make a difficult journey up here to rescue her. Even if she didn't need rescuing.

She looked up with a smile as the front door blew open on a gust of wind and snow, but her smile died the moment she saw Archer. He was soaking wet, his hair plastered to his head, his clothes clinging to him, dripping rivulets of water.

"What happened to you?" she exclaimed.

"F-found a c-creek. Un-d-der the s-s-snow. The h-hard w-way."

"You fell in a *creek*?" She leaped to her feet without waiting for his answer and rushed over to push him in front of the fire, where she commenced peeling off his wet clothes. Darned if he didn't look totally gorgeous with his hair slicked back from his face like that. The man really should be a model.

But then she got his sweater off and caught sight of his chest. It was unnaturally pale. And he was shivering violently. His hands were bright red and his fingertips were turning white. Good Lord. The beginnings of frostbite.

She dropped his sweater in a sopping pile on the hearth. "Good thing that's wool, or you could have really been in trouble," she groused, more worried than she cared to admit to him.

"Am in t-trouble."

"We'll get you warmed up in no time," she said reassuringly. "We just have to get all these wet things off you." She peeled his wet jeans down his hips and froze as she realized he'd gone commando this morning. And *hoo baby*, even cold as a Popsicle that man was *gifted by Mother Nature*. No wonder porn producers had propositioned him.

Resolutely, she leaned down, trying and failing to ignore his man parts looming less than a foot from her face. Were he not half-frozen, she would definitely have taken advantage of the moment in some inappropriate way. Doggedly, she dragged the wet denim down his muscular legs. God, his entire body was as perfect as the rest of him.

"Lift your foot," she ordered. As he complied and she peeled the sock off—jeez, even his foot was gorgeous!—she muttered, "It's really not fair for one man to be so hot, you know. Some other poor schmuck got no good looks at all because you double-dipped when God was passing out handsome."

He made a noise that might have been a laugh, but it was hard to tell over the chattering of his teeth.

"Other foot," she ordered.

When she had him buck naked, she raced for the bathroom and towels. She rubbed him all over briskly and toweled off his hair. He wasn't getting back his color, though.

"I think you're now getting hypothermic, Archer. We're going to have to warm you up another way. Come with me."

He followed her into the bedroom. "Turn your back," she ordered him.

He complied and, self-conscious, she stripped off her T-shirt to expose her bare chest. She'd gone commando this morning, too. It was his fault, of course. She'd spent all night dreaming about having sex with him and had been feeling inordinately naughty when she woke up. She kicked off her jeans and jumped into the bed, as embarrassed as she'd ever been in her life. Holding up the comforter, she finally looked up at Archer.

"What are you waiting for? Get in."

"C-can't."

"Yes, you can. And you need to. It's Girl Scouts 101 that skin-to-skin contact is the fastest and best way to warm up a hypothermic person. Surely, even you know that."

He stubbornly shook his head.

"If you don't get in here with me, I'm going to have to come out there and wrap myself around you, and then we'll both get cold. Now get your smoking-hot body over here and plaster it against me before you freeze to death!"

"W-when you p-put it l-like that…" He climbed in beside her and she gasped as his icy body rolled against hers.

"Omigod, you're freezing!" she squealed.

He buried his ice cube of a nose against her neck under her hair and muttered. "You're so hot."

She laughed. "Keep saying that. Maybe someday I'll believe you."

His arms went around her, and even though they were bands of frost, they pulled her tightly against him. In turn, she wrapped her arms around his lean, powerful waist. They lay like that for long minutes in silence, and slowly, slowly, his shivering lessened. Her own body went from warm to freezing, and slowly back to warm.

And then other things began to register. The ways the hairs on his chest rubbed against her breasts when he moved. The way his muscular thighs gripped one of hers between them. The way his hardness nestled against her belly...and was, um, waking up.

His hand, the one resting between her shoulder blades, drifted lower, following the inward curve of her spine to her waist, and then lower to the small of her back. And then lower, to the upper curves of her tush. His fingers plunged gently into the crevasse between her cheeks and slowly eased lower.

Why hadn't someone ever told her how totally erotic that part of her body was? She gasped and her hips undulated forward, toward him, as her entire lower abdomen melted.

"You're so responsive," he muttered into her hair.

His fingers slid even lower. Toward her hungry and pulsing lady parts. But then, infuriatingly, his hand stopped. What was it with him and getting right to the edge of spectacular things with her and then *freaking stopping*?

"Don't you *dare* stop now, Archer Archer," she warned him.

He lifted his head away from hers and leaned back

far enough on the pillow to stare down at her. "Marley, we shouldn't. *I* shouldn't."

"You shouldn't, or you don't want to?" she asked painfully.

"Are you kidding me?" he burst out. "I've been walking around with the mother of all hard-ons since the moment I met you!"

"Then make love to me already!"

"But…"

"But nothing," she cut him off. "I want you. You want me. And I did just possibly save your life. You owe me. So get with the program here!"

"Yes, but there are things we should talk about first…"

She threw him a narrow, withering look. "Are you seriously going to make me beg? That's not the slightest bit gentlemanly of you."

A smile started in his beautiful brown eyes and slowly spread to his mouth, his cheeks, and then his whole face. He was so breathtaking she could barely stand to look at him.

*This was it.* She was finally going to have sex. All the way. Her boldness deserted her and left her staring up at him without a clue as to what to do next.

"You're sure?" he asked. "I can't recommend me as a lover. I'm a head case on a short rotation stateside. I should have told you before."

"Gordon told me."

He snorted. "Bastard. Remind me to bust his nose the next time I see him."

"You should've been the one to do it."

"It didn't occur to me to tell you until I realized I was contemplating more than just a…temporary relationship with you."

* * *

Marley frowned up at him as if she didn't know whether or not to believe him. Fair enough. He deserved her skepticism. Hopefully it would be enough to back her off this whole sex-right-now idea. They really did have things to work out before they did this.

He wasn't sure he had the strength to turn away from her nakedness, her willingness to be in bed with him and her bodily throwing herself at him. He had the most honorable of intentions, but even his self-restraint had its limits.

"I want you," she whispered. "Temporary or not. Right now. Please, Archer. Make love with me."

He was still shaking his head in denial when she closed the distance between them and kissed him. It started slowly, just her lips brushing lightly across his.

"Please, Marley. Don't do this."

"Do you want me?"

A painful bark of laughter erupted from his throat. "You have no idea how bad I want you."

"So, we're both consenting adults. No one else will get hurt by us doing this. This is purely between you and me. I see no reason why we can't do this."

"Because I want it to be perfect. I want things to be good between us."

"Then do it right, Einstein. You're the expert at sex, after all. Show me how it's supposed to be done."

She pressed the entire glorious, naked length of her body against his, and he groaned, gritting his teeth until his jaw ached.

She kissed his jaw, his eyelids, his brow. Her hands roamed across his body, exploring and learning it. For a beginner, she was doing a spectacular job of finding all his most sensitive spots. Her breath against his belly button was steamy with the promise of things to come, and his entire body was stretched on a rack of desire and denial. She was torturing him. Or more accurately, he was torturing himself.

Before her mouth could slide any lower on his stomach, his fingers fanned out into her hair, and he lifted her up his body, rolling her onto her back. When she would have protested, he kissed her in desperation to silence her words.

Her tongue slipped between his lips, boldly exploring the contours of his mouth. "Please, Archer. Kiss me back." Aching need vibrated in her voice.

He couldn't deny her any longer. Couldn't do it to either of them. Couldn't hold out in the face of her full sexual onslaught. He surrendered.

Exultation roared through Marley when she sensed as much as felt Archer give up fighting against the idea of having sex with her.

Finally.

He kissed her, lightly at first, then more deeply as she plunged her fingers into his hair and pulled him closer. He supported his weight on one elbow, and slid his other hand around the back of her neck to lift her to him. His mouth opened against hers and she matched him thrust for thrust with her own tongue.

He groaned in the back of his throat, and in an instant the kiss shifted. Became carnal. Intense. Frankly, a bit intimidating. But this was Archer. He knew what he was doing. He had this under control.

She arched into him, handing over her body and her jittery nerves into his care.

"You taste like cherry pie," he finally murmured against her lips. "I could taste you all day long."

Immediately, her thoughts turned to that night in the truck when his amazing mouth had taught her things about pleasure she'd never known before. "That... sounds...wonderful," she replied between kisses.

He laughed low and husky, and her toes curled into tight little knots of excitement. Under the comforter, his hands roamed her back, and he did that sexy thing with his fingers again where he traced her spine all the way down to her tush and beyond. But, praise the Lord, this time he didn't stop just shy of her begging, swollen center of need.

"Been thinking about this, huh?" he murmured against her neck.

"You have no idea. Day and night."

He made a sound of humor against her skin. "I know the feeling, baby."

But then he kissed his way across her collarbone and lower, and any reply fled her lust-fogged mind. She shoved her hands into his damp hair as his mouth closed on her nipple, licking, sucking and tugging at it until she thought she might cry with the wanting it created elsewhere in her body.

His hand replaced his mouth, and his lips closed on her other nipple. And then his hand, the one that had been stroking her lower, returned, and his finger eased inside her. She was stunned at how wet and slippery she was.

"You're so tight." He sighed against her breast. "I can't wait to get inside you and feel your sweet body clenching around me."

On cue, her internal muscles tightened around his fingertip and clung tightly to it, willing it farther inside her. She ached to be filled, and her hips rocked forward eagerly against his hand.

But maddeningly, he withdrew his finger and rubbed the lubrication from it around her swollen flesh in a swirling motion that made her breath catch. "Do that again," she gasped.

He obliged, dipping just into her juices and then slicking them over her now wildly throbbing core. Every beat of her heart pulsed through her belly, and she hovered on the edge of the same miracle he'd shown her before.

"Don't stop, Archer," she panted. "Never stop."

"What do you want from me?" he asked low, his voice intense.

"Everything you're willing to give me."

He stared down at her intently. "Do you mean that?"

"Yes, yes," she cried out in desperation as his fingertip swirled slowly around her and then flicked once, almost but not quite hard enough to launch her into outer space. She felt his lips curve into a smile against her belly as he slid lower, his head disappearing entirely beneath the comforter.

He pushed her thighs apart and she was more than glad to oblige, opening her body to him completely in her excess of lust.

His voice was muffled, but she couldn't miss the note of satisfaction in it. "*Mmm.* Ready and willing. Just the way I like my woman."

And then his mouth closed on her and all thought blew away like a snowflake in the storm outside. In seconds, he had her hovering again on the edge of infinity, right there, teetering on the precipice. His fingers drifted lower, circling the epicenter of her lust.

His finger pressed into her once more. Just enough to force the muscles to relax and accept the intimate invasion. And all of a sudden, the tension in her body let go, opening for him, throbbing eagerly in anticipation of whatever debauchery he felt could perpetrate upon her lust-crazed body.

Another finger made its way inside her. He moved both fingers gently, along with his tongue, and she cried out as her body lurched up off the mattress.

"Like that?" he asked.

"Omigosh, yes," she panted.

His teeth closed on the peak of her breast, trapping it in his mouth, and then his tongue flicked back and forth across it fast, its slightly rough texture wet and relentless. She screamed as an orgasm ripped her apart from the inside out. She'd died. Gone to heaven. Space traveled. Heck, *time* traveled.

"*Voilà*. The screaming orgasm," he murmured against the inside of her thigh. "Want another one?"

"Yes. Oh, please, *yes*."

"Your wish is my command."

She laughed helplessly as he started the whole process over again, playing her body so she all but sobbed with need once more. This time when she came, he didn't let up. His fingers and tongue kept up that insane rhythm on her body and her orgasm stretched on and on, wave after wave of pleasure breaking over her, drowning her, then saving her, lifting her out of herself and onto another plane of existence altogether.

"I want you inside me so bad I can't stand it. I'm begging you."

His mouth kissed its way across her collarbone and up the straining column of her neck. Inch by inch, his magnificent body came into full contact with hers. His powerful thighs edged hers aside, and his washboard abs were rock hard against her belly. He braced an elbow on either side of her head, and he was gloriously heavy on her.

And then his body touched her *there*. If the rest of his body was hot against hers, his erection was white-hot steel fresh off an anvil. He pushed against her opening, and she couldn't help it, she tensed. It was supposed to hurt the first time. It didn't help that he seemed extremely well endowed, nor that she had no idea what to expect.

Frowning slightly as if he sensed her abrupt tension, he paused, shifting his weight onto one elbow so he could reach down between them. His finger unerringly found her core, which was still galvanized from that last, endless orgasm. It took only a few strokes and flicks with his fingertip to have her moving restlessly beneath him once more, her virginity eagerly seeking its destruction.

He eased a little farther into her and stretching fullness gave way to some discomfort. But the pleasure his hand was spinning so cleverly easily overwhelmed any pain. He pushed a little farther, and the pleasure and discomfort mingled in an intoxicating cocktail of surrender and possession. Never in her life had she felt so much like a woman. Who knew that sharing her body and soul wholly with a man could feel like this?

She started to shudder with another encroaching orgasm from his magical fingers, and just as it slammed into her, he pushed all the way home, seating himself to the hilt inside her.

She cried out in the most exquisite pleasure she'd ever experienced, bar none. She clenched and unclenched around him, and his eyes glazed over in lust and pleasure to rival hers.

"I have never felt anything so amazing in my entire life," he groaned.

She gasped when he moved experimentally, withdrawing partway, then easing back into her. She registered a dull ache, but in the overarching haze of magnificent passion, it was but one more ingredient in the heady mix, a reminder that she was now Archer's woman. Claimed and taken by him.

This part of her would always belong to him.

She was glad. She'd chosen well.

"Are you okay?" he asked tightly.

"I'm fantastic."

"Yes. Yes, you are." And then he grew impatient, and his body began to move more urgently inside her. She was shocked when her hips rose of their own volition to meet his, thrusting against him hungrily, milking his body shamelessly for all the pleasure it could give her. There was one more thing she sensed she was missing, and she sought it fiercely, surging beneath him like a wild thing.

He reached over her head to grab the headboard with both hands as his body slammed into hers with not quite gentle violence, over and over.

"More," she gasped. She wasn't sure what "more" was, but she sensed it just over the horizon.

"Marley," he groaned. His hips moved faster, harder, deeper, and she forgot to breathe.

"Yes. *Yes.*" This was it. That thing she sought.

His entire body clenched just as hers coiled for one last leap off the cliff. He gave one final, pounding thrust, all the way to her womb, and came with a shout that launched them both into a place of utter darkness and brilliant light. Of complete grounding and weightless free fall, their bodies spinning weightlessly through space in mutual release.

They slowly fell back into the grip of gravity together, his body shuddering against hers. She absorbed his release, the aftershocks of her own climax mingling with his as they collapsed against the mattress, breathing hard.

It took a while for any thought at all to register in her mind. At first only disjointed impressions came to her. *Wow. Incredible.* And then emotions followed. Amazement. Joy. And finally, blessedly, relief. It soaked into her bones and washed away long-held stress that had been part of her for so long she hardly knew how to relate to this deep sense of release from it. It was as if she had been born again, into a new life and a new self.

She'd had no idea she would feel such an intimate and powerful emotional connection with Archer. Most people talked about sex as if it was a purely physical experience. But for her, and for him, she thought, it had been more. When he'd gazed into her eyes and she into his, it was as if she'd been looking straight into his soul.

How could anybody do that casually? It was by far the most emotionally naked and revealing moment of her life. She'd been deluded to think she could share that with another person and then walk away from it as if nothing of importance had ever happened. It was the deepest and most powerful bond she'd ever forged with another human being.

Archer rolled over and gathered her against his side. She snuggled against his big, warm body, her hand resting lightly on his stomach. They dozed like that for a while, but eventually as the light began to fade outside, he moved away from her, rousing her to a half-conscious state.

"Back in a minute," he murmured against her brow. He dropped a light kiss on her forehead and slid out from under her, heading gloriously naked for the bathroom. She would never, ever get tired of looking at him.

Until he left her. In less than three weeks.

*Oh. Crap.*

# Chapter 10

Archer had been truly shocked a few times in his life, but nothing compared to what he was feeling at this moment. He'd been taken to school by possibly his most inexperienced lover ever. She'd taken him to an emotional place he'd never even guessed existed. She'd laid her entire soul bare before him. The courage that had taken blew him away.

Who would ever have guessed that shy, innocent Marley would throw herself into making love with such abandon? Not him, for sure.

He shoved a hand through his hair in confusion. He ought to be freaked out by the intimacy of what they'd just done. It had nothing to do with hot, impersonal sex and everything to do with romantic lovemaking. Hell, he *was* freaked out by what had just happened. But what he wasn't doing was running screaming. And why the hell not, he hadn't the slightest idea. His main urge was to crawl back into bed with her and do that again.

He turned around to do just that and...

Where did she go?

He looked out into the main room and saw her sitting in the big armchair in front of the fireplace, wrapped in a quilt, her shoulders bare beneath her tousled hair and so sexy his breath stuck in his throat. From the back, she could be Marilyn Monroe reincarnated. The resemblance was uncanny. Or maybe he was just going that crazy.

He followed her and busied himself for a minute piling more wood on the fire and stirring it up. He sat down on the hearth in front of her. The heat from the fire felt good on his back. "First things first. Are you okay?"

A cute little frown wrinkled the spot over her nose. "Gosh, I could have *sworn* you were in that bed with me. Yes, Archer. I'm fine."

"You're not...freaked out or anything? Upset? Overwhelmed?" *Damn.* He didn't even know what to be concerned about.

"Freaking out, no. Overwhelmed? Well, I *was*. In a good way. Did I do something wrong that I don't know about?"

"God, no!" he exclaimed quickly. "You did everything incredibly right."

"Then why the third degree?" she asked, tilting her head curiously at him.

Because, for once, he was unsure of himself. He didn't understand what had just happened between them and he felt a driving need to figure it out. But he didn't even know where to begin peeling back the onion and discovering the emotional layers to what they'd just done or how he was reacting to it. Not that he was about to admit any of that to her. Particularly not with her gazing at him, like he was some sort of conquering god.

A terrible certainty that she was going to realize what a fraud he was came over him. Soon, that look in her eyes would change and become hatred. Disgust. Rejection. Panic jumped in his gut at the idea. He had to distract her before she dug too much deeper into his psyche and saw him for the shallow, emotionally empty shell of a man that he was.

"Hungry?" he asked her, desperate to erase that adoring expression from her face.

"I don't know. I guess so."

He leaped up and headed for the cupboards in the kitchen, rummaging around and coming up with some canned stew. He dumped it in a pan and brought it back to the fire.

"So how did you fall into that stream?"

"It was covered with a thin layer of ice and a thick covering of snow. I went right through both."

"I've got the mechanics of how you fell in the water. My question is why were you stomping around in the woods where you could fall into a stream?"

He wedged the pan at the edge of the fire and turned to face her, frowning. "I thought I saw something. I went to investigate."

"What was it?"

His frown deepened. "I thought I saw someone in the woods."

"Out here? In the middle of a snowstorm?" she asked skeptically.

"I know. I didn't think it made sense, either. That was why I went to check it out."

"For all you knew, it could have been a bear. You shouldn't have taken such a risk," she chided gently.

"It wasn't a bear. It was upright. Moving on two legs. Definitely a person."

"Or Sasquatch," she retorted humorously.

"I thought some guy confessed to faking the whole Sasquatch thing a few years back."

She shrugged. "My TV station did stories on sightings about twice a year."

"The figure I saw wasn't that big. Or hairy."

"Who would have been dumb enough to be tromping around in the woods in this kind of weather?" she asked drily.

He rolled his eyes at her, and she grinned back unrepentantly. Okay, fine. He deserved that jab. It had been dumb to go out in a bad snowstorm. He redirected his thoughts to her question, which was a damned good one. "Do you know how close any neighbors are to this place?"

She shook her head. "Not sure. But I didn't see any driveways for the last couple of miles of the drive up here. I got the impression this place is pretty isolated. And the owner did mention to me on the phone that he owns several hundred acres of land up here."

A bad feeling took root in Archer's gut. The person he had seen would definitely have been on the property that went with this cabin, then. Why would anyone trespass out here in the middle of nowhere? The shadowy figure he'd seen flitting through the pine trees and falling snow hadn't been wearing an orange vest or appeared to be carrying a weapon of any kind. Not a hunter, then. Unless...

Unless the intruder hadn't been hunting deer.

"Marley, do you have any enemies that you're aware of?"

"That's a pretty random thing to ask. Where did that question come from?"

"Just tell me. Do you have any enemies?"

"Of course not. Why do you ask?" she persisted.

He sighed. "The person I saw was moving furtively. Like he didn't want me to see him. He was lurking fairly close to this cabin when I startled him into moving away into the woods."

"Maybe it was a squatter hoping to shack up here and ride out the storm."

"Was the door unlocked when you got here?"

"No. The place was locked up tight. But I got here before it started to snow, too."

Archer frowned, reconstructing that brief glimpse he'd gotten of the other person before he fell into the creek and had to give up the chase. The figure he'd seen had been bundled up warmly against the cold and the snow—not like a vagrant who'd gotten caught out unprepared for the storm.

Marley moved past him to give the stew a stir, and he snagged her around the waist as she headed back to her seat. He pulled her into his lap, reveling in her warmth and softness as she cuddled in his arms in front of the fire. He kissed her bare shoulder before pulling the quilt up over her satin flesh to keep it warm.

"I forgot to say thank you for helping me get warm earlier," he murmured.

She laughed quietly. "I'm happy to strip you down and go for a little skin-on-skin heat transfer with you anytime. Just say the word."

He chuckled against her temple. "I never would have pegged you for such a wanton under all that innocence."

"A wanton?" she exclaimed.

His smile widened. "And a hoyden."

"A hoyden, huh? Wow. I'm impressed that a stick jockey like you knows such a fancy word."

"We're not dumb jocks, thank you very much." Although he could see where she might get that impression from the rather locker room environment the stunt pilot crew fostered on set. "Most of us are totally domesticated. Guys get married, have a few kids, pick up a mortgage and a lawn to mow, and they settle right down."

Marley went very still in his arms. Damn. She didn't think he had just proposed to her, did she?

"That sounds kind of nice," she confessed. "I guess I'm more the domestic type than I wanted to admit. I had all these big dreams of exciting adventure and death-defying feats of camera work. But I like this." She looked around the cozy cabin and snuggled a little more closely against his chest.

Dammit, he liked it, too. And he'd spent most of his adulthood living exactly the exciting adventures and death-defying feats she was talking about. The woman was freaking *taming* him.

Appalled, he muttered, "You should go get some clothes on. It's getting colder in here. Temperature must be dropping outside. While you do that, I'll bring in more wood and build up the fire some more."

She dropped a quick kiss on the end of his nose and wriggled out of his arms, dragging the quilt with her. But it sagged enticingly off one of her shoulders as she sashayed into the bedroom and he half rose to his feet to follow her before it dawned on him that she had him dancing on a string like a green kid.

Stunned, he fell back to the hearth and stared into the fire in dismay. What was happening to him? What had she done to him?

They shared the stew in front of a roaring blaze. It was indeed getting colder outside. At this rate, it could be several days before it warmed up enough to melt off the worst of the snow. He didn't like being trapped here like this. If someone was, indeed, out there in the woods stalking Marley, he bloody well wanted to be able to leave. The sooner, the better.

After the meal, he announced, "I'm going outside to have a look around."

"But your coat isn't dry! You can't go out there in damp clothing or you'll get hypothermic again."

He swore under his breath. She was right, of course. He got up and fetched his wet boots, coat, hat and gloves, and spread them on the hearth to dry, as close to the fire as he dared put them without them catching on fire.

Marley asked in a small voice, "Are you in that big a hurry to get away from me?"

His head whipped around and he stared at her. She looked like a lost child, her arms wrapped around her middle and her big blue eyes hurt.

He surged forward onto his knees in front of her, swept her into his arms, ignored her protests and bent his head down to kiss her. Since he couldn't seem to express himself properly in words, maybe this would work.

His lips touched hers, and everything else went away. All that remained was the sweet, soft feel of her mouth beneath his, the way her lips yielded to his, the way she opened so readily for him and let his tongue inside to plunder her. That…emotional thing…moved again, deep within him. Possessiveness. Need. *Recognition.*

But of what? If he didn't know better, he'd say she was his soul mate or something equally inane. Granny Minerva and her damned kismet were at it again. Except Archer didn't do deep emotions. Ever. This had to be something else.

Maybe he was losing his mental grip.

Marley's slender arms slipped around his neck, and he dipped his hands under her sweater. Bare skin slid beneath his palms, silky and feminine, and hunger ignited in his gut. His male parts announced their approval of this method of communication with Marley, and his heart seconded the motion.

He lifted her out of the chair and into his lap where, in the dancing light and heat of the fire, he unwrapped her like a present to himself. Her breasts flushed rosy in the firelight, and he dipped his head to enjoy them like the luscious lollipops they might as well be. Her rib cage lifted, thrusting her flesh up into his mouth. As he gorged himself on her, she moaned, and he froze. He wasn't hurting her, was he?

Her hand plunged impatiently into his hair and pulled him back down to her breast, and he smiled around her rosy peak. *Ahh.* Well, then...

He half lifted her and slipped out from beneath her, depositing her back in the big armchair. He leaped to his feet and all but ran for the bedroom. His wallet was in his bag, and condoms were in his wallet. He might have been irresponsible with her once when he was half-frozen and taken by surprise, but he wasn't going to make the mistake twice. He grabbed a quilt on his way back to the main room and sprinted back to Marley as if he was afraid she would disappear before he got back to her.

He spread the quilt over the thick rug in front of the hearth and laid her down upon it. The firelight licked across her skin, just as his hands wanted to do, and she was all golden sex goddess reclining beside him. He let her go long enough to peel his shirt over his head and unzip his jeans, but then she was reaching for him again, murmuring about how perfect he was and how much she enjoyed looking at him.

"It's mutual, baby," he managed to get out before she raised herself on an elbow, dipped her hand inside his jeans and, holy cow, took his erection in her small, tight fist. Fast learner, much?

"You don't have to…" he started. But then she ran her palm down the length of him and back up, ending by swirling her fingertip with a flourish around the most sensitive part of his erection.

She leaned forward to kiss him, as well. Her mouth was all wet and lush and sexy, and words failed him as her tongue mimicked the stroking of her fingers. Her fist grasped him tightly and slid up and down the length of him, once, twice. All the while, her clever tongue darted in and out of his mouth, imitating the sex he was dying to have with her again.

His hips thrust forward of their own volition, driving him deeper into her fist. He tried to pull back— goodness knew the last thing he wanted to do was scare her. But she draped her leg over his hips and met the thrust of his hips with one of her own. The combination of fist, mouth and silky, naked body was insane, and he groaned as his flesh took on the characteristics of stone, so hard and heavy he could barely stand it.

She pulled back enough to smile up at him. "What *are* we going to do with this?"

"It's too soon. You'll be sore. We can't…" He broke off, groaning aloud as she leaned forward and took his lower lip between her teeth and gave a tug on it.

"Where did you learn to do that?" he gasped.

His brain was draining out his left ear as she kissed him and fondled him. He couldn't think with her doing that. Her fingertip rubbed in a slick little circle just at the base of his erection, and he about jumped out of his skin.

"Amazing the things a girl can learn on the internet," she murmured as her attention turned back to his mouth, licking and soothing the lip she'd just bitten.

He swore under his breath as he fought like crazy for control of his raging body.

"Any chance I can persuade you to do something naughty with me?" she inquired. "Maybe show me something I've never tried before?"

The idea of being the first to show her a whole host of sexy things all but did him in.

He groaned and barely managed to cobble together a semicoherent, "What, uh, did you, uh, *damn*, have in mind?"

"I thought I'd rely on your vast experience to come up with something interesting."

He laughed painfully. "If you don't stop squeezing me and kissing me like that, I'm not going to be able to think of anything at all."

She pulled back from him immediately. Relief in his brain warred with dismay in his body. "New and different, huh?" He considered her thoughtfully, now that he wasn't being driven completely out of his mind and could actually breathe. "You're sure you're not sore?"

"Well, maybe a little. But would you believe me if I said I kind of like it?"

A slow smile unfolded within him. "Well, then. That does open up some fascinating possibilities." As her face lit up, he added wryly, "Going to be the adventurous type, huh?"

She nodded at him, her eyes sparkling with anticipation. Her breathing sped up visibly as her breasts lifted and fell with her quick little gasps. *Good grief, she liked the danger*. The domestic-goddess wannabe had given way to this seductive siren.

His imagination shifted into overdrive. But before he acted on his fantasies, he wanted to hear hers. He slipped his hand lower, down the gentle swell of her belly and lower, relishing the limpid surrender in her as she buried her face against his shoulder and moaned a little in pleasure.

It took about two seconds to stroke her into a state of mindless lust. "Tell me what you want to try, baby."

"Um, I don't know…" A gasp as he plunged a finger inside her and withdrew it slowly. He repeated the process until she was panting in sexy little gasps. "I like this."

"So do I. Tell me what else you want me to do." He lifted his hand away from her hot, needy flesh.

"Archer!"

"Talk to me. I'm yours to direct as you wish."

Her cheeks went rosy with embarrassment, but he didn't break down and take charge. He waited until she started speaking hesitantly.

"I want to make love with you again. Now. In front of the fire."

"What else?"

Her voice dropped to a whisper. "And maybe try a few different positions to see what feels best."

"What would you like to try first?"

Her blush intensified, spreading down her neck and across the upper reaches of her breasts. "I have no idea."

"First, because you're fairly new to this and I don't want to hurt you, I'm going to suggest we make sure you're entirely ready."

"Meaning what?" she asked breathlessly.

He leaned down over her and kissed her long and

druggingly. "Meaning, that I'm going to make sure you're very turned on before we engage in any gymnastics."

She was so open and enthusiastic and trusted him implicitly. In turn, he trusted her to be honest with him. It added a dimension to sex play that he'd never experienced, either, and he reveled in the newness of it right along with her. *Huh.* Maybe there really was something to the whole soul-mate thing, after all.

He stopped their increasing frantic explorations abruptly. "Hold that thought," he ordered.

She wailed in frustration as he rose to his knees and lifted her up. Oh, she was going to be tons of fun to play with.

"I don't want you to get cold while we do this," he explained, guiding her hands to the warm stones of the raised hearth. He moved behind her, spooning her smaller body with his larger one. "Bend forward a little, baby."

"Oh," she murmured. "Oh!" He entered her slowly from behind, giving her body plenty of time to adjust to this new kind of invasion. She was so tight and hot around him he worried that he was hurting her.

He stopped, but Marley was having none of that. She drove her hips backward and down onto him in no uncertain terms.

"Oh, my." She sighed. "That's very nice."

"Nice?" he echoed indignantly. "I'm not going for nice here."

"Then stop holding back," she challenged him over her shoulder.

He chuckled and drove up into her more strongly.

"Mmm. Better. But not quite doing it for me."

His laughter took on a helpless quality. "You're incorrigible."

"I'm insatiable," she announced cheerfully. "And you're lagging in the sating department, good sir."

"I wouldn't want to let the lady down, now would I?" And with that, he commenced sating her with quite a bit more vigor and enthusiasm.

In seconds, Marley was arching back against him, groaning in pleasure and then crying out more sharply as an orgasm built deep inside her. He felt it in the way her internal muscles clutched at him more urgently, in how she met his thrusts with eager thrusts of her own, in the way her breathing caught in her throat with each cry of lust he wrung from her.

Without warning, she shattered around him, crying out and shuddering violently in her release, dancing upon his flesh like a faerie nymph in the flickering light of the fire. It was one of the most erotic things he'd ever seen. She was so totally open to him and held nothing back from him.

The rush of a woman giving herself to him so completely, body and soul, was intoxicating. Something deep in his heart—something angry and locked down— broke loose and floated away on her sighs of pleasure. In the past, he would have taken a certain dark satisfaction in driving a woman out of her mind while he retained a certain emotional detachment. But here… now…he only wanted to give Marley all the pleasure she'd ever fantasized about. He wanted to give her all of himself in return.

He stayed very still, reveling in the new orgasm building within her. It was exquisite. He didn't even have to move for her to come.

"Archer," she gasped. "What are you doing to me?"

Slowly, slowly, he moved in and out of her, counting each time she cried out and convulsed around him.

Finally, when she was a quivering mass of desire and her eyes were completely glazed with pleasure, he let go. Unclenching his jaw at last, he surged into her and, with a shout of his own, buried himself inside her sweet body one last time. She responded to that ultimate thrust with one last, apocalyptic orgasm of her own.

He took everything she had to give and, in return, poured everything in his heart into her. His entire being exploded into that climax, and it felt as if a giant, damaged chunk of his soul went with it.

He braced himself against the hearth with a hand on either side of her, panting like a racehorse. She was breathing just as hard and rested quiescently against him, spent.

"You okay?" he murmured.

"Better than okay," she breathed. She turned in his arms and he gathered her close, lowering her to the quilt and joining her upon it. "Thank you, Archer. That was…spectacular."

He pushed the hair off her face gently and leaned down to kiss her cheek "You were spectacular."

"Can we do something else new? Soon?"

Amazement soared through him. And joy. She was perfect. That was all there was to it. "Yes. Soon. I promise."

"Pinkie swear?" she replied in a small voice.

"Good grief, I've created a monster."

"Hopefully, a monster you won't mind feeding?" She smiled up at him over her shoulder, looking as pleasured and relaxed as any woman he'd ever seen. It was a beautiful sight. Something strange unfolded in his gut, like a flower opening or a butterfly unfurling its wings.

Except he didn't do butterflies and flowers. Yup, no doubt about it. He was losing his mind.

He laughed ruefully. "Baby, it's going to be a long time before I get tired of feeding your curiosity.

"I'd love to offer you a nice long soak in a hot bath, but until we get power back, there won't be any hot water—" he glanced around the cabin "—unless…"

He jumped up and went over to the kitchen cabinets to rummage around. *"Aha!"* He emerged with giant soup kettle. "It'll take a while to heat up the water, but I might be able to get you a hot bath, after all."

She dozed in the big armchair before the fire while he heated the water, but in an hour or so, he was able to fill the bathtub with hot water and then add just enough cold water to create a steaming bath for her.

"Wake up, sleepyhead. Your bath is ready."

She smiled up at him blissfully and he leaned down to kiss her softly. "You're perfect," he whispered.

*And she was his…*

Since when did he get possessive over a woman? Hell, he'd hadn't even been possessive of his toys as a kid! He installed her in the tub with a pile of towels waiting beside it and backed out of the bathroom with an admonition to her not to fall asleep and drown.

"I wasn't a Girl Scout for nothing, you know," she called after him as he pulled the door shut. "There's a merit badge for avoiding stupid ways of dying!"

He grinned at the closed panel. Something light and silly twisted in his gut. Damn, he was all over the emotional map today. Men didn't get crazy hormone surges, did they?

While she soaked, he carried in a few more armloads of wood. It had indeed gotten very cold outside, but the good news was the falling snow was finally starting to slow down. Upward of two feet of the stuff had come down already. Damn. They could be snowed in here for several days.

He took a long, hard look around the tiny clearing around the cabin. Nothing moved in the forest. He saw no sign of any intruder lurking out there, watching and waiting to harm Marley. But the flesh at the back of his neck still crawled. They had to get out of here before anything bad happened to her. He wanted Marley back in town, close to Steve and the other stunt crew members who were trained Special Forces types.

The sooner, the better.

Marley luxuriated in the hot bath, which felt as unreal and fantastic as the sex she'd just had with Archer. As flings went, this had to be just about the mother of them all.

Her bliss dimmed slightly. *If only this weren't just a fling.* If only this was the beginning of something wonderful and lasting. Then her happiness would be complete. But Archer would be gone in a few short weeks. She'd known that going into this affair, so it wasn't like she could blame him for it now. He was going to leave her as surely as the sun rose and set.

She sighed and sank to her neck in the water. It wasn't his fault she'd chosen to have her first fling with a soldier on leave.

No regrets, darn it. No second-guessing. She was finally rid of her pesky virginity, and if she played her cards right, he would divest her of a whole lot more of her inconvenient innocence, too.

Apparently, she had forgiven him for not trusting her before and not telling her about his temporary status stateside. She probably shouldn't have. Great sex didn't make his other bad behaviors acceptable. But dang, it was hard to see anything past the mind-blowing pleasure he gave her.

It wasn't as if he was going to stick around for a real relationship that would require them to work out their differences, though.

Except she really wanted to work things out with him.

*If only Archer wouldn't leave her.* The seductive pull of that idea, of Archer staying home, making her his, protecting her and loving her for a very long time to come...*oh, my.* She was getting a little breathless at the mere thought of it.

Fear, cold and insidious, abruptly clutched at her. She dared not fall in love with him for real. He would be here for a few more weeks, tops, and then he would be out of her life and off to fight his wars. She would be a total idiot to lose her heart to him.

At all costs, she must *not* get any more emotionally involved with this man than she already was.

Except she already was too far gone. When he left, she was going to be utterly and completely devastated. She could already feel the beginnings of the agony waiting for her in a few weeks. The mere idea of him going away provoked a hot knife of pain in her heart.

A sinking feeling that she'd done a bad, bad thing rolled through her. Like it or not, she was already a whole lot more than just infatuated with Archer.

This sucked. She wanted him forever. But he only wanted her for now. She'd chosen a guy for a fling far too well. He made no bones about the fact that he didn't stick around for long-term relationships. He freely admitted that he jumped in and out of bed with women, that he shamelessly used his good looks to get laid and that he wasn't looking for anything more than hot chicks and hotter sex.

An end to their relationship was not a probability. It was a certainty. A month from now, he would be halfway around the world in some danger zone flying choppers right on the edge of disaster and bedding every sexy female who crossed his path. And Marley would be just another notch on his bedpost, long forgotten.

If she were smart, she would cut her losses and run. Now. Before he saw beneath the Marilyn Monroe makeup and sexual adventurousness. Before he realized she was really as plain as white bread, inside and out, and dumped her cold. God, how humiliating would it be to watch him sleep his way through the other women in the cast and crew over the next two weeks? And it would happen right under her nose because they were all living practically on top of one another in that damned motel.

The shame of it, of having not been enough to keep him occupied for more than a weekend in the mountains, would kill her. But maybe…if *she* dumped *him* first, at least she would garner some sympathy and respect for having realized he was a shallow womanizer and gotten rid of him. She was so tired of being a joke to other people.

Not to mention, she was letting her imagination completely run away with her. Archer hadn't dumped her. He hadn't left her yet. And truth be told, he'd seemed as blown away by their lovemaking as she'd been. She owed the guy a chance to see where this thing between them went before she assumed the worst.

But a trace of the fear stayed with her as she climbed out of the rapidly cooling bath.

She jumped out of the tub, dried off and dressed quickly, shivering. If she knew what was good for her, she would limit her feelings to no more than a crush on him. She would keep their relationship as close to purely physical as she could. Just sex.

No attachments.

No strings.

No problem.

*No way.*

# Chapter 11

Archer looked up quickly as Marley emerged from the bedroom, her skin rosy and her hair curling in soft little blond tendrils around her face. She looked so sweet and innocent, but his firsthand knowledge of her voracious sexual appetite made that innocent look so sexy he could hardly stay in the armchair and not throw her down and ravish her all over again.

"Feel better?" he managed to murmur blandly enough.

"As good as new," she said brightly.

"I heated up some baked beans for us. They're not fancy, but better than nothing."

"Man, it seems like I'm eating continuously today," she groused. "I'm going to be as big as your truck by the time we get out of here."

"Oh, I can think of a few ways to exercise it off you. Besides, it's cold. Your body's burning extra calories staying warm."

She grinned at him. "Let's go with that explanation."

He offered his lap to her and she sank onto it readily. Satisfaction coursed through him that she was so comfortable with close physical contact between them. He fed her the beans, alternating taking spoonfuls himself.

"Who'd have guessed eating beanie weenies could be so nice?" she commented. "I gotta say, the Girl Scout handbook left this part out."

"I should hope so," he said with a chuckle.

They polished off the beans, and he set the pan aside. The fire hissed a little as snow dried off the latest batch of logs, and the silence was as deep as the snow outside. He couldn't remember ever feeling this much at peace.

"So, here we are with nothing but time on our hands," she said tentatively. "How about you tell me more about that last flight of yours before you came home? I swear on a stack of Bibles that I won't ever breathe a word about it to anyone else. Maybe if you talk it out with me you'll be good and over it before you go back to your unit."

Peace shattered. *Dammit.*

He tensed. "I'd really rather not."

She laid her palm on his cheek. "I understand. But I think maybe you need to talk about it. You get really uptight whenever you're reminded of it."

He stared at her, a sinking feeling in his chest. She was right. Besides, who else was there to talk to? He refused to come within ten miles of a shrink who could take his wings from him. And the other military pilots he served with were busy fighting their own demons. Not to mention, none of his colleagues wanted to hear the uncomfortable truths of their profession. Better to stay in a nice, safe state of denial, and pretend that good men and women didn't suffer and die in their line of work.

He sighed. "What do you want to know?"

"Not sure. What can you tell me without breaking the rules over classified material?"

"Not much." He considered his words for a few seconds and then began to speak slowly. "It was a rescue mission. In a place no Americans were supposed to be. Which meant neither the guys we were rescuing nor we were officially there."

"And it went bad, right? You got there and it was some sort of ambush for you, too."

He shrugged. Honestly, he wasn't sure if it had been an ambush for him, or an unlucky coincidence that he flown right into the teeth of a rebel stronghold to rescue that American patrol. "We got a distress call, and I was the guy on alert, so I responded."

The frantic radio call for help from the ambushed unit crackled in his head, and the sudden tension of a clock ticking on a bunch of Special Forces troops' lives tightened his gut.

"We came in for a landing and were hovering about thirty feet in the air over the team we were pulling out. That's when we got shot out of the sky."

A log broke in the fireplace with a shower of sparks and he jumped, startled. *Firelight. Cabin. Marley.* He was *not* in a helicopter hovering over hell's doorstep.

Her hand alighted softly on his arm, a look of concern in her eyes.

He shook his head. He was okay. And she was right. He did need to relive that night. To work through how he felt about it.

Grounded in the present once more, he continued, "We crashed, and my bird was a mess. Not gonna fly again. A hell of a firefight broke out as soon as we came down in the LZ, and we were suddenly in need of rescue, too."

She frowned. "LZ?"

"Landing zone." She nodded and he continued. "Rockets and bullets were flying all over the place. We were pinned down in a valley with rebels in the hills on either side of us. We were fish in a barrel. It was uglier than you can imagine."

Marley shivered against him and he tightened his arm around her waist a little. God, she felt good in his arms. A reminder that this other world, where people didn't shoot at and kill one another, existed.

"Before we went down, I got off a Mayday—that's an emergency call for help. We took hellish incoming fire for about the next half hour. We were running out of ammunition and medical supplies, and when, from over the ridge, I heard a chopper. That was just about the sweetest sound I ever heard."

"That must be how all the people you've rescued felt when they heard you coming," she murmured.

"I suppose so." He'd never thought of it in those terms.

"Go on," she urged gently.

"A pair of choppers came in first and made a strafing run. Softened up the rebels so a rescue bird could come in and land."

"By softened up, I gather you mean it shot up the rebels?" she asked soberly.

He nodded. "Lit them up like the Fourth of July. The second rescue bird landed practically on top of us. We loaded up the injured and piled aboard in about ten seconds flat."

He could see and feel it all again. The tracers and ex-

plosions too damned close to them. The smell of blood,
the moans of the wounded and the shouts of the others
to *Go! Go! Go!* He felt the rescue helicopter shaking
beneath him as gunfire raked its light armor.

"We flew like a bat out of hell and cleared the ridge.
Our helicopter took some hits but held on. We limped
home, but two more guys died in the back before we
could get to a field hospital. There was blood all over
the place. And there was nothing we could do to help
them. They both had internal bleeding that would have
taken a damned fine trauma surgeon to stop."

"So there was nothing you could've done for them,"
Marley stated.

Archer winced. And there it was—the inconvenient
truth he and all his fellow pilots tried so hard to avoid.
Sometimes, bad things happened to good people. There
was no fancy explanation, and it sucked rocks. Sometimes a combination of uncontrollable circumstances
just lined up wrong and killed people.

"There was nothing you could have done, right?"
she pressed.

"I could've been the one to take a bullet," he replied.

"Thank God you didn't," Marley retorted with a
world of empathy in her eyes.

He smiled a little in spite of himself.

"Seriously, Archer. What could you have done differently?"

"Nothing. The call would have come in and I would
still have gone even if I knew I was going to get shot
down. It was my job. Those guys on the ground were
depending on me to come get them. I had to at least try
to pull them out."

"There you have it. You'd have done the same thing
again. And the same thing would have happened. It

wasn't your fault, and you couldn't have changed the outcome."

There was something therapeutic in hearing someone else say the words, in someone else absolving him from responsibility.

"As crappy luck would have it," she continued, "some guys you were trying to help took unlucky bullets."

"About as crappy as luck can get."

"Nonetheless," she pressed, "we're talking about bad luck, not any specific mistake you made. Right?"

"Look. I know that in my head. But it's going to take a little time to convince my gut."

"Fair enough," she said calmly. "Have you grieved for the guys who died yet?"

He stared at Marley. "Come again? I didn't know any of them."

"That doesn't mean you can't feel bad over their deaths."

Right. Like he and the other guys sat around singing "Kumbaya" and boo-hooing every time some poor sod got shot and bled out in combat.

It was the pits. But it was war.

"I've had no time to even think about the mission, let alone grieve for anyone. As soon as I filed my written report on the incident, the flight surgeon put me on mandatory leave for a month. I packed my bags, got on a plane, and here I am."

"I'm no expert, but even I know you need some time to absorb what happened and deal with it. *Anyone* would feel guilty surviving under those circumstances. No wonder they made you come home for some leave. The flight surgeon must have known you would need time to work through this."

He stared at her. Was she right? Was survivor's guilt

the source of his problems? Was the cure as simple as making peace with those guys' deaths?

"You should talk with Steve Prescott."

He started. "Why him?"

"I heard he was a Marine. Some kind of combat commander. I'll bet he knows exactly what it feels like to lose troops he felt responsible for. Maybe he'd have some suggestions for getting past it."

He'd never thought of his brother in those terms before. As a kid, he'd looked up to Steve. Seen him as his invincible big brother. He'd never considered that Steve might have scars and emotional baggage of his own from his military career.

Archer turned over the idea thoughtfully, and abruptly he felt restless. Caged in. "I need to take a walk. Stretch my legs."

"Last time you went out for a walk you came back sopping wet and hypothermic."

"I know where the creek is now," he retorted drily. "And it's not like you could stop me. I outweigh you by a good eighty pounds, and I'm a lot bigger and stronger than you, pip-squeak."

She tensed indignantly. "Who're you calling pip-squeak?" Her gaze narrowed menacingly, and she held up the cutest, most ineffective fists he'd seen in a long time. "Call me that again. I dare you."

He grinned broadly at her. God, she was good for his soul. "How about you help me bundle up? You can check to make sure all of my clothes are dry and that I'll be sufficiently warm for you not to worry about me."

He had to admit, his heart felt lighter after their talk as he put on his coats, hats, gloves and boots—all vetted and declared dry by Marley. Maybe talking about the mission hadn't been such a bad idea.

What would he do without her? One thing he knew for sure: he didn't want to find out. His return to active duty in a few weeks loomed large in his mind as he stepped outside into the waning afternoon light to run a quick patrol around the cabin and check just how impassible the driveway was.

First things first. He had to figure out who was stalking Marley before he could even think about leaving her side.

Marley waited impatiently for Archer's return. The cabin felt empty and hollow without his huge presence filling it. She was relieved that he trusted her enough to talk about that awful mission with her. What must it be like to carry around terrible memories and pain and have no one to share it with? She shuddered to imagine it. It certainly put her stupid jinx into perspective. It wasn't worth obsessing over any more.

Meanwhile, no more silent suffering for him. She vowed to herself to be there for him whenever he needed someone to talk to. Although how she was going to pull that off when he went back to his unit, she had no idea. She supposed soldiers kept in touch with their families over the internet these days. It wouldn't be ideal, but she supposed it was better than having no contact with him at all.

Now, how to figure out if he was willing to give a long-distance relationship a try? Did she dare ask him outright? That seemed pretty bold, even for her.

She paced the interior of the cabin nervously while she waited for his return. Was this to be the shape of her future life, waiting and worrying about him for weeks or months on end? Was she strong enough to do it? For him? Would he wait for her, too? Could what they had between them grow into something strong enough to withstand the distance and separation? She desperately hoped so.

Archer stared down at the snow in horror. There was no doubt about it. Those were footprints. *Human* footprints. Right underneath the bedroom window of the cabin. And neither he nor Marley had been outside recently enough to have made the prints. The wind was still blowing fiercely, filling in the prints even as he stood there. Which meant whoever'd been peeking in the windows had done it very recently. Maybe recently enough that he could track and catch the bastard.

Quickly, he followed the line of tracks. It led around the back of the house and up onto the small back porch. Had the bastard tried the lock on the door? Attempted to get into the cabin? Or had he just stood there on the porch, peering in the door and spying on them?

Archer's skin crawled at the idea of being watched like that. Had the stalker seen them having sex in front of the fireplace? Fury on Marley's behalf ripped through him. It was the worst possible invasion of privacy to have their lovemaking spied upon.

No way could he tell Marley about it. She would flip out. He knew from his survival-school training that women took sexual invasions of their privacy much more personally than men.

He was going to kill this asshole when he caught up with him. Slowly and painfully. He followed the tracks around the far side of the cabin, past Marley's snow-covered car, in a circle around his truck and back into the woods.

He'd traveled no more than a quarter mile into the heavy stand of timber around the cabin before he lost the trail. A combination of rapidly shifting drifts of snow and pine needles carpeting the forest floor where there was no snow made the trail impossible to follow.

If it had been bright daylight out and powdery gusts of crystalline snow not been blowing in his face and obscuring his vision, he might have been able to track the trail. But as it was, he had a pretty good idea where the stalker had headed, anyway. The trail had gone more or less in a straight line back toward the main road.

He was fairly sure the intruder must have had a vehicle, maybe a snowmobile, parked on the road and driven away. It was too cold out here for anyone to make camp and hang out in the woods for any period of time. At least not without extensive cold weather gear that would've been difficult to carry in through the deep snow and miserable to camp in for long.

Who in the hell would sneak up to the cabin and peer inside the windows like that? He supposed it was technically possible that the stalker was after him. But frankly, he didn't think he had been back in the United States long enough for any enemies he might have to have caught up with him so quickly. Which left Marley as the target of this craziness.

He frowned. What if the accidents around the movie set had something to do with her? Steve had been clear that Marley had been close to all of the places where things had gone wrong either just before or at the time of the incidents. Had *she* been the target of all the near-catastrophes? He needed to get back to town. To talk it over with Steve. Look at the security footage of the incidents and see if Marley could possibly have been the target instead of the movie set itself. For that matter, he needed to check the footage and see if he could spot someone who might be stalking her.

They had to get away from this cabin as soon as possible. They were completely isolated out here in the woods and severely limited in options for self-defense.

He took a hike down the driveway, and it was a disaster zone. Drifts of snow nearly as tall as he piled across the drive, lined up one after another. He might be able to shovel through it all, but with the wind blowing like it was, any path he made would fill right back in, probably in a matter of minutes. They were stuck here until the wind died down.

He turned around and headed back to the cabin and Marley. He was not leaving her side again until they were safely back on the movie set and surrounded by Steve's stunt crew, most of whom Steve had recruited from the ranks of recently retired Special Forces soldiers.

He slipped inside the cabin, stripped off his coat and stomped the snow off his boots. He had suggested to Marley that she take a nap while he checked out the snow. Hopefully, she'd listened to him and was safely tucked under the down comforter. He stuck his head in the bedroom door and spied a riot of blond curls peeking above the covers. Relief coursed through him. She was safe. And, by God, he planned to keep her that way.

He piled more wood on the fire and laid out his snowy clothes to dry on the hearth, then headed for the bedroom and climbed into bed. Marley promptly rolled over in her sleep and draped herself over him. She came half-awake as her limbs wrapped around his. Hugging an ice cube probably would wake him up, too.

He murmured, "Go back to sleep, baby. I'll warm up in a second. And then I promise I'll hold you all night long."

She breathed on a sigh of total contentment and mumbled, "Best. Fling. Ever."

His hands stilled on her skin. A *fling*? He was really starting to hate that word.

Still, he was the last one who should be throwing stones. It had been his own MO for so long, he didn't know what the hell to do now that his perspective was changing. And he sure as hell didn't like that she was turning the tables on him.

He was spinning out of control, and there didn't seem to be a damned thing he could do about it. He was having all sorts of strange feelings piled one on top of another, and he couldn't stop any of them. This must be what it felt like to go crazy. It was by turns giddy and truly terrifying.

It was almost as if he'd become obsessed with Marley. Either that, or she'd invaded his mind somehow.

He was actually considering asking her if she would be willing to give a long-term relationship with him a try. He knew better than most just how hard those were for military members and their significant others to sustain. He'd watched dozen of men and women in his unit over the years try to hold together long-distance romance with their spouses, girlfriends and boyfriends. Some had succeeded…and some hadn't.

Poor Marley. He had no business inflicting all his crap on her. She had just wanted to gain some sexual experience. Not that he minded being the provider of that. But she'd never bargained on him turning out to be the one who wanted to turn their fling into something more. Something long-term. Hell, maybe even permanent.

As much as he might want more from her, a fling was probably the best thing for them. No deep emotional attachments, no obligation for her to wrestle through his deep-seated relationship demons with him. Yup. A fling was the thing.

On cue, the whole stew of weirdness in his gut flared up again. He couldn't even begin to name all the ingredients. Need. Longing. Anger. Abandonment. Grief. It was as if all the emotional crap in his life had picked this moment to come surging out of wherever he usually stowed it, and all of it was messing with his head. Nobody had ever warned him that falling for someone opened the floodgates to all the relationship issues amassed over one's entire life.

What the hell was *wrong* with him? He hadn't felt remotely this emotionally unbalanced even right after that last mission from hell.

Maybe it was the incredible, emotional sex with Marley throwing him off his game. God knew, it had blown his mind. The weird thing was he'd had hot sex with lots of women in his life, and none of it had ever had this kind of an effect on him. But Marley was different.

Warming to the mental topic, he postulated that maybe it was something about her inexperience making him unable to shake her from his thoughts. She'd made him feel unusually protective. *Yeah. That was probably it.*

Although it wasn't as if he was going to get to stick around to find out. He would go back overseas, and she would move on with her life. She would find a guy who was permanently stateside, who could offer her a stable life and the promise of a long-term relationship.

A hot knife of jealousy stabbed him at the thought of a lout like Gordon Trapowski getting to be with her, getting his mind blown on a nightly basis by Marley. God, what he wouldn't give to be that guy. It was almost enough to make him think about resigning his commission and staying stateside for good.

The random thought shocked his mind into stillness. He had never been the type who would give up his career for love. He'd always scorned those men and women, in fact.

But damned if Marley wasn't rapidly turning him into one of those love-struck idiots. This was nuts. He'd clearly lost his marbles. The hell of it was that it felt so damned good. He didn't want to wake up from this mad dream. At all.

Marley moved restlessly against him, and he gathered her closer, wrapping his arms and his heart around her protectively. She settled, cuddled even closer to him and drifted back into a deep sleep.

His last conscious thought was to register in vague shock that he felt a smile on his face. What kind of fool fell asleep grinning?

A fool just like him apparently.

Marley woke slowly, warm and lazy and in no hurry to go anywhere. A warm, muscular, entirely male chest rose and fell gently under her ear. Yup. This was just about perfect.

A chill in the air announced that she and Archer had slept through the night and that the fire in the main room had burned down while they slumbered. She ought to get up and feed it more wood, but she was too comfortable and cozy right here to summon the energy to crawl out of bed, put on cold clothes and go out into the icy main room to stoke the fire. In a few minutes...

The next time she woke up, Archer was gone and she heard a firing crackling and popping loudly in the living room. The bedroom was still cold, so he must have gotten up recently. She sat up reluctantly, keeping the comforter tucked up around her chin.

"Hey, sleepyhead," Archer said cheerfully from the doorway.

"Hey. What time is it?"

"Sadly, it's time to go. The wind has died down, which means I can shovel the snowdrifts and they won't build up again. I'm heading out soon to try to open up the driveway."

"That thing's a quarter mile long. No way can you shovel the entire thing!"

He threw her a mock scowl. "Hey. I'm a specimen of supreme physical ability, thank you very much."

She laughed gaily. "Well, then. Please forgive me for impugning your superpowers. You're not seriously going to shovel the whole driveway, are you?"

"Nah. I'm gonna use my truck to blast through the drifts. I'll only dig whenever it gets stuck. Hopefully, it'll knock out all but the worst of the drifts blocking our escape."

"Our escape?" That was a strange word choice. "You don't feel trapped by me, do you? I mean, I don't expect you to make any promises or to hold you to any long-term commitments because we, well, you know."

"Had smoking-hot sex?"

"Yeah. That." Crud. Her cheeks were getting hot. Worse, though, Archer was frowning for real now. What was that all about? What had she said to put that deep crease between his eyebrows?

He whirled and headed out into the main room. His voice, a bit on the clipped side, drifted into the bedroom. "Hungry?"

"Yes. I'll cook if you'd like."

"Nah. I got it. You get dressed and pack your stuff. I want to leave as soon as possible."

A hot, nasty little dagger of pain slipped between her ribs and fished around inside her guts. Little bastard found a number of soft, ready to bleed organs, too. Why was he suddenly in such an all-fired hurry to get out of here? Was he bored with her? Already? God, and to think she'd been fantasizing about a long-term relationship with him. Who was she kidding?

Glum, she climbed out of bed and shivered as the nippy air chilled her through in a matter of seconds. She raced to the bathroom, jumped into her warmest clothes, and packed as he'd suggested. It was sad to feel this magical interlude coming to a close. In a wistful frame of mind, she zipped her rucksack and carried it to the bedroom doorway.

Archer was sitting on the hearth, staring pensively into the dancing flames, as she approached him. What had him looking so serious? She had worked with enough guys to know better than to ask him outright. In her experience, men didn't like to talk about their feelings unless they initiated the conversation in the first place.

She sat down in the big armchair in front of the hearth and he silently passed her a pan that turned out to have hot oatmeal in it. Not her fave food, but it was warm and sweetened with plenty of melted brown sugar. She dug into the cereal silently.

He moved to the door and fished in his coat pocket, coming up with a jangly key chain. "My truck has an automatic prewarming and defrost feature. I'll get that going now, and by the time you're done eating, it'll be thawed enough for us to head out." He pressed a button on the key fob.

*Kaboom!*

A brilliant flash of light blinded her from outside the cabin and a concussion wave shook the entire cabin. The windows rattled, ash rained down from inside the chimney and the china rattled on the kitchen shelves.

The sound was deafening. It actually hurt her ears, as though someone had slammed their hands against each side of her head. Hard.

Something big and fast moving shot toward her. It grabbed her out of the chair and threw her to the floor, then smashed her flat beneath its weight.

Archer. He'd tackled her like an NFL linebacker. He was staring down at her like the end of the world was upon them and he was bracing himself for a fatal blow.

"What was—" She stopped. Huh. She couldn't hear herself talking. She tried again, louder. "What was that?" Her ears rang ferociously, and she could barely make out her own voice.

"Explosion," Archer answered loudly.

"Of what?" she demanded in disbelief.

"My truck. It just blew up."

# Chapter 12

"Stay down, Marley."

She stared up at him in dismay. *He* pressed up and away from her abruptly. She sucked in a deep breath as his weight lifted away from her rib cage. How on earth had his truck blown up? That was crazy.

Archer sidled up to the wall beside one of the windows as if he expected someone to shoot him if he showed himself. He must be having another one of those combat flashbacks of his. Curiosity to know how and why his truck had just exploded overcame her shock and she climbed to her feet to have a look out front.

Something was definitely burning out there. A bright glow flickered beyond the front porch. That and debris was starting to rain down on the cabin. It sounded like a storm of hailstones plinking off the metal roofing.

She headed toward the window and Archer, and he bit out, *"Get back!"*

But she'd gone far enough. She could see the source of both explosion and fire. His truck was, indeed, entirely engulfed in flames. The doors and roof of the cab were gone, the hood over the engine was nowhere to be seen and the remaining parts of the frame were mangled and twisted almost beyond recognition. Wow. That was some blast to have completely torn the sturdy vehicle apart like that.

"Oh, my God!" she cried. Horror flowed over her. Her breath and pulse accelerated, sending blood careering wildly through her veins. Her legs felt shaky and her knees were physically wobbling.

"Keep your voice down," Archer growled.

*What* was his problem? Shouldn't he be racing outside to put out the fire and see if he could salvage his truck? Instead, he was acting like a squad of terrorist commandos was about to break down the door and kill them both.

In an attempt to lighten the moment, she said drily, "Um, Archer, while that preheating and defrosting system is *incredibly* effective, I might not use it again until your truck's manufacturer works the bugs out of it a little more."

Archer snorted for a single instant of humor, but then he was right back to his terse, tightly wired self. "Get back from the window, for God's sake," he hissed.

Startled, she lurched and took a few steps away from the window and slid more behind him and the front door. "What in the world is going on?"

"Someone just blew up my goddamned truck. Tried to kill us. Bastard's probably out there right now, watching his handiwork."

Tried to kill them? What? No. She glanced out the sliver of window she could see from here. Archer's truck was a blazing fireball. No question about it. Had the two of them been inside it when that explosion happened, they would both have died. Surely it was an accident. His high-tech prestarting system had malfunctioned.

"C'mon," Archer muttered. "We've got to get out of here before the bastard moves in to confirm the kill."

She took one step to follow him and he glared back at her. "Get *down*. He can see in the windows. And if he can see you, he can shoot you."

All at once, the gravity of their situation penetrated the haze of shock that had come over her when his truck exploded. *Bomb. Killer. Shooting. Dead.*

Adrenaline slammed through her, making her entire body feel hot and cold by turns. They could *die*. What in the hell was going on? She dropped to her hands and knees, mimicking Archer.

He crawled to the bedroom door and grabbed her rucksack, then back over to the fireplace to grab his. That gave her enough time to mostly catch up to him and follow closely on his heels to the back door.

"What are we doing now?" she whispered, fully in panic mode now.

"We're heading into the woods. Whoever blew up my truck will be back, assuming they're not outside right now, getting their sick jollies watching my truck burn, presumably with us in it."

"They wouldn't know for sure that I would be in it with you. Why would someone try to kill you?" she asked, confused. Her mind just wouldn't seem to operate at full speed, and his logic escaped her. Or maybe it was just denial making it impossible for her to accept that someone was trying to *kill* her.

Archer ignored her question. Instead, he said tersely, "Once I open the door, don't make a sound. We're sneaking out of here as silently and covertly as we can. Stay right on my heels and hang on to my coat. I'm going to be moving fast at first. If you can't keep up with me, let go of my coat and I'll slow down until you catch up and grab it again. Got it?"

"Yes, but..."

"Hush, baby. We've got to go. Now."

He eased the back door open just far enough to slip outside onto the little porch. It was awkward staying low and sidling through the cracked door behind him. As soon as she cleared it, he eased the door shut behind her again. He checked to make sure it was locked and then he nodded grimly at her.

She nodded back, although she felt none of the readiness to head out into the woods that her nod conveyed. One second she'd been eating a pot of oatmeal, and the next second, someone had apparently just tried to assassinate her and Archer. The whole idea was so surreal as to border on absurd.

Crouching low, Archer darted into the woods behind the cabin. She followed, disbelief raging through her terror. She struggled to concentrate on even moving her feet, let alone keeping her balance, staying right on Archer's heels like he'd told her to and remembering to hang on to his coat.

He wasn't kidding. He did move fast through the heavy woods. Branches laden with snow whipped her in the face, dumping powdery snow all over her. It got in her hair and down the neck of her coat, into the crease between her mittens and coat sleeves. And it melted. And got cold. And miserable.

While Archer had been running around at high altitude in the mountains of the various war zones he flew in overseas, she was a sea-level baby. In a matter of minutes, she was huffing and puffing behind him.

It was a dilemma whether to breathe hard and have enough oxygen not to pass out, or to try to control the noise of her breathing so the hypothetical bad guy chasing them wouldn't hear them and shoot them dead. She alternated between holding her breath and panting like a dog on a hot day.

Her lungs burned and then her legs burned. She felt light-headed and spots danced in front of her eyes before she finally had to let go of his coat out of sheer inability to hold her fist closed any longer.

Archer stopped immediately. He pulled her down into a crouch under the spreading branches of a big fir tree. The snow was not deep under its thick canopy of branches. It took her an embarrassingly long time to catch her breath.

While she huffed and puffed, Archer tried his cell phone, but there was no signal up here in these isolated mountains.

Finally, as her respiration approached normal once more, Archer mouthed, "Ready?"

She nodded resolutely.

He headed out at a slightly more reasonable pace. But again, the altitude got to her eventually, and she had to let go again. They fell into a pattern of moving for about fifteen minutes and stopping for her to catch her breath for about five.

She thought of herself as a relatively fit and strong person. After all, shoulder-held cameras weighed upward of forty pounds and she had to be able to walk around with one on her shoulder, holding it steady with one hand and dragging around a power cord with her other hand. And she might be required to do it for hours on end with only short breaks for rest. But running around in these mountains while scared out of her mind was kicking her butt.

They must have run and walked through the woods for two hours before Archer finally halted under yet another huge pine tree. This pocket of shadow was almost entirely devoid of snow. Archer used his gloved hands to gather a big pile of pine needles together. He sat down on it and gestured her down beside him. She sank gratefully to the impromptu cushion and leaned into the crook of his arm that he held out for her.

He spoke in a low mutter that wouldn't carry five paces. "How are you?"

"Terrified. Who blew up your truck?"

"No idea."

"Are they following us?"

"I haven't heard the sound of any pursuit whenever we've stopped. I'm betting we bugged out of there much faster than the bastard thought we would. I think it's safe to assume we slipped away unseen."

She probably ought to feel relieved at his assessment, but she couldn't work up much of a sense of safety while hiding in the woods in the middle of winter in the mountains, far from civilization. She felt exposed and tremendously vulnerable out here. "Now what?" she asked in a small voice.

"Now we find civilization. Another cabin or a passable road where we can flag down a car and get a ride to somewhere with a working phone. Cell tower coverage is nonexistent out here."

She glanced around at nothing but trees and more trees around them. "How do we find a way out of here?"

His arm tightened around her shoulders. "I happen to have a decent sense of direction. We've been paralleling the main road the cabin was on. All we have to do is cut to our right and go a quarter mile or so, and we should hit the road. Then we follow it to another driveway or until a car comes along."

"How will we know the driver isn't the same person who tried to kill us?"

"We've been walking uphill, away from the nearest town. Odds are that the would-be killer headed back to town after supposedly frying us extra crispy. I don't see him driving higher into the mountains and higher into the snowfall line."

His logic made sense. Still, deep paranoia about any other human being overwhelmed her at this point. Although it wasn't like they could just stay out here forever. They rested for perhaps fifteen minutes this time, and it felt like heaven to relax her entire body like this.

But eventually, Archer murmured, "Ready to head out?"

"As I'll ever be." She sighed.

He helped her to her feet and they headed out again, blessedly at a much more sane pace this time. However, now they were cutting across the direction of the prevailing winds of the past few days, and they had to slog through drift after drift of snow. It was slow, cold and wet going, and all she had to do was follow in the path Archer made for her. She didn't envy him having to forge his way first through the chest-high mounds of snow. She did offer to take her turn going first, but he was having no part of that.

She didn't know how long they trudged through the snow. She just knew she was exhausted and hungry, and wet and cold, when Archer stopped so abruptly in front of her that she ran into his back.

Startled, she peered nervously over his shoulder.

There. Through the trees. A strip of relatively flat, white snow. With tire tracks in it. *A road.*

Archer eased forward slowly, and she followed behind, being as stealthy as she could manage on her limp-as-noodles legs. He stopped just under the cover of the last trees by the edge of the road.

"Now what?" she breathed.

"Now we wait for someone to drive by."

She got the distinct impression that he thought this could take a while. Great. If they stopped moving, she suspected the cold would catch up with them quickly and make their misery complete. But miserable was better than dead.

She was, in fact, shivering so hard her teeth physically chattered by the time Archer went tense and alert beside her. She clamped her jaw shut to hear past her tap-dancing teeth and listened hard. There it was. A rumbling noise in the distance.

It sounded like it was coming from above them on the mountain. Archer moved closer to the road after muttering to her to stay under the trees until he waved her over.

Tense, she waited where he told her to, watching the road a hundred yards or so to their left where it disappeared around a curve into the trees.

Her breath caught as a huge dump truck rumbled into sight, a snowplow blade mounted on its front bumper. Archer leaped out of the trees and into the road, waving wildly for the driver to stop.

The vehicle ground to a stop and the passenger window came open. "You folks in some trouble?" the driver shouted.

Archer waved her over and she stumbled through the snow frantically. It wasn't as if the guy was going to drive off and strand them out here, but she was so grateful to see another human being who obviously wasn't going to kill them and could take them away from this nightmare that she could cry.

In fact, as Archer hoisted her up the steps into the high cab of the truck, she did feel tears tracking down her cheeks, leaving icy cold trails behind. Archer piled in behind Marley and slammed the door shut gratefully behind himself.

The warmth in the heated cab struck her like a physical blow. It had been days since she'd felt room temperature air surround her. Ahh, the comforts of modern civilization. God bless them, one and all.

"You folks have car trouble?" the snowplow driver asked.

"You might say that," Archer answered wryly. "Any chance we could get a ride to town, or at least someplace with a working phone so we can call for help?"

"Yeah, sure. But I can plow your car out and give you a tow back onto the road if you want."

Archer shook his head. "Car's dead. Gonna need more than plowing and a tow, I'm afraid."

"Okay. Well, sit tight. It's gonna take me a little while to plow my way down this road."

She leaned forward to ask, "Has this road already been plowed? I see tire tracks."

"One of the guys went through here last night. Did the initial clearing and got one lane open. I'm opening up a second lane."

"What about the tire tracks?" Archer asked, obviously seeing where she was going with her line of questioning.

The driver downshifted as the road went downhill more steeply. "Some of the locals have been out on four-wheelers playing in the snow. Had to tow one out already today."

So. It was possible that their would-be killer had driven in on a four-wheel-drive vehicle, sabotaged Archer's truck and then driven out. She sincerely hoped the guy was long gone.

"Lean back," Archer muttered to her under his breath. "And turn your head toward me."

She did as he instructed, but looked at him questioningly. He had slouched deeply into his seat and pulled his watch cap way down over his eyebrows as she stared at him.

He murmured, "Your driveway's just ahead. In case our friend's watching the road, we shouldn't be visible."

Oh, God. She yanked her hood forward over her face and pulled her neck scarf up over her mouth and cheeks.

She couldn't see the driveway from her position, with her back toward the window, but Archer eventually released a long breath and sat up straighter. He grinned ruefully at her. "You look just like the guy who tried to run us off the road last week."

She scowled at him and pushed the hood and scarf off her face. A smell of wet wool filled the cab of the truck as her clothes and Archer's dried in the heat. It took a while, but finally she began to feel warm all the way through. Her fingers and toes thawed and dried out, and she even began to feel sleepy.

Gradually, as the truck plowed its way down the mountain, the amount of snow lessened, and the vehicle picked up speed. In maybe a half hour, she began to see houses more thickly clustered. And then a gas station, followed by a small strip mall.

"This good enough for you guys?" the driver asked.

Archer thanked the man profusely for his assistance and shook his hand warmly.

They climbed down out of the big truck and Archer led her to a diner next door to the gas station. While she ordered food for them, he made a phone call.

"Hey, Steve. It's me… Yeah, I found her. We've got a bit of a situation up here. We need a ride back to Serendipity… I can't get into it over the phone. Our friend from the set struck again, though… Nope. No kidding."

The call was very short after that. Archer told Steve where the two of them were, and then he hung up.

To Marley, he said, "He'll be here in an hour."

They ate their lunch at a leisurely pace and split a piece of apple pie between them before an SUV pulled up in front of the restaurant. A familiar, tall form climbed out of the vehicle.

"Steve's here," she announced.

Archer jumped up, took her arm and ushered her outside hastily. Apparently, he was as eager as she was to get back to the relative safety of the movie set.

Steve barely made it to the door of the restaurant before she and Archer met him and hustled him back toward his SUV.

"What's going on?" Steve asked sharply as Archer piled her into the backseat of the vehicle and jumped in the front seat quickly.

"Let's go. I'll explain on the road," Archer replied tersely. Steve nodded briskly and threw the vehicle into gear.

One thing she had to give these military guys credit for. They knew when it was time to stop and talk and when it was time to *move*. The little town had disappeared in the rearview mirror and Steve had driven with dispatch down the mountain, below the snow line, before he took his foot off the gas pedal.

"Okay, Arch. What the hell's going on? Why couldn't you drive your own truck back to town?"

"It blew up this morning."

"Come again?" Steve glanced across the front seat at Archer. From her vantage point, she spied the blank shock on his face.

"It blew up. Someone planted a bomb under it. I used the remote warm-and-defrost feature to start the engine from inside the cabin, and when I did, it blew up. As in kaboom. Big fireball. Engulfed in flames. Parts flying everywhere."

Steve swore luridly under his breath. He glanced cautiously at her in the rearview mirror and asked Archer, "Is it our saboteur?"

Archer took a deep breath. Exhaled hard. "As much as it pains me to admit this, I think you're right, Steve. I think Marley is, in fact, behind all the accidents on the set. And this is just the latest of the bunch."

# Chapter 13

"What?" Marley squawked from the backseat. "How can you say something like that? I would have died right along with you if we'd have gotten in your truck before you started it." Fury and terrible hurt wrestled for control of her emotions.

Even Steve's head snapped toward Archer like the announcement had taken him entirely by surprise. "How's that?"

Archer looked back and forth between both of them defensively. "I didn't say I thought Marley was the saboteur. But I do think she's the *target*."

Marley fell back against the seat in disbelief. He'd hinted at that once before. But it simply made no sense. She didn't have any enemies. And she certainly didn't have any stalkers who were crazy enough to blow up the truck she was about to climb into.

A sick suspicion that Mina might be crazy enough

to blow up a truck passed through her mind. As the rap sheet Steve Prescott had unearthed did demonstrate, her twin had a rebellious and even violent streak. But Marley dismissed out of hand the notion of Mina attempting murder. Particularly murder of her own sister. She loved Mina, and Mina loved her. Mina would never harm her. *Right?*

Surely, the explosion had been a result of a mechanical flaw in the truck's high-tech remote heating and defrosting function.

"When we get back to the hotel, the two of you are going to sit down and tell me every detail of your weekend at the cabin. Everything you saw, everything you heard."

Gulp. Surely Archer wouldn't tell his boss *every* detail of the weekend.

"You got it," Archer answered jauntily from the front seat.

She seriously considered crawling under her seat in the SUV and never, ever coming out. Her feet probed beneath her. Not enough space for her to fit, darn it. As soon as they got back to the hotel, she would find a nice big rock to hide under. Forever.

Unfortunately, Archer helped her out of the SUV and escorted her inside without giving her a chance to find that rock. Steve installed them in the living room of his suite, and she bought time by asking if it was possible to get some food sent up to them. While he ordered room service, she turned to Archer and whispered urgently, "Please promise me you're going not to tell him about us."

"You heard the guy. He wants every detail."

She did a double take and saw his eyes twinkling

with humor. Oh, thank God. He wasn't going to humiliate her with his boss.

"My grandmother taught me that gentlemen don't kiss and tell," he murmured under his breath.

Abject relief flowed through her. But she still swatted his knee for scaring her like that.

Of course, Steve came back into the room just as she slapped Archer's leg to find them laughing at each other, probably a bit too companionably. Rolling her eyes at Archer, she scooted farther away from him on the sofa.

Not that she thought they were fooling Steve Prescott for a second. The man was no dummy. Still, she was going to keep up the charade of being just coworkers until somebody forced her to drop it. The idea of the movie crew at large knowing all the sordid details of her love life made her skin crawl with embarrassment.

But Archer had her back. He wasn't going to let anyone humiliate her.

"All right," Steve announced. "Start at the beginning…"

Marley woke up slowly, sleepily. She was curled on her side around a pile of pillows, which was odd. She rarely slept with extra pillows in her bed…

*Oh!* Archer.

He'd taken her to his room late last night and installed her in his bed with orders not to leave the room and to get some rest. She and Archer had described the events at the cabin to Steve over and over in excruciating detail—blessedly leaving out all the parts that involved getting naked and having mind-blowing sex.

She hadn't been aware that Archer had spotted tracks around the cabin. And her horror factor had gone through the roof when he relayed that the tracks had come right up to the windows and back porch. Who in the world would spy on the two of them like that?

Steve and Archer had spent hours combing through first Archer's life, then hers, trying to figure who might have fixated on one of them with such obsession that it led to attempted murder.

She steadfastly defended Mina through the evening, insisting that her sister was too easy to blame because of her troubled past, and that Mina would never harm her. But she got the impression that Steve and Archer remained unconvinced.

Frankly, she thought the odds were much better that it was an ex-lover of Archer's than anyone in her life. She'd been such an introvert, so shy and disconnected from the people around her for her entire adult life that she couldn't fathom registering strongly enough on anyone's radar to merit a strong enough fixation to culminate in bombing Archer's truck.

Steve argued that she hadn't seen Mina in years and had no way of knowing what her sister's mental state was currently.

She countered by arguing that it was entirely plausible some woman had fallen in love with Archer and that he'd broken the poor girl's heart. This hypothetical woman could have heard he was back in the United States, snapped emotionally and come after him to get revenge.

When Steve and Archer measured the size of the footprint Archer had put his hand beside and snapped a picture of, the shoe turned to be only around a man's size five. And that was far too small for most adult men.

Which left her sister or an ex-lover of Archer's as the primary suspects.

She sat up in Archer's bed and glanced over at the alarm clock. Almost 8:00 a.m. Wow. She'd slept the whole night through. After she'd had a nice, long soak in a steaming hot bath and let Archer tuck her into bed, she'd crashed hard.

Where was he, anyway?

She spotted her rucksack sitting in the corner and rooted around in it for clean clothes. She pulled on jeans and one of her flannel shirts, and on cue her stomach growled loudly. Hmm. The daily breakfast buffet for the film crew would be in full swing at this hour. Should she hop down there and get a bite to eat or not? Archer had been crystal clear that he did not want her to leave the room until he got back. But had he meant that for just last night, or did the order still hold this morning?

Her cell phone had charged overnight, and she dialed his number. Her call went directly to voice mail. Dang it. She waited in the room, pacing back and forth impatiently as the minutes ticked past and the demands from her stomach grew more insistent.

Finally, as the end of the buffet loomed near, she gave up on waiting. She was freaking hungry, and she would be perfectly safe with a crowd of cast and crew around her. She would just slip into the dining room, grab a quick plate of food and bring it back to the room to eat. No harm done.

She headed downstairs to eat and had no sooner set foot inside the door of the big dining room when Tyrone called out at what must be the top of his lungs, "Marley Stringer! Where have you *been* all weekend? Have you been holding out on me? Who's your secret lover, girlfriend?"

That last question, delivered in a stentorian tone that

carried to the far corners of the dining room, made every single head turn in her direction. So much for making a quiet entrance, getting a bite to eat and slipping out.

Swearing under her breath, she pasted on a lame smile, loaded up a plate with an array of fresh food, none of which came out of a tin can, and headed over to Tyrone's table. If nothing else, she had to keep the man from shouting out the details of her love life to everyone in the damned room.

"Where have you been all weekend?" Tyrone started in immediately. "I noticed that Flyboy was missing in action, too. You guys finally hook up?"

"You are way too nosy to have as many friends as you do," she declared around a bite of pancake smothered in maple syrup.

"Yes, but I'm too charming to resist. Tell me all the gory details, grasshopper."

She scowled and shoveled in another oversize bite of pancake while she frantically tried to figure out how Archer and Steve would want her to handle this. Ultimately, the less said, the better.

"I had to get out of here. Spending all weekend staring at rain and the walls of my room was going to make me crazy."

"Oh, yeah? Where'd you go?"

"I rented one of those tourist cabins and spent the weekend sleeping and staring at my toes." And having hot monkey sex with the most gorgeous specimen of a man she'd ever dreamed of landing. The mother of all flings. But no *way* was she admitting that to Tyrone.

"Were you alone all weekend?"

She did her best to look insulted. "What are you insinuating, Tyrone?"

He threw up his hands in mock surrender. "I was just asking. You look too tired to have spent the whole weekend sleeping."

"I overslept this morning. Barely made it down here in time to get some breakfast." It wasn't entirely a lie, anyway.

"I heard you got snowed in with that hot stick jock. Is that true? Deets, girl!"

Marley squeezed her eyes shut. She *so* didn't want to give the guy details.

Thankfully, Tyrone leaned forward and said in a sincere voice, "Look. Tell me to mind my own damned business if I cross the line with you, sweetie. I'm just not used to being around nice, innocent girls. Not too many like you in Hollywood. You keep right on blushing when someone asks you about that man of yours."

"He's not my man!"

Tyrone just smiled knowingly.

Dammit.

"Look, I gotta go, hon. I'm due on set in a half hour."

Thank God. She couldn't survive too much more of his third degree without revealing the truth.

"A bunch of us are getting together at happy hour tonight. You have to come," Tyrone announced. "And if you even think about blowing off me and the other girls, we'll come up to your room and drag you down here by your adorable blond curls."

Reluctantly, she conceded that hiding in her room imagining that a killer was about to jump out of the closet and slit her throat might not be the best strategy on earth. Maybe getting out and being with other people was a better idea.

Where had Archer gone off to, anyway? And why wasn't he answering his phone?

\* \* \*

Archer stared at the computer monitor in dismay. "And you're sure the forensic reconstruction of this digital footage is one hundred percent accurate?"

Steve hovered over his shoulder studying the grainy image, as well. "Yes. Absolutely. Adrian hired the same guy the FBI uses to recover and restore partially destroyed digital data. He's the best there is. His stuff is considered accurate enough to use in courts of law as evidence."

Archer shook his head. "I don't care how good this guy is supposed to be. I'm telling you, Steve. That's not her. That's not Marley."

"How can you say that? Even I look at it and recognize her. That's Marley Stringer rewiring the charges that blew up the set of the fake city. She is a cinematographer and familiar with electronics. She would have no trouble learning how to do this."

Archer stared at the crouching figure. Whoever the security camera had caught on film was definitely the person who had sabotaged the set and caused the whole thing to blow up at once. And he conceded that the person did look shockingly like Marley.

But it simply wasn't her. It had to be her twin, Mina. Marley was going to be devastated to learn that her own sister had tried to kill her. No way was he mistaken. He knew her too well, knew her mannerisms, her way of moving and carrying herself, and there were subtle differences between this person and the woman he knew and loved.

*Whoa. What?* Scratch that. Lusted after, yes. Was infatuated with, yes. But in love with? Absolutely not.

"Look, Steve. This has to stay between you and me, but Marley and I are more than friends. We didn't just sit around roasting marshmallows and playing checkers all weekend."

"Tell me something I don't know. The electricity between you two is palpable. It's obvious there's a hell of a connection between you that isn't the result of checkers and marshmallows."

Archer sighed. "I *know* this woman. I feel her all the way down to my bones. I know every nuance of her movements, her facial expressions...all the things that make her Marley. And this *isn't her*. It has to be her twin sister, Mina."

"Jeez, you've got it bad, dude."

Archer snorted. "Like you don't feel this way around Olivia? C'mon. I've seen the two of you together. Talk about electricity flying—you two can barely keep your hands off each other."

Steve grinned unrepentantly.

"Okay. So you watch this footage and you're positively, no question about it, one thousand percent sure the person in these images is *not* Marley. Is that correct?"

"Correct."

"You'd swear to it under oath in a court of law?"

"Without hesitation."

Steve frowned deeply. "All right, then. Where is Mina now?"

Steve picked up the phone and Archer watched as his brother dialed the private investigator who'd been investigating her and asked for an update. Steve put the guy on speaker phone so they could both hear the answer.

"She's smart as hell. Has managed to avoid arrest or conviction for any of the more serious crimes she has been suspected of. Only stuff she ever went to jail for was the minor stuff."

"What kinds of major crimes has she been implicated in?"

"Theft. Breaking and entering. Boosting cars. Drug possession and trafficking. Even arson."

"Any violent crimes?"

"No convictions, but a couple people I've interviewed who know her have warned me not to cross her. They seemed to think dire consequences would follow."

Archer winced. How could Mina have gone so far off the rails when Marley managed to take the same childhood circumstances and turn her life into something so decent and loving and positive?

"Any idea where Mina's living now?"

The PI answered, "I tracked her to LA, but I lost her there."

"Los Angeles?" Archer exclaimed. "She's in California?"

"Last I heard. She's accused of stealing a credit card a couple months back, and the last place it was used before it went dead was East Hollywood."

He traded grim looks with Steve.

"How dangerous is this chick?" Steve asked the private investigator.

"She doesn't have any firearms convictions, but I think it would be safe to say she's armed and dangerous. The twin sister, Marley's, ex-boyfriend accused Mina of trying to kill him when I spoke to him."

Archer swore under his breath. "Are you saying Mina tries to take out any man who gets close to Marley?"

"Looks that way," the PI answered. "The guy I talked to went to high school with the Stringer sisters. He said rumor was that Mina would kill any guy who tried to get his hands on Marley. He also said that by junior year, word was out, and no guy would come within ten feet of Marley out of fear for their life."

"Does Mina escalate situations when she doesn't get her way?" Steve asked.

"Fits the psych profile I've built on her," the investigator replied.

"Thanks, man. Could you dig around Serendipity for her trail? We think Mina's our saboteur, and furthermore, she's been spotted on the set of our movie."

"I'll get right on it."

"Thanks." Steve punched the button to end the call. He looked up at Archer. "Well, that seems to answer the question of who's been trying to kill you."

"But what about the earlier accidents on set before I came back from overseas and got involved with Marley?"

Steve frowned. "I wonder if Marley moving into an exciting career in the movies triggered Mina's resentment."

Archer spoke slowly. "As a cinematographer, Marley would get to travel the world and meet a bunch of famous people. Over time, she could achieve success, financial security, and even win public recognition."

Steve nodded. "Before you got here, all the accidents were aimed purely at sabotaging the movie. But as soon as you showed up, the accidents switched to targeting you. Or you and Marley."

"Why would Mina target me that first time I flew with Marley in my helicopter? I hadn't shown any interest in her up till that point. I mean, I remember commenting to a couple of the other pilots that she had a nice body. But I hadn't met her yet."

Steve frowned back at him. "That's a good question."

"And how did Mina gain access to my helicopter in

the first place to screw with the flight controls? The airport is fenced and has twenty-four-hour security. She couldn't just walk in there. I realize she has a history of breaking and entering, but wouldn't some sort of alarm have triggered somewhere? Or at least a camera have caught her on tape?"

"Those are outstanding questions, little brother. Wanna take a ride over to the airport with me to check out the footage from the security cameras there?"

"I ought to go check on Marley…"

"I really need your help to look at the security footage. You're the only one who can tell the difference between Marley and Mina at a glance."

Archer sighed and nodded. Steve had a point. And besides. He wanted to catch this bitch and put her away before she could get lucky and hurt Marley. If they didn't anticipate Mina's next move and nab her soon, he was going to have to seriously consider leaving the movie set and physically distancing himself from Marley for her safety.

Even that might not be enough, though. If Mina was so angry at what she'd seen Archer and Marley doing through the window of the cabin that she was willing to blow up both him and her own sister in revenge, there might be no stopping her. He might have to do something drastic like turn himself into bait to draw her out.

He hated the idea of leaving Marley for any reason. But it was a hell of a lot better option than sticking around, Mina losing what few marbles she had left and her going house on her twin sister. No way could he live with the guilt of Marley's injury or death on his conscience.

He knew what he had to do. He waited until Steve

left the room to go deal with some scheduling crisis that had just come up on set, and then he picked up the phone and dialed a memorized number.

# *Chapter 14*

Marley waited all afternoon for a callback from Archer, but none was forthcoming. What in the world was going on with him? She supposed he and Steve were still trying to figure out who'd blown up his truck, and she told herself every time panic started to climb the back of her throat to chill out and trust Archer.

He cared for her. She *knew* it. He might not have said the words, but every time he touched her, every time he kissed her or made love to her, she felt it.

Was she deluding herself? God knew, she didn't have any other experience with lovers at all to compare these feelings to. Surely, she wasn't *that* naive. Or was she?

Her emotions waffled all over the place as the afternoon aged toward evening. The walls of Archer's hotel room closed in on her, and that happy-hour date with Tyrone and the other makeup artists started to sound pretty darned good.

She ran down to her own room, threw on some makeup and a sloppy sweater and jeans and stood back to survey her efforts. Not bad for an emergency rush job. She was getting the hang of the whole Marilyn look. A quick brush through her curls and a finger fluffing and that was about all the time she had for.

She hurried down to the bar and paused just outside, the way she had a scant week ago. *A lifetime ago.* Before she'd gotten snowed in with Archer. Before he'd opened up vistas of sexual and romantic connection between two people that she'd never dreamed possible.

Would the difference in her be visible to other people in the bar?

She snorted under her breath. It wasn't as if she'd worn that big red *V* around so obviously before. Right? *She hoped.* Taking a deep breath, she gathered her newfound self-awareness around her like a blanket of confidence and stepped into the bar.

Tyrone and the other makeup artists let out a shout and waved her over to their table. Smiling bravely, she made her way across the crowded room to them. *How odd.* Had the men on the crew looked her up and down like that last week, or was it happening for the first time now? Maybe they'd been ogling her before, and this was just the first time she'd noticed it. Or maybe they'd all heard she'd spent a weekend snowed in with the hottest guy on the entire set.

Either way, her body tingled from the heated looks getting thrown her way. If only it were Archer looking at her like that…

*Stop right there.* Archer was busy trying to figure out who had tried to kill the two of them. He would call her as soon as he got a free minute to pick up the phone. He cared for her a lot more than he had admitted aloud.

She made eye contact with several of her male co-workers and smiled a little at them. She was shocked at how they all but came off their bar stools in response. Had she always had that effect on men, or was this something new, too, now that she was an Experienced Woman? Thank goodness. No more boring and unexciting for her.

She reached the table and sank gratefully into the empty seat next to Tyrone. Under the din of cheering for the latest sporting event on the big-screen TVs, he leaned over and sang, "*Ooh, baby. You got la-a-aid. I can see it all over you.*"

She touched her fingertips to her makeup. "Oh, dear. Does it really show?"

"Honey, you look like sex incarnate. Marilyn would be proud of you."

As her eyes widened even further in alarm, he added, "Seriously. You look like a million bucks. That flyboy must have been hell on wheels in the sack. Tell me all about it."

Marley blushed so hard her hair was probably turning pink.

"*Uh-huh.*" Tyrone grinned knowingly. "Spill."

"A lady doesn't kiss and tell," Marley resorted to lamely.

He nodded. "Good for you. So what's your updated relationship status?"

"Um, no clue."

"*What?*" Tyrone squawked. His eyes narrowed. "If that man took advantage of you and then walked out on you, I am going to have *hurt* him."

"It's nothing like that. Thing is, he has to go back to his military unit in a few weeks. I don't know if he's willing to try to do a long-distance relationship with me or not. We haven't talked about it yet."

"If he doesn't go down on one knee and beg you to be his girl, you let me know. I know some guys who'll bust his kneecaps so he can't go overseas. You catch my drift?"

She rolled her eyes at him. "I appreciate the offer, but that's okay. I've got this." Although she wasn't at all sure she did.

Thankfully, the conversation around the table devolved into who was sleeping with whom, and Tyrone got sucked into the speculation-fest.

But then the speculation turned to what she and Archer had done to occupy themselves in that cabin all alone and snowed in for two days. Every eye at the table turned to her.

"Um, we played checkers, and talked. Roasted a few marshmallows and stomped around in the snow. And cooked over the fire. You'd be surprised how long it takes to warm up a can of chili without scorching it." She added hastily, "Archer was a perfect gentleman. He's actually a really nice guy. Smart. Interesting."

Yeah, this crowd wasn't buying it. Still, if word got around about their hookup, it wouldn't be from her.

*Oh, God.* She hadn't even thought about the fact that he might brag to his buddies about getting in her pants. Maybe *that* was why all the guys were looking at her like that. Yikes. But then her better instincts kicked in. Not Archer. Never Archer. He wouldn't even tell his boss about the two of them this afternoon. She could trust him. Right?

A little voice in the back of her head whispered, *Then why hasn't he called you all day or returned any of your texts?*

"I'm gonna head back to my room now, Tyrone."

"Girlfriend, what are you running away from?" He lowered his voice beneath another general shout. "Or should I ask who? Do you need to go somewhere and talk, honey?"

She reached across the table to squeeze his hand. "You're a good friend. But really, I'm fine. Thanks for your concern, though."

"You call me if you need anything. Day or night. You hear?"

She nodded, suddenly and inexplicably near tears, and slid out of her seat. "Thanks. I will. You're the best." And with that, she turned and fled. To hell with dignified exits. She didn't need anyone ogling her right now.

What she really needed was a nice long cry. And a nice hot shower. And some nice expensive chocolate. Maybe some hazelnut truffles would reassure her that everything was okay between her and Archer.

If only she didn't have such a long and disastrous history with men. Not once in her life had a relationship between her and any male gone well. Not once. Archer might have turned his nose up at the idea of a jinx, but she knew it to be entirely real. Had it finally gotten the best of her and Archer?

Lord, she hoped he was all right. Visions of him lying hurt in a ditch or worse flashed through her imagination until she was faintly nauseated.

When she woke up the next morning, she moped around Archer's room like a kicked puppy and couldn't for the life of her get enthusiastic about doing anything other than lying in bed staring at the ceiling. She had a terrible knot in her stomach and nothing seemed to get rid of it. She took inventory and ruled out disease or pestilence as the cause of her malaise.

Eventually, she headed downstairs for a late breakfast and was surprised to see the dining room half-full. The construction crew and set dressers were out working, and the electricians and grips had been called to the sets to test for short circuits due to all the water. But everyone else was hanging around here.

Marley dished up an anemic plate of fruit and yogurt and sat down at a table in the corner.

"Mind if I join you?" a male voice asked above her.

Startled, she looked up at Steve Prescott. "Not at all," she replied.

He sat down at the tiny table and leaned in close. His voice was low when he murmured, "Have you heard from Archer recently?"

"Great minds think alike because I wanted to ask you that exact same question."

The former Marine swore under his breath. "I was afraid of that."

"Afraid of what?" she echoed in alarm.

"He's gone. And so is Adrian Turnow."

She stared. "Gone where?"

"I have no idea. Although I can guess why."

"Share."

He sighed. I think Adrian has gone to Los Angeles to talk with the insurance company about shutting down the film and collecting the insurance money."

She frowned. She really, really needed this job if she was ever going to break into movie cinematography. Would the director actually take his money and run and leave the entire crew high and dry? He'd seemed like such a nice guy.

"Did Archer go with him?" she asked.

"Nah. Archer's convinced your sister is out to get him."

"Mina?" she exclaimed.

Steve frowned. "Didn't you know about her messing with the guys you dated in high school?"

"Excuse me?"

"My private investigator talked with a guy who went to school with you two. Kid said word was that Mina would mess up any guy who got near you. All the guys steered clear of you because of her."

She felt sick to her stomach all of a sudden. The isolation, the way the boys looked through her as if she wasn't there, it all made terrible sense now. It wasn't a jinx at all. Mina had chased them all off. But why?

Marley would like to think it had been out of a sense of protectiveness. But her roiling gut said that it might have been something darker. More sinister.

When they'd been little, Mina had often accused Marley of making everyone like her best. Had Mina carried that early childhood jealousy forward into their teen years without her being aware of it?

Had she carried it forward into adulthood, too? Was *she* responsible for Archer's truck blowing up? As much as she hated to admit it, Steve and Archer's theory that Mina was behind the attacks on the set was starting to look pretty good.

Steve was speaking again. "—possible Archer has either left the area because he thinks being near you threatens your safety. Or, if I know him, he's gone looking for Mina."

*Oh, no. No, no, no.*

"If you have a few minutes, there's something in my suite I'd like to show you."

She looked at Prescott sharply. A significant tone un-

derlined his seemingly simple request. Her first instinct
was to say no. She didn't trust anyone right about now.
Thing was, Archer seemed to trust this guy implicitly.
She tended to trust his instincts. "Um. Okay. Sure."

She followed him out of the dining room to an elevator. They were the only people to get into it. The
doors slid shut and she ventured to ask, "Do you know
Archer's full name?"

Prescott gave her a funny look. "Of course I do."

"His parents didn't really name him Archer Archer,
did they?"

That made him laugh aloud. "No. They named him
Archer Windgate Prescott."

"Prescott?" she repeated. "As in the same last name
as yours?"

Steve frowned. "Yeah. And as in Jackson Prescott.
The three of us are brothers. Didn't Archer tell you?"

Her jaw all but hit the elevator floor. Archer and
Steve…and the famous movie star Jackson Prescott?
Brothers? "Why in the heck didn't he tell me?" she de-
manded.

Steve shrugged. "We decided not to let people know
he was family so he could better investigate who was
behind all the accidents on the set."

Sonofagun. "Does he have any other huge secrets
he's not telling me?"

Steve threw up his hands with a broad grin. "I know
better than to touch that question with a ten-foot pole.
You'll have to take his secrets up with him. I'm not getting caught in the middle of your relationship."

As if she and Archer had an actual relationship to get
in the middle of. She could not believe he hadn't told
her who he was! Although, to his credit, he hadn't used
his connection to the star of the movie and part owner

of the whole freaking movie studio to get any special treatment from the crew. Lord, the women he could have picked up if the perky bimbettes bouncing around the set had known he was Jackson Prescott's brother...

Steve led her to his suite and waved her over to his desk. "Have a seat. Take a look at this and tell me what you see."

He opened up a laptop computer and clicked a few links before turning the screen to her. She peered at the grainy video on the screen. "That's the fake city set that blew up last week. Before it blew, of course."

"Keep watching," Steve said grimly from over her shoulder.

The footage ran a few more seconds, and then a figure came onto the screen. Slender. Wearing dark pants and a dark hoodie sweatshirt. The person hugged a fake wall and paused at a fake intersection to peer around the corner furtively.

The figure moved along the edge of the set, pausing at an electrical junction box mounted on the backside of a fake set wall. Marley winced as the figure deftly picked the lock and opened the box.

The hands were agile. Graceful. The figure's movements were all graceful. Quick. Like a dancer's.

She knew that figure. Knew the mannerisms. Knew the way of moving. Her heart vehemently denied what her head was telling her, though.

The person fiddled with the wires inside the box and then turned toward the camera. The image froze, the face in plain sight.

She was looking at herself. Blond curls peeked out of the hood. Big, round eyes that Marley knew to be bright blue looked around. The bone structure, the shape of the mouth, the line of jaw. She'd seen them every morning in the mirror for her entire life.

And she'd seen them every day, every time she looked at her twin sister, until Marley had left home.

"Mina," she breathed. "Oh, Steve. I'm so sorry. I had no idea she would follow me out here. I knew she had emotional problems, but I never dreamed she would do anything like this."

Steve spoke soberly. "This is serious stuff. She tried to kill you and Archer yesterday."

Her stomach gave a great heave that threatened to eject her breakfast from her body. "I think I'm going to be sick," she said thickly as she lurched upright and ran for the bathroom.

Archer parked his rented motorcycle at one end of the main drag of Serendipity, California, and made a big production of strolling the entire length of Main Street. The whole object of this exercise was to get the word out that he was in town. Or more to the point, to get word to Mina Stringer that he was in town.

Steve's private investigator had a description from a reliable source of a woman closely matching Mina's description staying at a motel in Serendipity. This woman had apparently been causing some trouble at a local bar the previous week. She hadn't been seen all weekend, however.

He had the name of the bar and would, of course, show up there tonight. But in the meantime, he flirted with every woman who would talk to him on Main Street—making sure to drop his name with each of them—and he went into various stores to chat up the clerks.

He stopped in the jewelry store and made a big production of picking out and buying an engagement ring. He actually found himself choosing the ring he thought Marley would love most. It was a beautiful diamond in a simple solitaire setting. A matching but separate surround added an arc of smaller diamonds around the central stone. The overall effect was a sun-and-moon motif. But it would allow Marley to dress up the stone and be all girlie and shiny or to remove the surround when she was working and opt for the simple beauty of the unadorned diamond. He guessed at Marley's ring size and made arrangements to pick up the rings later in the day.

He stopped in at a florist's to discuss doing flowers for an oceanside wedding at his grandmother's estate outside of town. He swung by the best restaurant in town to talk about catering a wedding feast. He even went into the men's clothing store to try on tuxedos and chat about outfitting his best man with a tux, too.

There. If everyone in Serendipity didn't know within the next hour that he was getting hitched to a girl named Marley Stringer, he gave up.

He made one more stop at a sporting goods store to make a purchase for the night to come.

Now, it was time to head over to the bar Mina had been seen at and set a trap for her. And then the waiting game would begin.

Marley was stunned that Mina had apparently been behind most of the problems in her life, and apparently behind the accidents on the set. She intellectually accepted Steve's evidence against her sister. But she just couldn't *believe* it. She was appalled. Embarrassed. She couldn't name all the other awful feelings churning around in her gut.

She looked up at Steve somberly. "I brought this trouble to your movie set. What can I do to help make it right?"

He frowned at her for long enough that she didn't think he was going to answer. But then he said, "There is one thing you could do."

"Anything. Name it."

"Archer and I think it's possible Mina has a co-conspirator in the crew. She used a code to get past a numeric keypad and into the airport hangars last week. That code changes every two weeks, and only the airport employees and the film crew have the current number. But we have footage of her walking right up to the pad and punching in the correct number sequence. No errors, no hesitation."

"You think someone on the crew gave it to her?"

"Yes. I do."

"Do you need me to ask around among the guys to see if anyone knows her?" Marley offered.

"I've got a better idea. How would you feel about impersonating your sister? Do you think you could pull it off?"

# Chapter 15

Archer paced his childhood bedroom in his grandmother's house, unable to sit still. For once, the rhythmic sound of the ocean pounding the rocks below her cliffside estate failed to soothe him. He couldn't think about anything but Marley. Never in his wildest dreams could he have imagined that a woman could so totally capture his attention and affection so fast. All of a sudden, his entire existence revolved around her.

A knock on the door made him about jump out of his skin. He was irritated to find his brother Jackson standing there. "Thought I'd stop by to say hi and find out what brings you to Gran's place like this in the middle of the movie shoot, Arch. You haven't been your usual playboy self since you got back from overseas."

*Ya think?* He shook his head. "I met a girl."

"So I heard?"

He shrugged. "How the hell did you hear about it?

You're over in the trailer camp with all the fancy movie stars."

Jackson laughed. "Hotbeds of gossip, movie sets. And you were big news when you showed up. The women, including those fancy movie stars, were dying to know all about the hot stick jockey who'd shown up on set."

Archer snorted.

"If you ever want to talk about your girl troubles, I'm around. And I won't carry tales. Just sayin'."

"What makes you think I'm having girl troubles?"

"You're here, aren't you?"

He scowled at his brother out of general principle.

"So how was your vacation with the Marilyn-look-alike cinematographer?"

Damn. The gossip mill on set really had been busy. And it made him even more certain that Mina had a co-conspirator in the crew. How else would she have known where to find him and Marley so fast last weekend? Aloud, he answered, "Up till the part where my truck blew up, it was fine."

"Your truck *blew up*?"

"Yeah. Probably a bomb. I remote-started it to let it thaw out because it was covered in snow, and kaboom. Flaming truck."

"What's that all about? Any idea who did it? Is this tied to the other accidents around the set?"

He filled Jackson in briefly on his and Steve's suspicions regarding Marley's twin sister.

"So why are you here in Serendipity, then?"

Good instincts, Jackson had. He knew Archer wouldn't just leave Marley alone back at the set with her psycho sister on the loose. "Steve's private investigator thinks Mina is staying here, in town."

"And you came roaring in like a conquering hero to catch her."

Archer grinned. "Well...yeah."

"Alone?"

He shrugged.

"For a smart guy, you can sure be an idiot sometimes."

He scowled at Jackson. "She doesn't know we're on to her. All I have to do is get her talking and get her to slip up. I'll be wearing a wire."

"And you think a psychopath like her is just going to up and tell you all about trying to kill her sister?"

"No. I think she's going to recognize me as the guy who's been shagging her sister and try to kill *me*."

"You're using yourself as bait to catch a known violent nut ball?" Jackson voice rose in sharp surprise.

"We don't have enough evidence to take to the police. It's all circumstantial at this juncture and points at Marley as much as it points at Mina."

"And you're sure you're chasing down the right twin?"

"Would you mistake Lyra for Shyanne?" Archer retorted. Marley and Mina were possibly even more different in personality than his and Jackson's twin sisters.

Jackson huffed. "Of course not. They're as different as day and night once you know them."

"So are Marley and Mina."

"This is a dumb idea, bro. Have you got any backup at all?"

"No, and I damned well don't need you volunteering. Your wife is going to have a baby any second, and I don't want you running around dark alleys behind bars playing ninja assassin. I'm the highly trained soldier, bro. I've got this."

Jackson's brows knit in a heavy frown, but he didn't argue.

"Speaking of which, where is your lovely bride? I haven't seen Anna since I got here. I want to meet her."

"She's eager to meet you, too. She's heard plenty of stories about you."

Archer groaned. "Great. Just great. She'll hate my guts on sight."

Jackson slapped his shoulder fondly. "You're family. And family sticks together. She'll forgive your unending attempts over the years to corrupt poor innocent me."

Archer snorted and followed his brother out of the room. Yeah, but would Marley forgive him for putting her twin sister—her only living blood relative—in jail for a very long time to come? It was one thing to know your sibling was a bad egg. It was another thing entirely to see your only living relative punished for it. He, of all people, knew how thick blood ran. The Prescott clan stuck together no matter what.

Marley sat in Tyrone's makeup chair facing the mirror. She studied his work with intent concentration. The heavy, black eyeliner was exactly like in the last picture she had of her sister, taken some years ago. The slicked-back hair and partially failed attempt to subdue the blond curls was exactly like Mina's hairstyle, too.

Still, Marley murmured regretfully, "She's harder than me. She has always lived harder than me, too. Is there any way to add a few wrinkles around my eyes?"

"Does she smoke?" Tyrone asked, studying her face.

"She did. I don't know if she still does."

"Open your mouth, then. I'm going to paint your teeth a little more yellow. And then I'll add a few crow's-feet around your eyes and a line around your mouth."

She waited patiently while he aged her prematurely, and then she studied the results. "That's getting very close. But it's still not hard enough."

Steve, who was observing her transformation, interjected, "It's the expression in your eyes. You still look like, well, Marley. What happens if you think hard, angry thoughts?"

She looked up at Archer's brother, surprised. "Like what?"

"Like Mina's about to hurt Archer, and the bastard you're talking to is going to help her."

Even the idea of Archer getting hurt at Mina's hands or those of her sister's anonymous accomplice made her spitting mad.

"That's it!" Tyrone exclaimed.

She glanced into the mirror and reeled at the effect. Angry and glaring, she did, indeed, look just like her sister.

Steve spoke up. "You know what to do, right? Just lurk in the shadows at the edge of the big barbecue Adrian's throwing for the crew tonight. Wait for someone to contact you. Don't make any overt moves. Okay?"

She nodded grimly even though she was scared to death. She could do this for Archer.

"My guys will have eyes on you every minute. As soon as Mina's accomplice makes contact and says something to incriminate himself, we'll move in and nab him. And speaking of which, it's time to get you wired for sound. Tyrone, could you help her with that?"

"Of course." The makeup artist deftly threaded the

wire from the battery pack around her stomach and up into the cleft of her bra.

It was awkward having some guy's hands down her shirt that didn't belong to Archer, but it was a lot less weird having Tyrone do this than Archer's brother. She was grateful to Steve for his consideration.

"That should do it," Tyrone announced. Under his breath, he asked, "Are you okay, sweetie? You're as pale as a ghost."

"I'm terrified," she confessed. "Whoever's helping Mina is a would-be murderer. This isn't going to be a nice person I lure out."

"Steve Prescott is a good man. I've worked with him on a couple of movies, and he's smart. Tough. Takes care of his crew like they're his own family."

What she wouldn't give to be actual family to Steve. She would love nothing more than to settle down with Archer, marry and have a bunch of kids. Assuming Archer could ever forgive her for Mina doing her damnedest to kill him. She wouldn't blame him at all if he just walked away from her and her crazy sister. He hadn't bargained for so much family baggage when he'd gotten involved with her, for goodness' sake.

"Okay, Marley. The barbecue is getting ready to start," Steve announced. "Let's do this."

Here went nothing.

Archer stirred his soda on ice idly and did his best to ward off the more aggressive females in the bar. No sign of Mina, however. It was still early, though. The bar was half-empty, and groups of singles were only now starting to trickle in to toss down a few drinks and check out the local talent. Tourist season was pretty much over, but a few new faces were sprinkled in among the regulars, who hadn't changed much since the last time he'd been in here, some five years ago. Last time he'd been home on leave…

A petite blonde paused in the entry. She was looking back over her shoulder at someone outside on the sidewalk. Saying something inaudible. It made her grin, whatever it was.

Mina.

The resemblance to Marley was eerie both for how much the two of them looked alike and for how very, very different they looked. Physically, they were dead ringers for each other. But there was a toughness about Mina, a vibe of "don't mess with me or I'll hurt you bad" that was entirely absent from Marley. It was laughable to think that anyone could mistake the sisters for each other.

He looked down at his drink quickly, lest she spot him staring at her. He figured she would hide as soon as she spotted him to watch him. Maybe wait for a chance to swoop in and do something dastardly to him.

He half turned away from her to face the guy on a stool beside him. "Buy you a drink, buddy?" he asked.

"Yeah, sure. Thanks."

Archer nodded. "What're you drinking?"

He kept up an inane conversation with the guy for a couple of minutes. Then, when he'd purchased plenty of liquid goodwill in the form of multiple rounds of Scotch on the rocks, he said low, "Hey, dude. Do me a favor. I think I saw my crazy ex-girlfriend come in a while ago. Could you take a look around the place and see if you can spot her? I don't want her to see me looking for her, or she'll think I want to get back together with her."

"No problem. What does she look like?"

"Short. Blonde with curls. Wearing black. Good-looking. Kinda like Marilyn Monroe if she were a biker chick."

"You mean that hot number dancing over by the juke-box. Crazy, you say? Too bad. She's a looker."

Archer risked a surreptitious glance toward the dance floor and spied Mina immediately. All she needed was a pole to complete the raunchy dance she was doing solo, apparently for the benefit of all the unattached males in the joint.

"Yup, that's her. Do yourself a favor and stay way the hell away from her. Bartender, another round for my friend here."

When his impromptu drinking buddy was lubed up enough to need help getting to the restroom, Archer hoisted him off his stool and guided the guy across the dance floor using the other man's body as just enough of a shield to explain Archer not seeing Mina full-on. But if she was half as alert and predatory as he thought she was, she would surely spot him.

He left bar-stool guy on his knees in front of a toilet, worshipping at the throne of the porcelain gods, and slipped out into the hallway housing the restrooms. It was a straight shot to the dance floor from here. He would lay odds Mina was in a position to watch him emerge into this hallway, but he didn't look back to check.

He turned and went the other way, out the back door into the alley behind the bar. This afternoon, he'd un-screwed the lightbulbs in the cages on either side of the back door. It was dark out here, quiet, after the blaring music and lights of the bar/dance club.

He slid to one side of the doorway and eased back against the brick wall in the deep shadow cast by the small porch overhang.

He didn't have long to wait. The door opened a tiny crack. A pause. It opened a few inches more. Another pause. Then the door swung open far enough to nearly hit him and a small, slender form topped by blond hair stepped out into the alley.

"Looking for me?" he asked from behind her.

Mina whipped around fast, a blade glinting in her fist.

*Aww, dammit.*

"Hey, Archer," she said affectionately. "Didn't think I'd find you in town tonight. I figured you would be at the barbecue with the rest of the crew."

Was she actually going to try to convince him that she was Marley? Shock rolled through him. Her voice was *just* like Marley's in tone, inflection and accent. And yet, he wouldn't have confused Mina for her twin in a million years.

"What the hell are you doing here?" he asked as jealously as he could manage. "I mean, I know things didn't go that great up at the cabin, but I didn't take you for a cheat."

Mina took a step forward, the fist with the knife disappearing into a pocket of her leather biker jacket. Her free hand came to rest on his chest. It was all he could do not to flinch away from her touch. It felt slimy. Dirty. The vibe coming off her was all *wrong*.

He decided to go with an angry act. No way could he act amorous toward this woman. "Why the hell are you dressed like that? You know I don't like you in tight pants or low-cut tops. You look like a whore in that heavy makeup, for God's sake."

Mina's stare narrowed angrily for an instant, but then smoothed out. Her eyes went wide and innocent in the darkness. "Why don't you come back to my place? I got a motel room in town for tonight. If you don't like my clothes, you can take them off me."

She rose up on her tiptoes and leaned in to kiss him. He braced himself to pretend that he wasn't repulsed at the idea of kissing her. Funny how, in spite of all the women he'd kissed over the years, he couldn't fake enjoying a kiss with this woman.

Her lips nearly reached his. Her breath was warm on his face and smelled of rum. He could do this. Just. One. Kiss.

Something sharp and hot stabbed his gut. It took a millisecond to register that the pain was an actual knife. The bitch had stabbed him!

He wrapped his right arm around her neck and slammed his left fist down on her forearm with all his strength. The worst of the fiery pain in his side subsided. He must have knocked the blade out of her hand and out of his side.

She fought like a tiger to escape his grip, kicking and biting and scratching anything and everything she could reach. He finally managed to turn and trap her against the wall of the bar, using his superior size and weight to subdue her, but it was only a partially successful maneuver.

And then he felt something hard and cylindrical in almost the same spot she had stabbed him.

"Let go of me, you son of a bitch, or I'll shoot you dead right here. Right now," she growled.

He tsked in her ear. "But there are security cameras at both ends of the alley."

"I disabled those weeks ago," she snapped scornfully.

"I hooked them back up, this afternoon. You should have destroyed the cameras and not just unplugged them…Mina."

He jumped to one side just as the gunshot exploded. The noise was tremendous in the brick canyon of buildings. The pain in his side magnified by several orders of magnitude, and Mina leaped away from him.

She raised the pistol in both hands and pointed it directly at his face. "You've gone and done it now, you stupid bastard."

He registered a small caliber handgun. The kind that fit in a woman's purse. Not a lot of stopping power, but enough at this range to mess him up bad. "You gonna kill me?" he rasped. "Why? Because I love Marley and not you?"

A muzzle flash banished the night, and the next gunshot was even louder than the first one. The last thought that passed through his mind was a single word. *Bitch*.

# *Chapter 16*

Marley moved around the edges of the party, sticking to the shadows mostly. It was hard to keep remembering to channel Mina. To walk and slouch like she was a badass biker chick.

She used to imitate her twin in high school in front of the bathroom mirror in hopes of gaining a little of Mina's confidence and assertiveness. The results had always looked silly to the point of absurdity. But she gave it her best shot tonight. Archer's safety might very well depend on finding Mina's accomplice.

She could do this.

She stumbled around in the dark for nearly an hour, and her feet hurt like hell. Mina had always hated being short and worn stupidly high heels. Even her biker boots had been wedges that added several inches to her height.

Not to mention Marley felt weird wearing leather pants like this. They clung far too revealingly to her thighs. Although it wasn't like the black tank top under her leather jacket left a whole lot to the imagination, either.

"What the hell are you doing here?" a male voice hissed from behind her.

Marley whirled to face the big tree behind her. A big, bulky form lurked in the shadows beyond it.

"I told you never to make contact with me, you idiot. I'll make contact with you when I have information for you."

Marley's jaw actually dropped open for a moment. *Gordon Trapowski?* He was the insider?

She improvised fast. "Yeah, well, I've got a problem. Marley knows I'm here. I have to get her away from here before she tells anyone."

"You were supposed to *kill* her. Little whore couldn't wait to spread her legs for that damned Army prick."

*Channel Mina. Be Mina.* She said sarcastically, "You're just pissed off she didn't go for you."

"Hey, I'm screwing the hot sister, anyway. It was your idea for me to go after her, not mine. It was a good idea, too," he chuckled. "Pissed off Archer Prescott to no end."

Marley felt filthy. Used. She'd just been a pawn in Mina and Gordon's scheme...whatever that was.

"Speaking of which," Gordon murmured in what she gathered was supposed to be a sexy voice, "How about a quickie? It's dark and there's no one around."

Ohgod, ohgod, ohgod.

"C'mon, baby. I've done everything you wanted me to do to mess up the movie. I heard a rumor today that Turnow's even thinking about shutting down filming. We won. We screwed over the people who took the studio away from my family and we cost your sister her job. After I'm done spreading rumors about her being behind the accidents on his shoot, she'll be poison in Hollywood. No one will ever hire her. Just like you wanted. So how about it? Show Gordon a little sugar." He leaned down like he was about to kiss her her.

"Not a chance." The words were out of Marley's mouth in her regular tone of voice before she could call them back.

Gordon glared at her, peering closely at her in the dark. "You look different tonight..."

He lunged, slapping a hand over her mouth and dragging her into the jungle of trailers just beyond the tree line. He swore in a continuous stream under his breath as he bodily carried her through the trailer park at a heavy run. The guy was massively strong and she struggled for all she was worth to break free or at least get her mouth free of his huge hand so she could scream for help. But to no avail.

Steve's men were watching her. They had the feed from the wire. They would know Gordon had recognized her. They would come for her. Save her. Right?

Archer blinked up at the night sky. Someone was kneeling over him

"Wake up, Archer!"

"Jeez. I'm awake. Quit shouting at me," he groused up at his brother Jackson. His head was pounding and his ears ringing. "What the hell are you doing here?"

"Covering your back, you lucky bastard. The cops are here, too."

"Mina?" He lurched and tried to sit up, but a guy wearing a medic's jacket shoved on his shoulder and held him down.

"In custody. Sheriff Thomas shot the gun out of her hand and then his guys moved in and arrested her."

"How did they get here?" he asked. Man, his brain was foggy.

"I called them, nimrod. No little brother of mine was walking into an ambush with a psychopath alone. The sheriff and his guys have had the bar staked out all evening. Apparently, you talked at some length with an undercover deputy at the bar. Got him pretty drunk, too."

"Huh. Thanks for the backup, bro. She talking?"

"Nothing worth repeating. She's been calling you some pretty creative names. I may have to write a few of them down to use in my next movie."

"What about actual names? Has she dropped the name of her accomplice? She has one on the movie set, and I really need to know who it is."

"Dunno. I can ask the sheriff, though."

To the medic, Archer asked, "Can I sit up now?"

"I'm almost done bandaging your side. You have a puncture wound. It's not deep. You're lucky you had that flak vest on. It stopped most of the blade's penetration. And, of course, it stopped the round she tried to put into your heart."

Jackson grinned. "You were wearing a bulletproof vest?"

The medic glanced up at Archer's brother. "How else do you think he survived that point-blank gunshot? He's going to have a hell of a bruise on his chest. Might even have cracked a rib or two. But he'll make a full recovery."

"I have to talk to her. Let me up," Archer demanded.

The medic lifted his hands away. "I'm done. And you're welcome."

"Thanks, man. Seriously."

Archer took Jackson's hand and let his brother hoist him to his feet. "Where is she?"

"Over there."

Archer strode over to the nearest working streetlight where the sheriff and two of his deputies were talking with Mina. Or trying to. She had her mouth stubbornly shut and didn't look interested in answering any of the questions they were peppering her with.

She glared murderously at Archer as he strode up to her.

"Yet again, you failed to kill me," he commented lightly.

Her glare intensified.

"So. Are you going to tell me who your accomplice on set is, or should I just call my brother and ask him? He knows who it is by now."

Mina spat an epithet at him and then, "Your brother's a dead man. And so are you. He'll kill you all."

Archer was startled. "What does your accomplice have against Steve?"

"He'll kill all you damned Prescotts."

Archer's gaze followed her glare. Huh. She was giving Jackson the evil eye now. "What have you got against the Prescotts?" he asked.

She ignored his question. "I want a trade. My freedom for the name of my stooge."

Her stooge, huh? So it was definitely a man. "Not a chance."

"That bitch always got everything. Everyone liked her better than me. She was always the *good* girl. Teachers liked her. Boys liked her better. Hell, our parents liked her better. She always got to do whatever she wanted while I was always grounded and in trouble and getting punished."

"Maybe that's because she wasn't running around trying to *kill* people," he retorted.

"I'll kill you. Kill her, too. I'm coming for you. All of you! I'll get even. You wait and see!"

He stared down at this madwoman who looked like a bad parody of the woman he loved. "You're genuinely crazy, aren't you?"

Mina lunged against the hands holding her arms and growled like a rabid dog.

Archer looked at the sheriff in distress. "She's clearly mentally ill. Violent and unstable. Keep a close eye on her, will you? I'd hate to see her harm herself. Her sister would be heartbroken if something bad happened to her."

Mina's growl rose in pitch until it was a feral scream of fury.

Whether it was fury over being caught or fury at the idea of Marley still caring for her, Archer couldn't tell. And frankly, he didn't care. Marley was safe now. That was all that mattered to him.

"You think you've won!" Mina screeched. "But I've got a surprise waiting for you, Flyboy…" Her words devolved into mad cackling.

*Damn.* Now what did she mean by that? Had she sabotaged something back at the movie set? Something that would hurt Marley? Oh, God. What had she done? His blood literally ran cold in his veins as fear streaked through him. Marley. He had to warn her and Steve. What on earth did she have planned? Frantic, he struggled to think clearly. Mina used the word *flyboy*. Was her "last laugh" directed at him and flying, maybe?

Terrified, he reached for his cell phone to warn Steve and Marley. But just as he fished it out, his phone rang.

He answered it quickly. Marley had been leaving messages on his phone for much of the day.

"Marley, baby. I've got good news for you."

"It's Steve, bro. And I've got bad news for you..."

Jackson drove, which was just as well. Archer was so freaked out he'd have had trouble keeping a car on the road. He'd been stunned when Steve told him the identity of Mina's accomplice. And he'd nearly lost his supper when Steve told him that Gordon had apparently kidnapped Marley.

Where in the hell had the bastard taken her? And why was Gordon Trapowski, of all people, trying to destroy the Prescotts? What had they ever done to him?

Steve told him that Gordon had made a reference to the Prescotts stealing Serendipity Studios from him and promised on the phone that he would have his private investigator look into it. But in the meantime, Steve and all of his entire crew were searching the set frantically for Gordon and Marley.

Every time Jackson's sports car topped a ridge and they momentarily got decent cell phone coverage, Archer called Steve. Finally, after nearly an hour and only minutes away from the set, Steve had news for Archer.

"A helicopter just lifted off from the airport the studio rented out. With its transponder turned off. And I've already verified with Adrian that no flying was scheduled for tonight."

"Are you tracking the bird on radar?" Archer asked tersely.

"Air Traffic Control has been notified, but if he gets down in the valleys they won't be able to track him by skin signature."

Archer swore. Mina had alluded to doing something

to harm him and his flying. Was this what she'd been talking about? Or did she have something else cooking? "I'll be at the airport in ten minutes."

"I'll meet you there," Steve replied. "And don't do anything stupid if you get there before me."

Archer disconnected the call without bothering to answer. "Floor it, Jackson."

Minerva was gone. Apparently, Gordon had decided to emphasize his victory by not only taking Archer's girl, but also taking his helicopter.

While Archer didn't give a flip for the bird, it made his blood run cold to realize how much hatred Gordon must harbor for him. Enough to take out the whole Prescott family? Damn. The guy must be at least as crazy as Mina.

The first thing Archer did when he leaped into one of the studio's other helicopters, a model identical to Minerva, was turn on all the radios. The battery had plenty of power to run them until he got the engines going. He skipped ninety-nine percent of the usual preflight checks and went straight for a combat start. His hands flew across the controls and his thumb jammed the ignition switch. The rotor overhead started to turn ever so slowly, taking a gradual, freaking lifetime to spin up.

A tall figure sprinted out of the hangar toward his passenger door. Steve jumped in the aircraft with a grim nod and buckled his seat belt while Archer finished powering up the last systems.

Over the headsets, Steve asked, "Do you have any idea where you're going?"

"Just up into the mountains."

"The Sierras are pretty damned big, bro."

"I have to find her. I *have* to."

They lifted off and banked north and west into the mountains. Archer followed the valley in which the airport was situated, on the assumption that Gordon would have wanted to stay below radar coverage immediately after his takeoff. Had Steve not alerted the authorities already to be on the lookout for an unscheduled take-off, Gordon likely would have gotten away unnoticed, too. As it was, the local air traffic controllers had only caught a glimpse of Minerva on radar before they'd lost the helicopter.

He flew for perhaps ten minutes, setting up a loose search-and-rescue pattern to crisscross the terrain. Steve used binoculars to scan the valleys below them.

Abruptly, the emergency radio crackled to life. "Oh, my God!" a female voice exclaimed.

*That was Marley.* Panic ripped through him like a tornado. Archer transmitted urgently, "Where are you Marley? Say your position!"

*Silence.*

"Talk to me!" Archer transmitted urgently.

The radio crackled again. "There's smoke!" Behind Marley's scared voice, Gordon was audibly swearing. He sounded like a pilot in trouble.

Archer's adrenaline spiked off the charts. Gordon and Marley were in the helicopter *he* usually flew. Had Mina done something to it? Sick certainty that she had took hold in his gut.

"Trap, take your bird back to the airport. Or back to the valley where we've been shooting the combat scenes. They're big and open and you can set down safely. Mina sabotaged that helicopter because she thought I was flying it next. I won't call the police, man, I swear. You can walk away. You have my word on it. Just put the bird down on the ground now." He was begging, but he didn't care. Gordon couldn't kill Marley. He *couldn't*.

"I think I see smoke," Steve reported. "It's over that ridge off to our right."

Archer pointed the helicopter where Steve indicated. He jammed the throttles forward and trees sped by. But it was taking forever to get there.

A dozen endless seconds ticked by. A year fell off Archer's life for each one that crawled past. Marley! What the hell was going on with her? If he lost her, he'd curl up in a ball and die.

"The engine is on fire," Marley cried. "We're spinning around!"

Only the lap belt stopped Archer from coming out of his seat as he bit out to Steve, "They've lost power. They're autorotating." He chanted in terror, "Damn, damn, damn."

Autorotations were bitches at best, and controlled crashes—or worse—when they went badly. People often died in them. Particularly when they had nothing but trees to come down in.

A long, drawn-out scream came across the radios. *Mother of God.* That was Marley screaming her head off. He'd never heard anyone sound so terrified.

He keyed his mike frantically. "Talk to me, Marley. What's going on?"

"Omigod. We're going down. We're going to die! Archer!"

"Is there smoke in the cockpit?" he demanded sharply.

"We're spinning around! We're falling! I don't want to die!"

*Dammit.* Marley wasn't screaming now. She was moaning in raw, animal fear over the radio.

"It'll be okay, baby," Archer lied in desperate calm while he died a little with each of her moans.

"I'm going to die," she wailed, "and I never told you."

"Never told me what?"

Her voice rose to a frantic cry. "I love you, Arch…"

The radio cut off. Only static came across the channel.

Archer yelled, "They've gone down!"

Steve snapped sharply, "Keep flying your own bird, Archer. You can't save her if you crash yourself."

He fought back the panic enough to scan his flight controls. His bird was okay. Steve dropped into terse, calm, crisis mode beside him, which helped him to do the same. Sort of. "I'll call the FAA. Request search and rescue. You just fly, Archer."

Marley had crashed. She might be horribly injured. In need of immediate airlift to a hospital.

*C'mon, c'mon, c'mon!* He urged his aircraft to go faster. *Hang on, baby. I'm coming.*

# Chapter 17

Archer's heart was beating so hard it about exploded out of his chest.

Desperation clawed up his spine and lodged in his throat. He shoved down an urge to puke. *Focus*. Marley needed him. Her screams still rang in his ears. No doubt about it, he would be hearing that sound for a long damned time to come. He topped the ridge and did a hard turn to start a run down the valley that opened up at his feet.

"C'mon, c'mon. Help me out here," he muttered. "Send up a flare or a signal of some kind, Trap, you bastard."

Agonizingly, the pass yielded nothing. He turned back again and started a second pass over the thick tree cover that was a sea of black at night.

*I love you, Arch...*

The words echoed in his brain like a death knell.

She couldn't be dead. She loved him, dammit! Marley could not give him the Holy Grail in one second and then die in the next.

"Keep her alive for me, Trap," he growled at the universe in general. He banked into a third pass, and cold, hard terror began to overtake him. If she was hurt, bleeding, and he didn't find her soon…

He couldn't complete the thought. She loved him, dammit, and he couldn't lose her!

*There.* A small clearing. A broken helicopter lying on its side. Tail snapped off. Rotors bent to hell. *Oh, my God.* Marley had been in that? How was she still alive? Images of blood and broken bodies crashed through his mind, horrifying him into near-catatonia.

"Can you put us down close to it?" Steve bit out.

The clearing was tiny. There was barely room for one helicopter, let alone two. "Hell, yes, I can," he declared. Concentrating fiercely, he descended, placing his bird in the one spot far enough from the trees and the crash site not to foul his rotors and kill him and Steve, too.

The skids bumped into the ground and he chopped the power. He leaped out of his seat and crashed frantically through the weeds to the downed helicopter.

*Don't you die, don't you die,* he repeated over and over in his head. He raced to the mangled bird and saw a female form lying beside it. Blond curls. Female curves. Blood. *Oh, God.*

"Marley," he groaned. He fell to his knees beside her. Something hot streaked down his face. Her eyes were closed. He felt under her chin for a pulse, praying like he'd never prayed before. *Thud, thud, thud.* Her pulse beat strongly, if terribly fast, against his fingers.

*Alive.* Thank God. But unconscious. His hands

skimmed over her body in search of broken bones or obvious injuries.

He vaguely heard a voice intoning, "Nonononon-ono," and realized from afar that it was him. "Wake up. Fight, dammit!"

Marley's eyes fluttered. Opened slowly. He reeled, light-headed with relief. "How do you feel?"

"Okay, I guess," she mumbled.

"What hurts, baby?"

"We hit hard. Knocked the wind out of me. Think I fainted."

He heard a groan nearby and looked up. Steve was crouched over Gordon, and Trap was just coming to.

"You got here fast," Trapowski rasped.

"You had Marley," Archer retorted sharply.

"Didn't think you'd take too kindly to me killing the girl you love."

Archer turned his attention back to Marley. "Fingers and toes. Can you feel them? Move them?"

She nodded, and he walked her through a quick injury assessment. Apart from a shallow cut on her forehead that had bled all over her face and made her look on the verge of expiring, she seemed unharmed. A miraculous act of God he would be giving thanks for forever. He tore off a strip of his shirt and wrapped it around the cut. He used his sleeve to mop away the worst of the blood from her face.

"Can you sit up?" he asked gently.

"If you help me."

With a supporting arm around her back, he eased her to a sitting position. She blinked her eyes hard and looked a little dizzy, but then steadied. "I knew you'd come for me."

"I'll always come for you."

Overcome by his emotions, he wrapped his arms around her and drew her into his lap for a desperate hug. He put into the embrace all the panic and fear and relief in his heart that he could not put into words.

Marley cuddled against Archer in shock. His heart beating hard in her ear was just about the greatest thing she'd ever heard. An undeniable affirmation that she was alive. Really alive. She'd been certain her number was up when the helicopter started spinning wildly out of control.

"Gordon wants to kill everyone in your family," she eventually said against his chest. "Mina was sleeping with him. She helped him sabotage stuff around the set in return for him helping her sabotage my life."

"I know."

"He said your family stole the movie studio from him."

He stared down at her. "Steve mentioned something about that. But Jackson and Adrian Turnow bought it from Z. K. Tripp."

"Zacharius Trapowski," Gordon rasped from the ground.

"Relation of yours?" Steve asked drily.

"My brother."

"The way I heard it, Tripp had the studio up for sale, and Jackson and Adrian bought it fair and square."

"I set up a hostile takeover…was supposed to get half the money…" Gordon wheezed. "Z.K. sold it out from under me…got nothing…I'll kill him…kill you, too. All of you…"

"Easy, there, Trap," Steve urged. "Looks like you've got some busted ribs. Sounds like you've punctured a lung and collapsed it, too. Just lie still and breathe slowly while I put this zip tie around your wrists."

"You went after Mina, didn't you?" Marley accused Archer without much heat.

He nodded down at her apologetically. "I did. She's in police custody in Serendipity. She tried to shoot me in front of a bunch of cops. I'm afraid she's going away for a very long time, baby." He added in a suddenly fierce tone, "But she won't be hurting you again. Ever. I'll see to it personally."

She caught the first hint of relief on his face since she'd opened her eyes. It was still hard to compute that she was alive. She'd been so sure she was going to die. "You mean that?" she asked in a small voice.

"I've never meant anything more." He took a deep breath and then said cautiously, "About what you said on the radios before…"

"You mean shouting at the top of my lungs that I love you?"

"I realize people say things in the heat of the moment when they think they're going to die…" His voice trailed off.

She reached up and laid her hand on his cheek. "Oh, Archer. I didn't say that because I thought I was going to die. I said it because I wanted you to live. I figured if you knew that a woman had genuinely loved you in her lifetime that you might let another one love you someday."

He frowned down at her, processing her words. He had no frame of reference in which to comprehend what she was saying. She cared about him enough to think more about his welfare than hers? Even in the last moments before she died?

Something tight that had been squeezed into a little

corner of his heart for a very long time unraveled, un-furling like a newborn butterfly's wings. *This* was what real love was. Willingness to throw oneself into the line of fire on behalf of the person one loved. The way he'd gone after Mina without a second thought for his own safety. The way she'd thought of his future happiness over hers even as the helicopter fell out of the sky. She loved him. Really *loved* him.

And moreover, he loved her. He was capable of real love, after all. His past had not broken that part of his heart, after all. It had just taken the right woman to come along and show him how to love. The knowl-edge sank into his soul like cool rain after a long, hot drought.

"I don't deserve you..." he started.

She pressed her fingers over his mouth. "There will be no more talk like that, Archer Prescott."

A smile tugged at the corners of his mouth. "You found out my last name, huh?"

"Remind me to get mad at you later for not telling me."

"You got it." A pause. "I love you, too, Marley."

Something shifted in the air between them and in the ground beneath him. It was as if the entire world tilted a little on its axis. She let out a long, slow breath. "But my sister tried to kill you."

He shrugged. "My family's enemy tried to kill you. I'd say we're about even on that score. Wouldn't you?"

His mouth curved up in the most beautiful smile she'd ever seen. He leaned down and kissed her so sweetly her heart could hardly hold all the joy that erupted inside it. "I'll never get enough of you, Archer."

"You can have me as long as you want me."

She pushed back in his arms enough to stare up at him. "You mean that?"

"I do. I'm yours, Marley. Body and soul. Marry me, baby."

She swallowed hard. Did he really mean it? "Um, okay. I mean, yes. Yes! Oh, *yes*."

He'd given her the stars and sky, the sun and moon, and in turn she gave him her heart right then and there. All of it. Forever. With the silent, majestic mountains standing witness to it around them.

"Oh, wait. I picked up something for you when I was in town today." He fished around in his jacket pocket and fished out a little velvet box. "Let me do this right."

He set her on her feet and knelt down in front of her. "Marley, would you make me the happiest man in the world and do me the great honor of marrying me?"

Tears filled her eyes. "The answer is still yes. Ring or no ring, you wonderful man."

He surged to his feet and wrapped her in a hug so tight she could hardly breathe. And she totally didn't care.

Eventually, Archer called out without loosening his hold on her one bit, "Hey, Steve."

"Yes?"

"Am I correct in thinking, now that Gordon's going to be spending a lot of quality time in a federal penitentiary, you're going to be down a permanent stunt pilot on your crew?"

"That is correct. You know of any hot stick jockeys who might be looking for a job stateside?" Steve asked drily.

Marley stared up at Archer, stunned. He would give up his military career for her? "I don't mind being a military wife and doing the separation thing."

He nodded firmly and answered without hesitation. "Yeah, well, I mind the separation thing."

"Are you sure?" she breathed.

"Absolutely. I'm not leaving you again, baby. Ever."

His face lit with a smile, and her heart lit with an even bigger one. He wanted to stay with her?

Archer grinned. "Stunt flying is fun. Keeps me on my toes. And it's steady work. Good for guys raising a family."

"A family?" she echoed. She wrapped her arms around him, hugging him tight. She was never, ever letting go of him.

"Hey, Steve," Archer said again.

"Yeah?"

"Once the medics clear Marley to fly, any chance Adrian would let me borrow one of the studio's helicopters for a few hours, seeing as how I'm going to be his newest full-time employee?"

"What have you got in mind, little brother?"

"Marley and I need to fly to Reno." She stared up at him, sensing where he was going with this but not quite believing it.

Steve answered warmly, "I'm sure Adrian won't have a problem with that."

Archer grinned down at her. "So, baby. How fast can you be ready for a wedding?"

"For my wedding to you? Ten seconds to brush the grass off my clothes."

He gathered her close and murmured for her ears only, "No shenanigans while I'm flying us to Reno, though. You and I are both living to a ripe old age so we can have lots and lots more sex. Got it, Mrs. Prescott?"

"Got it, Mr. Prescott. You did promise me a wild ride, though."

He kissed her hard and fast. "Hell, yeah. Strap in tight, baby. This is going to be the wildest ride of your life."

Lord, she hoped so.

* * * * *

# MILLS & BOON®

## Want to get more from Mills & Boon?

Here's what's available to you if you join the
exclusive **Mills & Boon eBook Club** today:

✦ *Convenience – choose your books each month*
✦ *Exclusive – receive your books a month before
  anywhere else*
✦ *Flexibility – change your subscription at any time*
✦ *Variety – gain access to eBook-only series*
✦ *Value – subscriptions from just £1.99 a month*

So visit **www.millsandboon.co.uk/esubs** today
to be a part of this exclusive eBook Club!

# MILLS & BOON®

## Need more New Year reading?

We've got just the thing for you!
We're giving you 10% off your next eBook or
paperback book purchase on the Mills & Boon
website. So hurry, visit the website today and type
SAVE10 in at the checkout for your exclusive

# 10% DISCOUNT

## www.millsandboon.co.uk/save10

# MILLS & BOON®
## INTRIGUE
### *Romantic Suspense*

**A SEDUCTIVE COMBINATION OF DANGER AND DESIRE**

# MILLS & BOON®

## Why shop at millsandboon.co.uk?

Each year, thousands of romance readers find their perfect read at millsandboon.co.uk. That's because we're passionate about bringing you the very best romantic fiction. Here are some of the advantages of shopping at www.millsandboon.co.uk:

* **Get new books first**—you'll be able to buy your favourite books one month before they hit the shops

* **Get exclusive discounts**—you'll also be able to buy our specially created monthly collections, with up to 50% off the RRP

* **Find your favourite authors**—latest news, interviews and new releases for all your favourite authors and series on our website, plus ideas for what to try next

* **Join in**—once you've bought your favourite books, don't forget to register with us to rate, review and join in the discussions

Visit **www.millsandboon.co.uk**
for all this and more today!